THE
INDIAN ROPE
TRICK
and
OTHER
VIOLENT
ENTERTAINMENTS

THE

INDIAN ROPE TRICK
and
OTHER
VIOLENT
ENTERTAINMENTS

BY
TOM MEAD

Introduced by Martin Edwards

Crippen & Landru Publishers
Cincinnati, Ohio
2024

Tom Mead stories copyright © 2024 by Tom Mead.

Introduction is copyright © 2024 by Martin Edwards.

For information contact:

Crippen & Landru, Publishers
P. O. Box 532057
Cincinnati, OH 45253 USA

Web: www.crippenlandru.com
E-mail: Info@crippenlandru.com

ISBN (softcover): 978-0-936363-89-6
ISBN (clothbound): 978-0-936363-90-2

First Edition: November 2024

10 9 8 7 6 5 4 3 2 1

Contents

Introduction

The Indian Rope Trick and Other Violent Entertainments is a single-author story collection focusing exclusively on locked room mysteries and other puzzles concerning apparently impossible crimes. Excitingly, all the stories have been written in the past few years, demonstrating just how much life there is in this popular sub-branch of traditional detective fiction.

In recent years, the term "locked room mystery" has been much misunderstood. The phrase has come to be used widely—especially, it must be said, by publishers who (unlike Crippen & Landru) lack a deep understanding of classic forms of the mystery—to denote all kinds of stories in which there is, typically, a limited pool of suspects: such as the guests at a country house party or visitors to a small island, to take two very familiar examples. These stories are better described as "closed circle mysteries."

Tom Mead, whose stories are gathered in this book, shares with me the view that the locked room mystery, correctly understood, involves as a crucial and indispensable ingredient some degree of apparent *impossibility* about the crime. This element of the strange, the bizarre, the seemingly miraculous, has attracted writers—and readers—from the earliest days of detective fiction. Poe's "The Murders in the Rue Morgue"(1841), widely acknowledged as the first detective story, was a locked room mystery. Even before that, Sheridan Le Fanu's "A Passage in the Secret History of an Irish Countess"(1838) featured a murder in a locked room, while E.T.A. Hoffman's novella, *Mademoiselle de Scuderi* (1819) might also be claimed for this branch of fiction.

The delights of this type of story were celebrated by John Dickson Carr in Dr. Gideon Fell's famous "locked room lecture" in *The Three Coffins* (1935, aka *The Hollow Man*), a novel which is many readers' favourite example of the form. When Fell says, "I like my murders to be frequent, gory and grotesque. I like some vividness and colour flashing out of my plot," he is speaking for his creator, who remains the outstanding specialist in locked room mysteries. Fell acts as Carr's mouthpiece, arguing the merits of this kind of story with genuine passion, whilst acknowledging that some critics regard the locked room mystery as flawed because of the inherent implausibility of so many of the storylines.

Writers (and admirers) of traditional detective stories which rely for many of their effects on ingenuity of plot have long feared that the well of ideas would eventually run dry. As long ago as 1928, Dorothy L. Sayers suggested in a much-admired essay which introduced her first anthology of short stories that: "There certainly does seem a possibility that the detective-story will some time come to an end, simply because the public will have learned all the tricks." In another widely-quoted and influential passage, from his preface to *The Second Shot* (1930), Anthony Berkeley suggested that "The detective story is already in process of developing into the novel with a detective or a crime interest, holding its reader less by mathematical than by psychological ties." And in his generally authoritative history of the genre *Murder for Pleasure: The Life and Times of the Detective Story* (1941), Howard Haycraft was unequivocal in his depressing advice to would-be detective novelists: "Avoid the Locked Room puzzle. Only a genius can invest it with novelty or interest today."

Certainly, the post-war era was a thin time for locked room fans and continuing developments in technology and forensic science seemed to mean that much of the old trickery was seldom feasible. Carr remained an enthusiast for what he called 'the grandest game in the world' and continued to publish novels until the early 1970s, but by then the old magic had faded, and it is significant that much of his later work was set in the past. In 1963, Ellery Queen complained in *The Player on the Other Side* (a novel ghost-written by Theodore Sturgeon) that: "There's no wonderment left in the real world any longer." and although the prolific short story specialist Edward D. Hoch wrote a large number of impossible crime stories for *Ellery Queen's Mystery Magazine*, many of which have now been collected in books published by Crippen & Landru, he seemed to be swimming against the tide.

Crime writing is, however, as susceptible to the fluctuations of fashion as any other form of entertainment, and from 1997 onwards the popularity of David Renwick's TV series *Jonathan Creek*, in which a magician's assistant demonstrated a flair for solving impossible crimes, offered encouraging evidence that this form of mystery still had plenty of life in it. There were several reasons why the series enjoyed great success, but the key reason was the originality of Renwick's treatment of the plot material. Even if there are few absolutely new ideas, familiar concepts can, in skilled hands, be refreshed so effectively that, instead of yawning, we applaud. One enthusiastic young viewer of *Jonathan Creek*, incidentally, was Tom Mead.

In recent years, we've seen an increasing number of writers relishing the challenge of reinventing the locked room mystery for a contemporary fan base. Plenty of authors—myself included—dabble in the field with great pleasure from time to time but there are several writers who have established specialist reputations in the sub-genre of impossible crimes: examples include Japan's Soji Shimada, France's Paul Halter, and America's Gigi Pandian.

And now we must add to this list the name of Tom Mead. In a short space of time, he has carved a niche for himself as an accomplished exponent of the form, his admiration for Carr, to whose memory his first novel, *Death and the Conjuror*, was co-dedicated. That book was the first full-length case of Joseph Spector, who has subsequently returned in *The Murder Wheel* and *Cabaret Macabre*, having previously appeared in short stories, starting with "The Octagonal Room," first published in an anthology in 2018.

Spector appears in all but two of the stories in this collection; the exceptions are "Invisible Death" and "The Wager." Three stories— "The Three-Minute Miracle," "The Problem of the Velvet Mask," and "Lethal Symmetry," are previously unpublished.

In his essay "The Method and the Effect: Conjuring the Impossible Crime," included in *Writing the Murder*, edited by Dan Coxon and Richard V. Hirst (2024), Tom Mead argues that "impossible crime tales require particular meticulousness in their construction" and highlights the connection "between magic and impossible crime… Both involve the mystification of an audience by a lone performer… But where the two art forms differ is in the resolution. Unlike a stage illusionist's audience, readers of impossible crime tales are 'looking for deliverance from the incredible'."

He proceeds to make the bold and thought-provoking claim that writers of this kind of story "are more acutely aware of the psychology of their readers than in any other genre. Because the construction of a fair-play puzzle with a satisfying solution relies on an understanding of the gaps in our perception of the world, and the knowledge of how to exploit them." And he gives a fascinating explanation of his own method for constructing a locked room mystery: "I tend to construct two parallel timelines, consisting of *what the reader* thinks *happened* and *what actually happened*. Observing where these twin timelines diverge and converge is an interesting exercise in itself, and helps enormously with the creation of suspense, the planting of clues, and the development of characters. To my mind, it is also a reflection of those two key principles of prestidigitation: the method and the effect. One timeline reflects the method for the trick; the sleight-of-hand under the audience's nose. The other is the perceived effect: a seemingly impossible phenomenon which is in fact the result of deception."

Tom Mead is, like Carr, a storyteller who is committed to entertaining the reader. It will be interesting to see how his career develops from here; in the meantime, it's a pleasure to introduce these stories to a wider readership.

Martin Edwards
www.martinedwardsbooks.com

The Indian Rope Trick

The Indian Rope Trick is a perfect illusion. According to ancient lore—mostly oral histories transcribed in Sanskrit—the trick requires a rope suspended in air, hanging from nothing. The magician's assistant, usually a young boy, then climbs the rope to the top, where he promptly vanishes. The original version of the trick features a brutal *coup de grâce*, whereupon the vanished assistant's disembodied limbs tumble magically from the sky, to be collected by the magician and mystically reassembled.

Perhaps this description makes it easier to understand why the trick has yet to make its appearance on the London stage in unadulterated form. It must be performed outside, in beaming daylight. The assistant must vanish in mid-air. The limbs, too, are an impractical addition.

The man who called himself Joseph Spector had long ago given up professional magic, and ceased to concern himself with humbugs like the Indian Rope Trick. Since the Great War, he had found himself a much more lucrative sideline as a spirit medium, which was not all that different.

But just because he had given up professional magic did not mean he had lost his passion for a nicely executed trick. Now entering his eighth decade, his sleight of hand was as sharp as ever. He was an historian and all-round scholar of illusion. The shelves of his funny little house in Jubilee Court were lined with leather-bound volumes; histories and scientific analyses. Some people dream in colours and sounds; Joseph Spector dreamed in magic.

He was one of the few surviving founder members of the London Occult Practice Collective, a prestigious and selective society for illusionists who met monthly in the upstairs room of The Black Pig in Putney. When he overheard a conversation between the conjuror Ferdinand Le Sueur and the mesmerist Doctor Gupta, in which Le Sueur claimed to have finally devised the perfect mechanism for the Indian Rope Trick, it is perhaps easy to understand how Spector's attention was caught.

It was summer 1933, and Spector was at a luncheon given in honour of the London chapter of the Collective. For an afternoon (and sometimes long into the evening) that brightly lit function room was peopled by a colourful array of performers. The hat-rack hung with capes, cloaks, and top hats, the room itself cluttered with magic boxes, wavering funhouse mirrors, even a guillotine. Two doves nuzzled each other on the chandelier above, and a lone rabbit darted friskily across the wooden floor. At the long dining table sat thirty or forty magicians, chattering amiably, some demonstrating card tricks or practicing hypnotism with gold fob watches.

Spector sat at the head of the table, nearest the window. Sunlight beamed in onto the plate in front of him, on which sat a steaming pea-and-ham pie. Spector studied this disconcertedly, and lit himself a cigarillo. Nearest to him sat Ferdinand Le Sueur (real name, Roderick Raskin), a young upstart who had been getting on everybody's nerves for the past year or so. Le Sueur was in heated debate with Doctor Gupta (real name, Charles Wetherby).

"Nonsense," said Gupta, "it can't be done."

"Of course it can!" protested Le Sueur. "This is the twentieth century, chum."

"The closest anyone ever came was Devant. No one will ever better his effort."

Le Sueur leaned back in his seat, smugly satisfied. "Well. Perhaps you'd like to bet."

At this point, looking for any distraction from his meagre repast, Spector joined in. "A bet?" he said. "What's at stake?"

"Professional credibility," said Le Sueur.

"Le Sueur has a foolish idea about the Indian Rope Trick. He claims he's come up with a perfect mechanism for working the trick. Something no one has ever thought of before."

"Well," said Spector, exhaling smoke in the faces of the two rivals. "I'm happy to serve as arbitrator."

*

And so the bet was made. It was essentially a contest between the two magicians, to see whose interpretation of that hoary old illusion was the most convincing. The following Saturday, Spector took a cab out to the Richmond Theatre, the use of which Dr. Gupta had secured for his part in the bet. Spector entered the auditorium and found the place eerily deserted, save for two figures onstage. Gupta himself, and Le Sueur. They seemed to be conversing cordially, but at the sight of Spector both men stood bolt upright like children caught misbehaving.

"Our esteemed judge," said Le Sueur, springing from the stage and shaking him by the hand.

"Good morning, boys. Where shall I sit?"

"Front row centre," said Gupta from the stage. "Where else would be fitting for the maestro?"

The stage was bare, save for a black back-cloth. With a flourish, Gupta introduced Ada. Her role as assistant had been cordially agreed upon by both parties. She was discreet and professional. She strode out from the wings and Spector was surprised to see she wore her conventional skimpy assistant's costume. These fellows were evidently taking their bet very seriously.

She took a little bow and then produced a coil of rope, which she laid in the centre of the stage.

Gupta began to work his magic, flourishing his hands. Then, slowly the rope began to rise. Eventually it stood rigid, reaching up into the rafters. At this, Spector and Le Sueur burst into spontaneous applause.

Gupta raised a hand to silence them. "But that is not all," he said. He turned to Ada. "Now: climb!"

And climb she did. Wrapping her legs around the rope, she began to shin her way up to the top. She paused just below the stage's proscenium arch and turned a blinding smile on the audience of two.

Gupta was grinning. "And now…"

He gave a flourish and a flap of his cape. There was a flash of light and a plume of smoke. Then Ada was gone.

Spector and Le Sueur stood. Their applause and cheers echoed high in the empty theatre. Gupta stepped forward, clicked his fingers, and the rigid rope swiftly collapsed. "And now, if you please…" he said, directing their attention to the rear of the auditorium. The two men turned, and there stood Ada, grinning.

"Now you have seen how it should be done," said Gupta.

"*Au contraire*," Le Sueur cut in. "Now you have seen *how it has always been done*. If you will permit me, I will show you how it *should* be done."

"Now?" said Spector.

"No," Le Sueur chuckled. "My colleague has been permitted to choose the site for his demonstration. Will you grant me the same courtesy?"

"Yes, yes," said Gupta, impatiently leaping off the stage to confront them. "But where did you have in mind? The Garrick? The Pomegranate?"

"I shall provide you with the address in due course. I will perform the Indian Rope Trick for you exactly a week from today. And what's more, I shall do it *outdoors*."

*

And so, a week after Gupta's competent yet unimpressive demonstration of the trick, Spector found himself in the back of another cab, being ferried to an altogether different location.

At his home in Jubilee Court, he had received that morning a telegram from Ferdinand Le Sueur. It contained an address he did not recognise, but as he sat in the back of the cab he saw that their destination was well out of London.

Eventually, they reached a small cottage set in pleasant green gardens. It was in a patch of isolated countryside perhaps ten miles out of London.

"Is this the place?" said Spector.

"It's what it says here," said the cabbie, wafting the telegram.

As Spector climbed out of the car, he was greeted by Doctor Gupta. "Glad you made it, Spector! Funny sort of place, isn't it?"

It was indeed. A most unassuming little cottage. When he got the chance to speak with Le Sueur he would ask him how he had come to choose it.

Gupta led him through to a sitting room at the rear of the property. It was plushly furnished, with wide French windows that opened out onto a wooden veranda. In the centre of the sitting room, close to the fireplace, Le Sueur was making himself ready.

"Mr. Spector! And right on time." He produced from his inside pocket his trademark collapsible top hat, which he assembled with a flourish before placing at a dandyish angle on his full mane of black hair. "There are two seats on the veranda. If you would care to step outside, we are now ready for the Indian Rope Trick."

*

The midsummer sun beamed, with only a wisp of white cloud to mar that perfect sky. Once they were settled in their seats on the veranda, Le Sueur emerged from the house. He passed round a coil of rope. Each man examined it in turn, before Spector returned it with a good-natured nod. Rope in hand, Le Sueur stepped onto the lawn. He marched out a few paces, so that he was more or less in the centre of that little garden. Then, in a swift underarm motion, he threw the rope. The guests watched it unfurl in mid-air, suspending itself upright and taut from the ground up, stout as a maypole. Cue polite applause from the assembled company.

Ada the assistant stepped onto the grass, clad in her traditional scanty garb. The sequins gleamed in the sunlight. She wrapped her legs around the rope and began to climb. Le Sueur stood grinning with childlike pride as she neared the top of the rope; that abyss in the empty air. Then he clicked his fingers and, at once, the rope burst into flame.

Even Spector was startled by the sudden flare. The rope immediately dropped like a corpse. Reduced to a small heap of ash on the grass. Ada the glamourous assistant was nowhere in sight. Le Sueur stood expectantly, his arms behind his back. Each man now stood from his seat and burst into rapturous applause. Spector was the loudest of the pair.

Le Sueur raised his hands for silence. "Gentlemen, forgive me but you look a little stunned. Could it be that you doubted your old friend Le Sueur's abilities? Perhaps a refreshing drink will calm your jangled nerves."

A maid entered with a silver tray of lemonade. It was only when each man had helped himself to a glass that the maid cast aside the tray like a discus and removed her cap to reveal that she was none other than the vanished Ada, back in the realm of the living again. She grinned and curtsied to more uproarious applause.

"Le Sueur, I take back everything I said," gushed Doctor Gupta. "It's a resounding triumph."

Le Sueur inclined his head in false modesty. "You're too kind. And what did you make of it, Spector? You are after all our arbiter. How does my effort compare?"

"I… I don't know what to say. It's a noble effort. Very clever indeed."

"Did you work out how it was done?"

Spector sipped his lemonade. "I'm afraid it's too much for my feeble old brain."

Gupta seized Le Sueur's hand and pumped it furiously. "Congratulations, my friend. Congratulations indeed."

The unlikely quartet headed indoors, and Ada poured for them all stronger drinks.

"Well," said Le Sueur, "a toast to the Indian Rope Trick."

They clinked their glasses.

"A toast to you, Le Sueur," said Gupta. "You pulled it off when I didn't think it could be done."

They clinked glasses again.

"Yes, it's a neat little trick, isn't it? But let's not forget Ada's part in all this."

Ada, slightly embarrassed at being singled out for praise, gave a curtsey.

"You're quiet, Spector. Don't you approve?"

"On the contrary," said Spector. "I'm rather astonished."

"Here's to that," said Le Sueur, and downed his drink.

The perfect sky darkened as the afternoon wore on. Spector feared they might be in for that summer storm after all.

It began to rain at around three o' clock.

"Honestly, Le Sueur, why did you have to pick a cottage out in the middle of nowhere?" Gupta protested jovially.

"Fear not," said Le Sueur, "there's plenty of room for you all in my car. We have a lovely canopy to keep the rain off."

Now all vaguely drunk, they drank a final toast to the canopy and began to get ready to leave. "Of course," Le Sueur said absently, "we could always spend the night here. I've rented the place for the weekend."

This idea was met with little response, so he set about packing up his trunk of paraphernalia.

Spector, seated on the sofa, saw Ada approach and whisper to him, "I can't go like this. I need to get changed."

"You can use one of the bedrooms upstairs," Le Sueur murmured, grappling with the padlock on the trunk.

"No," said Ada, slightly worried, "my clothes are in the car."

Le Sueur stood upright and sighed. "Very well. Behold, gentlemen. Chivalry is not dead."

The conjuror looked out the window and, with a look of disdain, put on his top hat. Then he went out into the hall. His three guests heard the front door open, and the pounding rain as Le Sueur jogged out to his waiting car. They waited a moment, looking at each other with slight awkwardness.

"I don't suppose," began Gupta, "you'd care to share the secret, Ada?"

Ada, laughing, shook her head. "More than my life's worth," she said. "Besides, I think you'd find it quite disappointing."

"Oh, I've no doubt. But I should still like to know."

They waited a few minutes more—perhaps two or three—and Spector lit a cigarillo. "Would anyone care to join me?" he offered.

The others declined. "I think I'll see where Ferdinand has got to," said Ada. She stood and ambled out into the hall. Spector watched Gupta, who was watching her go.

It was perhaps five seconds later that they heard her scream.

The rain had stopped by now. Ada stood in the muddy driveway beside Le Sueur's car, her hands over her mouth, speechless with horror. At her feet, face down in the dirt, lay Ferdinand Le Sueur.

Things happened very quickly after that.

Ada was swiftly dispatched to telephone for the police. Gupta and Joseph Spector stood over the fragile and pitiful corpse of the magician. He was face-down in the mud. Beside him, pathetically, his top hat lolled.

After a moment's thought, Spector reached into the back of Le Sueur's car—beneath the rain-drenched canopy—and retrieved the bundle of Ada's clothes. He traipsed back into the house and found Ada using the telephone in the hall. He handed her the clothes.

"I'm waiting for a connection," she explained.

"Ask for Inspector Flint," Spector advised.

Flint arrived within the hour, accompanied by his subordinate Jerome Hook and a retinue of uniformed officers. A perimeter was quickly established around the grounds of the cottage.

Spector and Flint's acquaintance was long-standing: each man bore a grudging respect for the other. So Flint, bemused and truculent beneath his damp bowler hat, drew the elderly illusionist aside.

"What the hell's this all about, Spector?"

Spector did not meet his eye. "I am not ashamed to admit, Flint, that I haven't a clue."

Flint sighed. "Cause of death: strangulation. Nasty, too—neck completely snapped. Marks on the throat indicate a length of rope, average thickness."

"But that's not all," said Spector.

"No," said Flint, massaging his forehead, "it's not. This dead magician—Roderick Raskin or Ferdinand Le Sueur or whatever—he stepped out of this cottage for, what, five minutes? And somebody strangled him quickly and brutally. You three were in each other's company the entire time, so it couldn't have been any of you… but then, it couldn't have been *anyone*, could it?"

Spector nodded with a half-smile. "So you noticed."

"Oh, I noticed. The entire driveway is caked with mud. But apart from the three of you, there's only one other set of footprints. Le Sueur's. The three of you dashed out to examine the body after he was dead, so that explains that. But *somebody* strangled him. And whoever it was, how did they get away without leaving behind them a single footprint?"

The corpse was cordoned off, but the fact was that all the footprints in the mud were accounted for: they were made by Le Sueur when he walked out to the car, then by Gupta, Ada, and Spector when they came out and examined the corpse. One set of prints each.

Optimistically, Flint ordered Le Sueur's car to be towed away and examined in case a killer had stowed himself in there somehow.

But the car was empty now, and investigators were still no closer to explaining how the killer had vanished without leaving a trace.

Ada and Doctor Gupta were to be taken in for questioning, but Flint offered to drive Spector back into London himself. As he drove, they talked.

"So what's this business all about?" demanded Flint.

"Good question, Flint. It started as a bet about the Indian Rope Trick. But now it seems to have turned into something else altogether."

And he explained the circumstances: how that curious quartet had come to be present at the cottage that day.

"So Gupta showed you his version of the trick last week?"

"Yes. At the Richmond Theatre. It was quite arbitrary: the rope itself was hollow. One of Gupta's confederates in a hatch beneath the stage fed a steel rod up through the rope so that it appeared to grow rigid. As Ada climbed, a black front-cloth was lowered to blend in with the identical back-cloth. Then, when Ada reached the appropriate height, Gupta set off the squibs, creating a momentary distraction for Ada to climb up into the rafters, concealed behind the invisible front-cloth. That's the textbook version of the Indian Rope Trick. It's the version that has been performed for years."

"But Le Sueur's version was different?"

"Not only different—revolutionary. He managed to perform the trick out of doors, which is something no Western illusionist has ever accomplished."

"So how was it done?"

"That's just it. *I don't know*. And I can't help but feel that if I can work out how the trick was done, I can work out how he was killed. Of course, the location is significant. Superintendent, what do you know about the cottage?"

"Only that it was rented for the weekend in the name of Roderick Raskin."

"No trick doors or mechanisms?"

"Letting agents didn't know of any."

They were back in London within the hour. Flint deposited Spector on the kerb outside his ramshackle little house in Jubilee Court and watched the old man mount the steps with a sullen slope in his shoulders and disappear inside.

*

Spector passed a restless night in his study. Surrounded by candles, he pored over his notebook, mapping out the trick from beginning to end.

First, Le Sueur stepped out onto the lawn, rope in hand.

There was a little flourish with the collapsible cane and hat... a clue there, certainly.

Then the rope, growing rigid.

The girl climbed...

But where did she go?

Of course, it couldn't be coincidence that the audience was carefully positioned on a veranda, of all places. And yes, it *would* have been possible for Ada to spring from the summit of the rope to the roof over their heads. But she couldn't have done it unseen...

Clotilde, Spector's housemaid, tapped anxiously on the study door.

Spector sat upright. He glanced at the clock: close to six in the morning. He must have dozed off. "Come in, Clotilde."

She entered with a cup of tea on a silver tray. He thanked her and she turned to go.

"One moment," he said. "Bring me the telephone, will you? I need to place a call to George Flint."

Flint agreed to meet him at The Black Pig that afternoon. The rain seemed to have exerted a purgative effect on the city. The steamy, putrid heat of the summer had been quenched. Now, the sky was bright and fresh. The clouds were white and benign.

Spector got to the pub and found Flint waiting for him. They went inside and Spector ordered drinks. He then looked hopefully at Flint, who, with a sigh, paid for them.

They found a little table in the snug. "So this is where the bet was made?" said Flint.

"Upstairs," said Spector. "The Collective has its luncheons up there."

"So? Why did you want to meet me? Have you worked out what happened?"

"I'm close. Very close. But I wanted to warn you: do not let Ada and Doctor Gupta out of your sight. I can tell you for certain that they were responsible for this."

"But how? From what you say they were the only two who *couldn't* have done it. They were with you when Le Sueur was strangled. Ada only left the room for five seconds before you followed her out."

"I know that," said Spector, shaking his head. "But I also know that we are dealing with several layers of illusion. I think it all comes down to how the Indian Rope Trick was performed."

"Well? How was it done?"

"The rope itself is simple enough. The clue came from Le Sueur's collapsible top hat. The rope was not a "rope" at all—it was a metal roller chain, rather like a bicycle chain. Except of course, this would be specially reinforced to take the weight of a fully-grown woman. Like the collapsible hat, the interlocking segments of the chain could click together in one swift motion, creating a rigid pole. Le Sueur must have prepared the terrain somehow, perhaps digging a small hole into which the pole could be inserted, anchoring it so it would not topple over. It could have been coated with some flammable substance which he triggered at the appropriate moment, reducing the rope to a blackened mass."

"You think the rope was used to kill him somehow? Remotely, when he was out of sight?"

Spector scowled and chewed his lip. "Possibly," he conceded.

Flint slapped the table with his palm. "Come on, Spector! Time is against me here! You say Gupta and Ada killed him—perfect. But if you can't tell me *how* the thing was done, then they are going to get away with it."

"I need to think. I just need to think...."

Spector produced a silver cigarette case from his pocket. From it, he removed a single cigarillo, which he slipped between his lips and lit with a long match. Leaning back in his seat, he watched the smoke plume out in front of him. He glanced toward the window, at the rolling white clouds. Then he began to chuckle.

"What is it?" said Flint.

"We need to go back to the cottage. And we need to bring Ada and Doctor Gupta with us."

*

The atmosphere in the cottage was much less convivial the second time around. The rooms seemed small and dark. Black thunderclouds converged overhead, as though nature itself sensed the approaching end.

Ada and Doctor Gupta (who, denuded of his "Indian" accoutrements was plain old Charles Wetherby) exchanged a few glances as Superintendent Flint led them into the lounge. Joseph Spector was waiting for them.

"Thank you for coming," Spector said.

"We didn't have much choice," said Wetherby.

"No," chuckled Spector, "I suppose not. I just wanted to congratulate you—*both* of you—on two near-perfect illusions. But I'll not beat around the bush, I know you're busy people. First, let's take the Indian Rope Trick.

"This trick was not so different from your own, Wetherby. But as an illusion it depended not on Le Sueur's prowess, but on *yours*, Ada. Because, and correct me if I'm wrong, won't you, *you* are the one who devised it."

This caused the briefest stir between the two accused. Spector was quick to elucidate. "Your own interpretation of the Indian Rope Trick, Wetherby, was sadly lacklustre. It was obvious from the first that the rope was induced to tumescence by a magnet in your signet ring, until it reached sufficient height that it could be coaxed to rigidity by a steel pole inserted from below the stage. Then Ada simply shimmied up and out of sight, in front of the black back-cloth, but *behind* an invisible black curtain, which was lowered at an opportune moment."

"Was it really that obvious?" said the erstwhile Dr. Gupta.

Spector smiled. "But whereas in your case the vanished Ada was concealed between two curtains of identical shade, in Le Sueur's interpretation, the shield was somewhat less tangible.

"Le Sueur invited us out onto the veranda. But I remember finding it a little odd that he stayed behind a moment. It was only when I examined the fireplace that I realised the reason why. He had dropped a pellet of slow-releasing smoke into the grate. This would gradually emerge from the nub-like chimney, creating a plume of white in the sky above the cottage. In the glare of the midday sun, we would simply mistake it for distant cloud. You forget that, because of our careful positioning on the veranda, we could see the centre of the lawn, but we could not see directly above our heads. This was essential. Once the whiteness of the smoke had blended sufficiently with the miasma of cloud that was already insinuating its way in front of the sun, Ada, perched atop the rope, could use her gymnast's prowess to spring onto the roof of the veranda. This took place when we were momentarily distracted by Le Sueur's somewhat garish, yet effective, misdirection: the burning rope.

"So you see, the conditions were essential. The sunlight, the south-facing veranda, the nub-like chimney. Even the breeze, to ensure the smoke would disperse appropriately above us. Correct me if I am wrong, Ada?"

Ada did not say a word.

"In the moment of misdirection, Ada leapt from the rope to the roof above our heads, shielded by the white smoke which appeared to us to be a fug of distant cloud. Her bare feet landed softly on the wood. She could then swiftly scramble through the attic window, perform a quick costume change, and descend just in time to make her reappearance as the maid. And now we come to the murder itself. I can tell you how it was done, but I cannot say *why*. That is a matter for your own consciences. All I know is that between you you conspired to murder Roderick Raskin, and to place me as a witness to your innocence. When the truth is you were the only ones who *could* have been responsible."

Wetherby collapsed on the sofa beside Spector. He stared glumly at the floor, chewing his bottom lip.

"I knew it had to be the both of you, in collusion. But what reason could you have had to dispatch poor Roderick Raskin? I think if we dig deep enough we will find the roots are monetary. Raskin, like all magicians, was a swindler. I presume that you two shared a grievance which you sought to amend. The motive, to be frank, is immaterial. The question was not why but *how*. For I knew it could only have been the two of you, working in tandem, with myself as your unwilling dupe."

Inspector Flint scoffed. But he had learned not to interrupt Spector mid-performance.

"The Indian Rope Trick, ironically enough, was an elaborate misdirection. The broken neck was enough to convince us that he was strangled. But I think a post mortem examination will indicate an altogether different cause of death.

"You recall I mentioned Raskin's collapsible top hat? Well, when I retrieved said hat from the ground beside his corpse, I gave it a little tap with my hand and to my immense surprise it failed to yield. The collapsible hat had been switched for an ordinary top hat. What could be the reason for that? Perhaps there was something incriminating tucked in the dead man's hat? We may never know, for I do not doubt that the collapsible one has now been destroyed. But it gives us the clue that we need. An undetectable means of murder, concealed in a magician's hat—perhaps a pinprick of poison?

"Bearing in mind the alacrity with which said poison would need to work, I should say Antiaris Toxicaria is the most likely culprit. It is typically introduced *through the skin*, and has been used historically to coat the arrowheads of Malaysian and Burmese warlords. Perhaps a hat-pin coated with the stuff somehow insinuated its way through the brim of Le Sueur's top hat, so the point of it scraped his skull when he put the hat on to venture out in the rain? An examination of the dead man's scalp will tell us one way or the other.

"It is an immensely fast-acting poison, attacking the central nervous system and causing immediate paralysis and cardiac arrest. As such, it would have caused Le Sueur to keel over face first into the mud within a matter of seconds. But he was not necessarily dead. Rather, he would have had the *appearance* of death when we dashed out to examine him.

"Let us for now assume that you, Wetherby, switched the hats at some point during the afternoon when we sat inside the cottage. Then, when the rains came and Raskin went outside, he put on the macabre death-cap, fatally introducing the poison into his bloodstream through his scalp. He would have been conscious of the merest twinge. He then went outside into the rain and the mud, where he promptly collapsed and died."

"But," Flint cut in, "what about the broken neck?"

"That was the work of moments. All it would take is a noose fashioned from the same material as the trick rope: an interlocking roller chain. During a moment when my attention was distracted—perhaps talking to Ada—Wetherby could place the rope-chain over the dead man's head, snap the neck and then retract the rope instantly. This would automatically send us in the wrong direction when attempting to pinpoint a cause of death."

There was little more to say. Joseph Spector sat quietly as Ada and Charles Wetherby were escorted wordlessly away. The sky above the cottage was bright, but a shadow hung over the sallow faces of those two murderers. The looped serpentine snare of a noose.

The Octagonal Room

"Let us calculate the motion of bodies, but also consult the plans of the Intelligence that makes them move."
—Pierre Louis Maupertuis, *Accord de différentes loix de la nature qui avoient jusqu'ici paru incompatibles* (1744)

I

But why *this* house?

Simon Eldridge was an American who came to England in middle age. His new home nestled in a clutch of woodland beside the River Dee: in the eighteenth century it had served as a watermill, but now, in 1931, it was disused and dilapidated.

Rumours about the place have circulated for over a century. Strange meetings and robed figures, bonfires blazing in unoccupied rooms, evil chants echoing through the trees. The mill seems cursed. No villagers venture there.

In the early 1850s, the surrounding land was bought by a merchant banker from London. "Most disappointing," was the banker's verdict to the villagers. "There seems to be nothing untoward about the place. The only feature of *mild* interest to me is the octagonal room."

Off the blank looks of his audience, he grew uneasy. "From a purely architectural perspective," he felt obliged to qualify.

"But sir," said the publican, "*what* octagonal room?"

The original architectural plans were duly consulted. And true enough, on those sketches there was no sign of an octagonal room. But forces had been at work, constructing an eight-sided turret on the north face of the mill. And at the top of the turret, a room: a fresh, albeit purposeless room, with eight walls and seven windows. So where did it come from?

An empty upstairs room, eight-sided, whose origins were shrouded in mystery. For those who know his writing, Simon Eldridge's name is synonymous with satanic rites and vengeful spirits. But what few know (and what I had the misfortune to discover) is that his fevered imagination was not "imagination" at all. He really believed all the strange fantasies he conjured in his fiction. And that is why he came to occupy the house known as the Black Mill.

II

He moved in during a rainstorm in April 1931. As the nearest neighbour, I walked out to the Mill to introduce myself. Simon himself came to the door, and I was surprised at how affable he seemed in person. He was inordinately tall; gaunt would be the word, with long arms swinging at his sides.

"How do you do?" he said with a gentle smile, offering his hand. I shook it. The skin had a warm, soft texture. He led me into the vastness of the Mill. The walls were hung with pictures and papered gaily. By daylight the horrors were not apparent to the naked eye.

"Come in," he said, ushering me through to the salon. He pushed open a wooden door and two black cats streaked out between his feet.

"Goddamn these cats!" yelled a female voice.

"My wife, Samantha," Simon explained. She was a thin-lipped woman with her hair scraped into a painful-looking bun.

When she saw me, she gave a broad, unconvincing smile. "Oh! Company!"

"This is our new neighbour, dear," said Simon.

"How are you settling in?" I asked.

"Marvellously well," said Simon, "this place is remarkable."

"Isn't it just," said Samantha, without emphasis.

Simon Eldridge was a soft-spoken man who sat in a wingback chair as we talked. One of his cats nestled in his lap. Samantha, however, was a gregarious hostess, who worked a little too hard at being charming. She perched on the edge of the sofa, leaning towards me in a faintly predatory manner. Simon merely smiled through it all.

Eventually, conversation turned to the Mill itself.

"We've only been here a few days, but I can tell you now what's wrong with the place," Samantha explained. "There's something here and it's…"

"Malevolent," Simon supplied.

Samantha sipped a cup of hot, strong tea, and I noticed a slight tremor in her hand.

"Have you seen anything?" I said.

"It's that room," she said hoarsely.

"You mean the octagonal room?"

"Yes! There's something up there."

"But of course there's something up there," said Simon. "That is why I bought this place."

"I hate it. Explain, please Simon, exactly what you have got planned for that room?"

"Ah!" beamed the author. "Well, I'm going to find out the truth. Why it was built, who built it, and what it's for."

"Well," I said, "I'm intrigued. If anyone's going to find the truth, I'm sure it'll be you."

Samantha turned on me. "This is supposed to be a *home*," she spat, "not a goddamned history project."

Simon went on: "We have two gentleman coming to stay with us. One is a research student called McIlwaine. The other is a real-life occultist and scholar. He wrote an excellent monograph on the Pittenweem witches. His name is Joseph Spector. He's coming down next week. We'll just see what they make of the place, shall we?"

III

The following Monday I had my first encounter with Mr. Spector. I was walking along the path beside the house when I spotted a ghostly old man in a black overcoat (with fur collar) and a homburg hat. He studied the Black Mill from afar.

"Good afternoon!" I called.

He turned to me, his face creasing in a smile. "Good afternoon, sir," he said, and his voice was disarmingly soft. "You are a local, I take it?"

"I am, I live in a house just along the trail there."

"My name is Joseph Spector," he said.

"Ah, the occultist! Mr. Eldridge has told me about you. He said he had invited you to look at the fabled octagonal room."

Spector's face had the appearance and texture of a charcoal drawing: ghost-white skin, etched with shadows and creases. Two pale blue eyes studied me as I spoke. "Yes. I've heard much about it but never seen it with my own eyes. Are you going up to the Mill?"

"That's right—I was going to pay a visit to Mr. Eldridge."

"Wonderful. I'll walk with you then, if I may." We strolled up to the Mill.

"Looks like someone has beat us to it," said Spector.

A figure stood at the front door, rapping authoritatively on the wood. When this figure turned to look at us I saw that it was a young man, studiously clad in a tweed blazer. He was perhaps twenty-eight, very tall but inclining to a paunch. He had a round, babyish face and a mop of Byronic hair. "Hallo there!" he bellowed. "There doesn't seem to be anybody home. How do you do, I'm Benjamin McIlwaine."

"The research student! Yes, Simon mentioned that you would be here. So you're preparing a piece on the octagonal room?"

"It's actually a wider piece of work encompassing witchcraft and folklore in the region. But of course, the octagonal room is one of the few genuinely unsolved mysteries I've come across…"

"Well, hullo there!" called Simon. We three turned and spotted him coming around the side of the house. In each hand he held a bottle of wine. "Forgive me, I was just round in the pavilion. Samantha's down by the river. Sunning herself no doubt."

"Pavilion?" I said. This was the first I heard of such a place.

"Yes, it's really a glorified out-building on the south side of the house. It's where we keep the wine."

Introductions were made and we meandered around to the far side of the Mill. The river babbled gently and Samantha Eldridge sat in a sun-lounger, reading a book. She did not look up to greet us. We sat at a table in the centre of the lawn and Simon Eldridge cracked open the first bottle of wine.

"A wine annexe," I said, "how decadent!"

Simon chuckled. "Well, it was either that or let the place fall into rack and ruin." He pointed, and I saw, concealed between two trees, the pavilion. It was fashioned from squat, grey bricks. It lurked with ominous inconsequentiality between the branches.

We sat in the sun and drank and chatted. Benjamin McIlwaine told us of the various ghost stories and folk tales which were the central focus of his study. Joseph Spector was quiet for the first part of the discussion, only springing to life when the octagonal room entered the conversation.

"It's fascinated me for years," he said. "A room apparently without a purpose. Why was it built? Who built it?"

"I think the moment has arrived," said Simon, flicking his wineglass with his fingernail, "for us to pay a visit to the octagonal room."

I, for one, was eager—in all my years I had never dared go there. But there is a certain frame of mind one adopts in agreeable company on a sunny spring day. I felt emboldened.

"Are you coming, Samantha?" said Simon.

"Thank you, no," said Samantha, not looking up from her book. "I've been in that room plenty."

Simon Eldridge led his three guests into the house and up the stairs. "This way," he said. As we drew near to the door, I confess to a tingle of fear.

Simon threw open the door and one by one we climbed the spiral staircase. The room at the top was large, spacious and light. The floorboards creaked underfoot, but otherwise the place was still and silent. The ceiling was plastered white. There were no panes of glass in the windows, but each was spliced by vertical iron bars. These created a patchwork of shadows across the bare wooden floor. There was no furniture in the octagonal room. Just the floor, the walls, and those seven barred windows.

I had hoped that when I stepped into the room that I would *feel* something. But I felt nothing. Spector and McIlwaine were silent. Simon surveyed our reactions with quiet amusement. After a moment, he spoke. "It has quite a feel to it, doesn't it?"

"Indeed it does," said the studious Mr. McIlwaine. Spector did not speak.

On leaving the octagonal room, we returned to the garden. Samantha was still reading. The sun shone and the river babbled. But now I realised something had changed; for the first time it dawned on me that the spectre of death hung over the Black Mill.

IV

Two weeks later, Spector and McIlwaine had more or less taken up residence at the Black Mill. I was walking to pay them a visit one morning, and as I strolled up the driveway my eye was caught by a moving silhouette in the trees. I stopped to look. I picked out the shadowy outline of a pair of legs dangling between the branches of a nearby oak tree. My first thought was a macabre one: I pictured a hanged man, swinging in the breeze, his dead feet knocking against the trunk. But as I approached, I saw that the figure in the tree was very much alive.

It was a boy, sitting on a branch. As I drew nearer, he dropped down, landing with a thump on the ground in front of me. He looked at me with a sullen, downturned chin and creased brow. He must have been around fifteen. Threaded around his hands was an elaborate cat's cradle. "String," he said.

"I beg your pardon?"

"He wants you to pull the string," said a man's voice. I turned. It was Carl, the gardener. Carl was a youthful and handsome fellow with curly hair and sun-baked skin. "You'll have to forgive him, he's not all there. He's my little brother. His name's Gordon."

"Hello, Gordon," I said.

"String!" cried the boy. I took the string which hung taut between his fingers, and plucked it gently. With this single gesture the whole intricate construction came apart as one; the single thread unfurled.

"Well done, Gordon," I said, "that's very clever."

"I know," said Gordon, still grinning. He was a thin and sad-looking boy. In his half-lidded eyes there gleamed a spark of unruly intelligence, as though his brain were too large for his brittle frame.

"He likes hanging about the Black Mill," Carl explained. "He likes to hear the scary stories."

"Witches live here," said Gordon, "they live in the octagonal room."

"Yes," I said, "so they say."

"It's true," asserted Gordon, "I've seen them."

"And what did they look like? Were they scary?"

Now the boy was smirking. "I wasn't scared," he said. "Carl's scared, but I'm not."

"That's enough," Carl said.

"He double-locks his door every night. Keeps a gun by his bed. Says he wouldn't work here if he didn't have to, but he's the only gardener who'll come within miles of this place...."

"*Enough*," snapped Carl. "I'm sorry about all this, mister. He's not normally this talkative."

"That's all right," I said. "But I must be going now. It's been good to meet you, Gordon."

Gordon wasn't listening. He whirled on his heel and ran full pelt toward the house. Carl gave an apologetic shrug.

When I got to the house myself, nobody answered the door. I waited a few minutes, then strolled around the side. Finding the rear garden deserted, too, my eye was caught by the outline of the pavilion.

Drawing nearer, I saw two people moving between the trees. My first instinct, I'm sorry to say, was fear. But this sensation soon gave way to an ungentlemanly curiosity when I saw who these people were, and what they were doing.

It was Samantha, of course. The man with her, though... I could not see his face. But I knew instantly it was not Simon Eldridge. When he spoke, my suspicions were confirmed: it was the student, Benjamin McIlwaine.

"I was lying awake last night," said McIlwaine in a low voice, "and I was thinking about the two of you. And I hit on the perfect solution to our problem."

"Mm, and what was that?"

"We could kill him."

Samantha looked at him a moment, and there was a fearful emptiness in her eyes. Then she laughed. "Benjy, you're a card."

"I'm serious. I've hit on the perfect method to use."

"But Benjy, why would we need to kill him? If we wait long enough the *house* will do it for us!" And they both laughed and kissed each other.

I looked around me. The place was deserted. Without a sound, I slipped away.

V

A week later Simon invited me for drinks. Joseph Spector was still very much in evidence—he had left ancient, dusty books scattered about the place, as well as assorted oddments from his occultist trade: shrunken heads, clattering tiger-tooth chains, tarot cards. But he did not surface from his work, and remained in the study while Simon escorted me out to the table on the lawn.

"And where is Mr. McIlwaine?" I inquired.

"Not sure," said Simon, not quite meeting my eye. "He'll be around somewhere."

And he was. No sooner had we taken our seats than Benjamin McIlwaine wandered into view from behind the pavilion. But he was not alone. He held hands with Samantha Eldridge. They seemed oblivious to us, and before I could call out, McIlwaine had leaned over and planted a kiss on Simon's wife. It was an angry kiss. When it was over, they continued toward the house.

Only at the last moment did Samantha register our presence. "We shan't be in for dinner," she called out. McIlwaine, head bowed like a naughty schoolboy, did not say a word.

Simon watched them go. "No," he said quietly, "I don't imagine you shall." There was a look on his face then which terrified me. It was not malice; nothing so tangible. It was a quiet and insidious madness.

VI

That night, I was woken from a fireside nap by an insistent rapping at my door. Stumbling out into the hallway of my cottage, I saw a dark silhouetted figure through the glass. "Who's there?" I called.

"Joseph Spector," came the soft-voiced answer.

"I'm sorry to trouble you at home," he began, as I led him through to the lounge. "It concerns Simon Eldridge," he commenced. "I understand you and he are friends."

"I like to think so. I was one of the first acquaintances he made when he got to England."

"Indeed. I wonder, then, if *you* have perceived a sudden deterioration in his mental state?"

"His mental state?"

Spector steeled himself. "Mr. Eldridge's interest in the octagonal room is… not healthy. I think his mind is deteriorating."

I considered this. "You might be onto something there." And I told him the whole story—Samantha's infidelity with McIlwaine, the 'plot' I'd overheard, and the terrifying look in Simon's eye.

When I was finished, Spector sat back in his chair. "This is troubling," he said. "Samantha tells me he is spending his nights in the octagonal room. That he barely sleeps, but when he does, it is only within the confines of the octagonal room, with the door closed and locked."

"What is he *doing* in there?"

"Writing. He sits cross-legged on the bare boards, the papers splayed out in front of him. I hear him pacing at night. Sometimes he seems to speak with someone."

"Who?"

Spector looked at me strangely. "With each day he seems more obsessed. I'm afraid soon he won't leave the octagonal room at all. I believe it may all end very badly. Come to the Mill tomorrow. We have to act soon."

VII

I headed out to the Black Mill the following lunchtime.

It was a day choked by muggy, languid afternoon heat. I passed the gardener, Carl, who was trimming the topiaries. "Excuse me," I said, "where is Mr. Eldridge?"

"Not here," said the gardener. "The old man took him into the village."

"Spector took Simon into the village? How did he manage that?"

Carl shrugged. "Magic, I suppose. The missus is round back."

I pressed on, marching around to the rear garden. Benjamin McIlwaine had draped himself awkwardly over the sun-lounger and looked to be snoozing. But as I approached, one beady eye snapped open. "If you're looking for Simon he should be back soon."

"The gardener tells me Spector managed to spirit him away from the octagonal room."

"That's right. Taken him into the village to look at some etchings or something."

I shuffled my feet. "And what about Mrs. Eldridge?"

"In the house somewhere. I'm not sure."

I paused. "Benjamin... I think what you're doing is dangerous."

He sat up and looked at me. "What's that supposed to mean?"

At that moment Spector and Simon Eldridge returned. Simon came towards us with a great beaming grin on his face. "Wonderful news! My ingenious friend Spector may just have cracked the mystery of the octagonal room. My mistake was focusing on the *walls* when what really matters is the *ceiling*... But I have to get back up to the room. I'm so close...." With that he marched back toward the house.

Spector looked worried. "I thought if I got him out of the room I might be able to convince him somehow. But I failed." He, too, marched back toward the building.

I followed him into the Mill via the newly-installed French windows, which took us straight into the dining room. En route, we bumped into Samantha. "Well, aren't you a pair of busy little bees," she said blandly. We ignored her and pressed on into the building. We marched up the stairs and along the passage to the doorway which led up to the octagonal room. The door was closed.

Spector rapped on the heavy wood. "Simon, open up. Please, Simon, let us in." He tried the handle. It rattled in his hand. "Locked," he said.

"Simon!" I called. "Simon, can you hear us?"

No response.

As we headed back downstairs, the air was shattered by a woman's scream. My heart stopped.

"Quick!" the old man spat, darting on ahead of me. We dashed out through the French windows again.

Samantha and McIlwaine huddled close together on the lawn. I followed their gaze into the trees at the far end of the garden. There, a satanic orange glow blazed. Grey smoke coiled upward.

"It's the pavilion," Samantha told us.

"How did it happen?"

"No idea," said McIlwaine. "We were just talking, and then..."

"We need buckets," said Spector. "We can fill them from the river."

The sky was racked by an explosion. Then another.

"What on earth...?" McIlwaine burbled.

"It's the wine bottles," said Spector. "We need to get this under control, or the trees will catch light."

Carl soon rushed to help. In each hand he held a tin pail.

Then the boy, Gordon, appeared and joined in the excitement. It took us what felt like hours, but slowly—bucket by bucket—we wrestled the blaze into submission.

"How did it happen?" Carl demanded.

"I don't know," said Samantha. "I just… don't know."

I looked at Spector, who was studying the remains of the pavilion. It now resembled a blackened stone shell. I was out of breath and my body still coursed with adrenaline, but Spector seemed calm. "What are you thinking, Spector?"

"I am thinking," he said, "that somebody ought to look for Simon."

VIII

En masse, we laid siege to the octagonal room. The door was still locked and our hammering on the wood yielded no response. "Simon!" bellowed Samantha, "Simon, there's been a *fire!*"

"It's no good," said Spector. "We're going to have to break it down."

It took us ten minutes. When finally we heard the doorframe crunch loudly, we then exploded through the door as one, and bounded up the staircase.

What we saw up there defies description. I will try to lay it out for any weak-stomached readers in as methodical a manner as possible. Simon Eldridge sprawled on his side in the centre of the octagonal room. Beside him lay an overturned wooden chair, and around him a vast pool of blood bloomed like a dark flower. His head—I feel nausea rising in my throat as I write—his head had been severed. It too lay on its side, facing away from us.

The body, chair and head were ensnared by a shape, drawn on the floor in some kind of white powder, later identified as salt. It did not take an occultist to recognise the mark of the pentagram. But this was not all. Looking upward, we were faced with a truly monstrous spectacle. Above, the virginal-white ceiling was daubed with an image: a face. A snarling, yellow-eyed face that watched us with venom in its stare. The devil's face.

IX

We gathered in the dining room downstairs to wait for the police. Nobody spoke. McIlwaine sweated and twitched. Samantha sat insensate as a stone. Joseph Spector was deep in thought, a philosophical gleam in his watery blue eyes. Carl and Gordon hovered by the door.

When the police arrived, time seemed to speed up. We were taken aside individually and questioned in various corners of the Black Mill. None of us saw Simon's body removed.

It was late evening when the inquisition ended. The superintendent—the only man present not in uniform—informed us that a police presence would be maintained at the Mill. When I asked if I could go home he told me *no*, I would have to spend the night here.

Chastened, I retired to the lounge. Spector sat staring into vacant space. "It's all wrong," he said softly.

"Where are the others?" I said.

"I just don't know," he responded, but it was as if he were answering a different question altogether.

X

Dawn rose over the Black Mill. I was awake to see it, in a chair in the lounge. Joseph Spector was at a desk behind me, scribbling away on his notepad. The place still crawled with uniformed police.

"What are you doing?" I finally asked.

Spector did not answer.

The door creaked open and the superintendent slipped into the room. "Gentlemen, a word. Something has been happening in this house and I don't know what it is. People don't die by violence alone in locked rooms. And that face on the ceiling…"

"Yes," said Spector thoughtfully, not looking up from his notes, "the face…"

"I want to know about the face. Who put it there?"

"At a guess, the image is some two hundred years old. Part of some puerile black magic nonsense. Plastered over recently, I'd say. Mr. Eldridge has apparently been at work uncovering it."

"And what does it mean?"

"Pure hocus-pocus. But I'm afraid Mr. Eldridge took it all a little too seriously."

The superintendent narrowed his eyes. "Looks like he wasn't the only one. Between ourselves," he went on in hushed tones, "I can't see how the deed was done. And if either of you fellows knows anything that might help, I want to be told. Understand?"

"I think, Superintendent, that *I* might have something," said Spector.

The superintendent's eyebrow twitched. "Well?"

"May I ask," Spector began at length, "have you found a murder weapon?"

The superintendent produced his own notebook and flipped through the pages. "Something thin and razor sharp, that's all we know."

"Then I'd like to make an observation. Namely that the pentagram on the ground was the work of the killer, not the victim. I'm sure you noticed that the shape—in salt, wasn't it?—had been drawn *on top* of Simon's blood. Obviously *after* the murder."

"But why? Devil worship, you mean? Some kind of sacrifice?"

Spector gave a little half smile. "A tempting conclusion. But I would have to say no. A crime like this... it reeks of artifice. I think the salt served a particular purpose."

"And what's that?"

Spector looked the superintendent in the eye. "Answer that, and you have your solution. Now, take me to the octagonal room."

It was perhaps four o' clock in the morning, but I had never felt more awake as we headed for the octagonal room. The superintendent led the way; behind him Spector scuttled up the steps like a spider.

The body was gone, but the room still reeked of death. Early morning sun streaked through the windows, between those iron bars, and made the blood gleam. Spector, carefully sidestepping the edge of the bloody pool, made for one of the windows. The superintendent and I watched as he commenced running his fingers around the edge of the window frame. "No glass," he said, "no *glass*..."

"But it makes no difference," said the superintendent sullenly. "The bars are completely impenetrable."

"All of them?"

"*All* of them."

Joseph Spector smiled. "Good."

XI

Samantha and McIlwaine sat shell-shocked in the dining room. They did not look at each other.

The superintendent stood poised with his notepad and pen. "I have a question," he began, "about the fire."

Silence. The couple looked at each other, as though hoping the other would pipe up with the answer. "I could smell the smoke," said McIlwaine. "Samantha and I were talking and I smelt smoke."

"And you didn't see the cause?"

McIlwaine and Samantha shook their heads as one.

Spector had another question. "Have you worked out what sparked the flame?"

"Oil and match," the superintendent supplied.

"Arson, then?"

"Undoubtedly."

While Spector consulted the superintendent, I drew Samantha aside.

"I want to tell you something," I began, "I heard you that day. You and McIlwaine. I heard what you were planning."

"What? You heard *what*?" She snorted. "My husband is dead. And no, before you say anything, I'm not sad about it the way I'm supposed to be. But if you think I *killed* him, you're mistaken."

Benjamin McIlwaine inched over to us.

"Oh, get out of here, Benjy," said Samantha. "Can't you see it's all gone wrong?"

"Samantha," said McIlwaine, "I just wanted to tell you that as soon as we're free to leave I am going home. I can't stay here. And I think I should warn you that, when I leave, things will be over between us. I'm sorry. I never meant for this to happen."

Now Samantha gave a harsh, barking laugh. "Well, isn't this wonderful? You know what you are Benjy—you're a *coward*."

McIlwaine lowered his voice. "Things have got out of hand. Listen to me: destroy the octagonal room. Have it dismantled, brick by brick. Seal it up so no one can go there ever again."

Samantha was giggling now. "You're a fool," she said.

I edged over to Joseph Spector, who sat by the window. "Let's go outside," he said to me. "The air is rather thick in here."

It was true that the Black Mill felt a little crowded. Its walls echoed with the booted steps of uniformed officers. Outside, we saw them conducting sweeps of the nearby woodland.

"What are they looking for, do you think?"

"They want to know who started the fire," said Spector. "Of all the assumptions they've made, this is the only correct one: that the fire and the murder were linked. The superintendent is a good man, I can tell. But he will insist on taking the folklore and moulding it to suit his own ends." Now, the old man turned to me and fixed me with a steady glare. "I can tell you one thing for certain. This was not a crime of flimsy, intangible philosophy, but one of cold, hard *science*."

"You know how it was done?"

"No," he said quickly. "I'm afraid that's the one thing I still do not know."

"Then you know who?"

Spector did not answer. He was looking at something. A wheelbarrow. Seated in it, gracefully licking the inside of the steel barrow, sat a black cat. Spector studied it. "I wonder what will happen to these cats," he said.

"Samantha despises them," I commented.

"Yes. Sad. She will most likely simply stop feeding them. Look at this little fellow. He's so hungry." Spector watched the cat for a moment, but it continued to lick the wheelbarrow and did not register his presence.

Spector noted idly: "It seems the relationship between McIlwaine and Mrs. Eldridge has soured."

"Yes. But I can't bring myself to believe that either of them would have felt the need to *kill* Simon. They were kissing right in front of him. It was as if he didn't even exist."

"Yes," said Spector. "As if he didn't exist. Tell me, my friend, when you first stumbled on the two of them together in the woods, are you sure what you told me was accurate? That those are *the exact words* spoken by the two of them?"

"Oh yes. I have an excellent memory."

"They talked of murder."

"Yes. But I don't believe they were serious."

"No, I'm sure they were not. And yet…" At this, the old man seemed to snap awake. I followed him as he headed for the ruined pavilion.

"All this talk of gods and devils clouded my mind. But I can see now that this was a meticulous crime, with one fundamental and crippling flaw. Namely, that it killed *the wrong man*."

The boy, Gordon, had seated himself on a heap of blackened bricks. He looked up from his cat's cradle as we approached.

"You see," Spector went on, "I've just realised something. This was a crime committed by someone a little cleverer than any of the grown-ups." He paused. "Wasn't it, Gordon?"

"Yes!" the boy exploded gleefully.

"Shut up, Gordon!" snapped Carl, emerging from between the trees.

"It's all right, Carl. I mean no harm to Gordon. All the same, I would like to check if my assumptions are correct. Would that be all right with you, Gordon?"

Gordon, beaming, nodded.

"It was the string which tipped me off. I asked myself what somebody with your dexterity and skill could accomplish with a length of *razor wire*, and a mind to kill.

"Because you did plan to commit murder, didn't you? But your target wasn't harmless old Mr. Eldridge. It was young, nasty McIlwaine. That interloper. Obstacle to your brother's happiness."

"How... did you know?" said Carl, slumping down on the bricks beside his brother.

"A conversation was overheard between McIlwaine and Samantha. In it, they talked about a man who was 'in their way' and whom they jokingly plotted to murder. From the brief snatch of dialogue overheard by my friend here, it was to be assumed that their proposed victim was Simon Eldridge. But it wasn't. It was you, Carl.

"You and Samantha were having an affair long before McIlwaine arrived, weren't you? And this was where the problem began: Samantha didn't care if her husband knew of her infidelities. She paraded her lovers in front of him. Killing Simon would not have occurred to her, even as a joke. But when McIlwaine turned up, she found herself in a quandary. Two lovers, *and* a husband, in such close proximity. It was unsustainable. Not so much a love triangle as a love quadrangle. This was why, when that conversation in the woods was overheard, the lack of context made us think Simon was the target. But when McIlwaine said to her the damning sentence: "I was lying awake last night thinking about the two of you, and I believe I have a solution to our problem," he was talking about Samantha and yourself, Carl.

"But nobody who overheard that conversation could have taken what they were saying seriously. The only problem was, someone *did*."

"No," I protested, "there was no one around. Just the three of us."

"On the ground, yes. But what about in the trees?" Spector smiled. "You were in the tree that day, weren't you, Gordon? High above my friend's head. You heard the same conversation, but you *knew* they were talking about your brother. And you took what they said at face value. You genuinely saw McIlwaine as a threat to your brother. That was why you decided to commit a murder."

"Listen," said Carl, "he didn't mean harm to anyone. He's not got it in him."

"Oh, I appreciate that. But all the same, he killed Simon Eldridge.

Your plan, Gordon, was marred by a single, fundamental miscalculation. You had set a trap for *the wrong man*. Your vantage point in the tree that day meant you could not see the man who spoke. From a distance, Simon and McIlwaine were similar in appearance: very tall and dark-haired. You never heard Simon's voice; your closest contact with him was a vision in silhouette through the lighted window of the octagonal room. You thought you were killing McIlwaine. It was, I'm sorry to say, an easy enough mistake.

"It was obvious all along that this crime was the product of a unique mind. The morning of Simon's death, you set it all up, didn't you, Gordon? That was the only time he was away from the octagonal room. You knew about the devil-face which the recent renovations had plastered over. You knew it could be used as bait for a victim. So, when you got up to the room, you peeled its covering away. Once it was revealed in all its hellish glory, you set your trap.

"You brought with you a reel of razor wire—the kind used around the village for penning in the livestock. And with it, two large sacks of salt. Once you got started, it did not take you very long to construct your death trap in the octagonal room.

"Threading the wire in and out of the seven windows, much as you would thread string between your fingers, you created a 'cat's cradle' of razor wire up in the rafters of the octagonal room. One end of the wire trailed out of the northernmost window, weighted down by a heavy bag of salt. The other end of the wire trailed from the southernmost window, tied to the second bag of salt. This second bag, however, remained stowed on the window-sill. This was to keep the cat's cradle slack and loose, creating a wide circumference around the centre of the room. When Simon Eldridge entered the room and, as he was supposed to, spotted the image on the ceiling (which *you yourself* had carefully uncovered), he behaved precisely as you had expected, didn't he, Gordon? Although he was a remarkably tall man—the same height as Benjamin McIlwaine—he still had to pull up a chair to examine the mural. He was so enthralled by the image that he failed to notice the near-invisible wire. This was when your murder weapon came into play.

"Like so many boys your age, you own a catapult. It's a common enough toy. And you used it to commit your murder.

"You saw your victim through the window. You saw that he had slipped his head unwittingly through your noose of razors. So, positioned in a tree on the south side of the octagonal room, you fired a rock from the catapult up at the bag of salt to dislodge it from the window-sill. When the bag fell, the counterweight of the second bag on the northern side pulled the razor wire taut across the room. When the wire snapped into its new position, it did so with sufficient force to slice through the air and any obstacles in its path. The only obstacle, of course, was Simon Eldridge's throat.

"But the job was only half-complete. Because, for all your ingenuity, Gordon, you didn't really think about getting away with it, did you? That was Carl's handiwork."

Now Spector turned to the gardener.

"*Your* first instinct, Carl, when your brother came to tell you what he had done, was to remove the wire and salt bags. But because the bags were perfect counterweights, each hanging some ten feet above ground, they were out of reach. Simon Eldridge was locked in. The house party had gone their separate ways. This was when you hit on the idea that salvaged the whole scheme. Gordon mentioned that you are equipped with a gun of some kind. All you had to do was puncture one of the salt bags with a bullet, so its contents would trickle out and the weight of the bag decrease.

"This would lead to a heap of salt in the waiting wheelbarrow below, an almost-empty bag being dragged *through* the bars as the cat's cradle unravelled, then pulled out the window on the opposite side by its counterweight. (It would also, incidentally, explain the pentagram in salt laid out on top of the blood—the drained bag trailed back and forth across the floor as the wire unravelled through each successive window, creating that blasphemous shape on the floor.)

"But you predicted—correctly—that the sound of a shot would draw unnecessary attention. You needed a cover. Thus: the fire. Exploding wine bottles were more than enough to cover the sound of a single revolver shot in the furore."

Spector said nothing more. He studied these two young men. Carl was staring dead ahead. Gordon, smiling absently, played with his string.

XII

By midnight I was in my own bed. As of this writing the investigation remains on-going.

Samantha returned to Boston soon after. She did not set foot on English shores again. McIlwaine now occupies a perfunctory academic post at one of our lesser universities; his work on the octagonal room remains unfinished. I never saw Joseph Spector again, nor Carl and Gordon. I do not know what became of them.

These days on my walks I do not venture as far as the Black Mill. The truth is, in spite of Spector's efforts to lay its ghosts, the place still seethes. A presence walks and breathes there. Often I sense a pair of eyes rooted on me, with venom and hatred in their glare, peering out from the barred windows of the octagonal room. On the rare occasions I find myself close to that terrible place, I keep my gaze fixed on the path in front of me: the narrow dirt trail which leads to home.

Incident at Widow's Perch

"The plain rule, is to do nothing in the dark, to be a party to nothing underhanded or mysterious, and never to put his foot where he cannot see the ground."
—Charles Dickens, *Bleak House*

The letter arrived on cheap paper, almost thin enough to see through. It was from Silas and he wanted me to go out to Widow's Perch.

Something about the whole thing troubled me. Silas was our family solicitor and to me he was always such a reassuring presence. Yet here came a letter that crackled with urgency—it was unnerving. Even the handwriting seemed cramped and knotted like a noose.

I can picture Silas now—his creased and kindly face, his voice rippling like mountain water, his fingers gently folded across a protuberant belly. This letter was not the Silas I knew. The problem was Margot of course; the problem was always Margot.

It was the summer of 1934 and the English countryside blazed in the sun. I drove my little Austin like a demon, the windows open and the soft, sunny air gusting around my ears. The house at Widow's Perch nestled on a crag of granite in the Lake District, a summit so desolate it was accessible only by cable car.

The house itself was built into the peak, as though carved from the rock, its cable car terminal the sole link to the outside world. The car itself was an "art deco" construction, a steel framework, panelled all around with glass to double thickness. The whir of its cables echoed around the valley.

The house was built in the eighteenth Century, and has been in the Latimer family almost that long. Until recently it had been occupied by my first cousin, Giles Latimer. Giles was a gentleman in the classic English tradition; to meet him was to be ineffably charmed by him. He was older than me by a good fifteen years. My last visit to Widow's Perch was for his forty-seventh-birthday celebration, an all-night gala affair in December of 1933.

Less than three months later, Giles was dead.

His wife, Margot, was the one who found him. She returned from a trip to London, and glimpsed through the glass floor of the cable car his broken body sprawled on the rocks at the foot of the cliff. Poor, dead Giles wore his smoking jacket and a look on his face as stark and blank as the stones on which he lay.

For a short while, questions were asked. But interest in the death lasted only as long as the tabloids could perpetuate a whiff of scandal. This was not long. Three months on, Giles lay beneath his marble headstone, dead and forgotten as if he had been gone a hundred years.

*

I stood at the foot of the mountain, gazing up at the immensity of rock. The cable car whirred its way slowly toward me and I glanced once again at Silas's letter. Framed in late afternoon sunlight, disquiet loomed over the house on Widow's Perch.

No sooner was I seated than the cable car jerked away from the ground. The view was dizzying and a little queasy-making. As I drew nearer to the summit of Widow's Perch, I got the feeling I was being carried towards an uncertain destiny.

A young woman waited for me at the top. "I thought it was you," she called. She was a sprightly creature swathed in a silk sundress. "Am I to assume," she went on, "that Silas has been writing to *you*, too?"

Stevie Sparling was Margot's sister (Half-sister? The distinction was never made clear.) She was a Knightsbridge *bonne vivante*, part of a tribe of wastrel artists and musicians who drank their way through short yet pleasurable lives.

As we walked from the terminal to the main house, Stevie explained that Margot was about to emigrate. The Latimer family heirlooms currently languished in packing crates; soon they would be shipped to some continental villa, never to be seen again. And Widow's Perch would lie empty once more.

Stevie was still telling me this when we got to the entrance hall. There, Silas stood waiting amid a ghostly assemblage of towering wooden packing crates. He came over to greet us, his face creased with worry. "Gerald, you're here at last."

"Where is Margot?" I demanded.

"She's upstairs. I'm sorry to say this but she is making a very dreadful mistake. If you let me explain…"

But I did not stop to listen. I thundered up to the first floor, where the door to Margot's bedroom hung open. The lady herself sat at her dressing table, applying perfume and admiring herself like some preening cat. She did not turn to look at me.

"Gerald," she said, "I see the old man has been writing another of his letters."

"What's this about, Margot? How dare you empty the house without informing me? These are Latimer heirlooms! They go back generations."

Now she spun round, eyes sparkling. "So Silas didn't tell you?"

"Tell me *what*?"

"Gerald, I could swear you were angry with me. *Tell* you, of course, that someone is out to kill me."

*

We gathered, all four of us, in the drawing room downstairs. With its immense and sublime view of the lakes and distant hills, the backdrop was disarmingly serene. Margot draped herself over the couch.

She was dressed in a loose, crystal-blue rayon dress. Her half-lidded eyes and long hair gave her a languid, sultry appearance. The walls around her were entirely bare, with only the ghostly outlines of frames which had once hung there. "I don't mind telling you all this," said Margot, "because I'll be out of this godforsaken country soon enough. The fact is that someone is trying to murder me."

"She refuses to take precautions," Silas cut in.

"What precautions," she countered, "would you have me take? Someone has tried to kill me once. And I know for a fact it's the same person who killed Giles."

"Now hold on!" I said. "Giles died in an accident."

"Gerald," said Silas carefully, "we cannot know that for sure."

"Listen to Silas," Margot cut in. "All we know is that my poor husband took a tumble from Widow's Perch. But you and I both know how *careful* Giles was. Accidents, especially fatal ones, were not his forte."

I collapsed onto the sofa, defeated. "You think someone pushed him?"

Margot smiled without humour. "As you know, I was in London when Giles was killed. But what you may *not* know, because it is a fact I did not present to the police, is that I can prove Giles was not alone here when he died."

She surveyed her audience grimly. "I smoke Xanthia cigarettes. They have a lovely refined taste which suits my palate. Giles smoked only a pipe—a wretched object which made the furniture smell. But when I arrived back here, I found the ashtray heaped high with brown cigarette stubs—nasty little Turkish ones which neither I nor my departed husband ever smoked. So you see, I *know* someone else was here with him when he died. That someone killed him, and now—because I know his secret—he is out to kill me."

"That's all very interesting," I said, "but I've heard a lot about this plot to kill you with nothing in the way of evidence. Care to elucidate?"

"You don't believe me, Gerald? Silas, you tell the story."

I turned to the old lawyer. "I'm afraid it's true," he said, "an attempt was made on Margot two nights ago."

"Oh my darling!" yelped Stevie, dashing to her sister's side.

"I, ah, was not present myself," Silas went on, "but I have seen the evidence and I cannot dispute it."

"Evidence?"

With a sigh, Silas delved into the pocket of his blazer. He then produced and unfurled his fist. Lying on the flat of his palm was a small copper-coloured object I recognised as the spent shell of a .38-calibre bullet.

"When did it happen?" said Stevie.

"After midnight," Margot explained. "I was alone in this room, and you know how I cannot abide an empty house. But, as it turns out, I was not alone after all. I heard footsteps out in the corridor. The next moment, I glimpsed a figure in the doorway. The pistol was raised—" she demonstrated with her thumb and forefinger—"and *bang*."

"Oh, darling, you must have been terrified!" Stevie snaked an arm around her sister.

"Bang?" I said. "What does that mean?"

"What do you think? He fired!"

"A single round, which missed you entirely?"

At this, Margot scoffed. She swiftly pulled up the left sleeve of her dress to reveal a tightly knotted bandage around what appeared to be a messy wound, caked with dried blood. "He fired once, but I assure you it was all that was required. I dropped like a stone and the madman no doubt thought I was dead, so he dashed out. I heard his running footsteps.

"You see what's happened? The killer thinks I know his identity. But of course, he's mistaken. All I know about the man is that he smokes Turkish cigarettes and that he has a penchant for gunplay. *That* is why I'm getting out of the country before any more trouble comes my way."

"When are you leaving?" Stevie demanded.

"Today. I think that's why poor old Silas summoned you here. To try and talk me out of it."

"But," I chipped in, "why did you want me here, Silas?"

"Because you of all people, Mr. Latimer, might be in a position to identify your cousin's killer."

I poured myself a scotch from the decanter on the sideboard. It tasted like acid, sizzling on my tongue. "Now let's just think about this a moment. Margot was in London. Somebody—we do not yet know who—visited Widow's Perch. He smoked several Turkish cigarettes (did he do this with or without his host's knowledge?) before hurling poor Giles from the summit, down a sheer cliff face to his death. He then vanished. Several weeks later, perceiving that Margot here had determined his true identity, he returned with a revolver, fired a single shot into his victim, and retreated once more. Is that the proposal you are issuing?"

Silence. "If he escaped without anybody seeing him," said Stevie, "why did he leave the cigarette butts behind? They were the only evidence that anyone else had been here at all."

"Yet another unanswered question," said Margot, springing to her feet. "Oh, don't look at me like that, Gerald. I knew you wouldn't believe a word of it. That's why I forbade Silas from contacting you. And yet, mysteriously, he did so all the same. Well, I don't need your help and I don't want it. I'm leaving this house and never coming back."

"But Margot…" Stevie spluttered, "what about your luggage? All your little trinkets?"

"They will be collected on my behalf. I, for one, cannot bear another moment on this wretched mountain." With that, she was gone, out into the corridor, her heels clicking spectrally on the stone.

"Stop her, please!" Silas urged.

I ran out and along the hallway. Margot had already flung open the front door and headed toward the cable car terminus. Before I realised it, Stevie was at my side. Silas puffed along behind. "We have to stop her," he wheezed. "She shouldn't leave here alone."

Margot paused before stepping into the cable car. She turned and bellowed back at us, "Don't try and stop me. When I make a decision, I stick to it." With that, she flicked a switch on the control panel beside the car. Then she stepped inside and pulled shut the glass door.

I made to run after her, but felt Stevie's small, warm hand on my elbow. "Let her go, Gerald. She's a wilful little thing."

With a throbbing electrical drone, the cable car jerked away from the terminus and began its descent. I watched the outline of Margot, framed in the glass window. Her back was to us, but she did not move.

"She's alone, Miss Sparling, that's what concerns me," said Silas.

We three stood in the terminal, watching the cable car glide downwards from the peak. I squinted as sunlight gleamed on the glass, but I promise you now that the car was never out of my sight.

The cable car, now dangling limply mid-way between solid ground and the peak of Widow's Perch, was swallowed by a great pluming ball of orange flame.

I remember Stevie, screaming. I remember Silas, the old family friend, silent at my side. But most of all, I remember the sight of that burning cable car.

The interior of the car itself was scorched black. Margot's remains sprawled face-down. The hideous truth was that she could no longer be recognised as human. She was just a heap of charred flesh, from which plumes of smoke curled upward in the soft summer air.

*

A week later, when I presented the facts of the case to my acquaintance Joseph Spector, I paused at this point to let him digest the details. In a piquant instance of nominative determinism, Joseph Spector was by trade a spiritualist medium. By vocation, however, he was a criminologist. Spector had a certain knack for peeling away layers.

We were seated in a snug, low slung alcove of The Black Pig in Putney. As an alehouse it was one of Spector's favourite haunts—not for the drink but for the privacy. He sipped a mysterious green concoction from a sherry glass and then turned his soft, watery blue eyes to me.

"Spontaneous human combustion," he said, chewing each word. "Quite a thing, that."

"But there's no other explanation," I heard myself say. "Police found no flammable substance on the inside of the cable car. Nothing that could have caused a spark."

We had been talking since lunchtime; it was now close to four o' clock. But the staff at The Black Pig were used to Spector's consultations, and knew to leave well alone.

"Nothing…" he repeated, gazing through me.

"I don't suppose," Spector said idly, "either Miss Sparling or old Silas Critchlow smoke Turkish cigarettes?"

I shook my head. "Silas smokes a pipe, like Gerald. And Stevie smokes whatever she can get her hands on."

"And yourself?"

"I don't smoke. I suffered a lung disorder as a child. I'm prone to infection."

Spector digested this. "I see. Giles, you will think me at best highly unorthodox in my reasoning, and at worst a lunatic. But I think I know the identity of the person who visited Giles on the night of his death."

Spector, sensing my confusion and delighting in it, changed tack. "How would you describe your cousin? A careful man, I think you said."

"That's how Margot described him."

"What was his profession?"

"He was a financier in the City. But when he came into his inheritance he had no further need to work."

"But he retained a keen eye for business?"

I shrugged. "I can't really say, Spector. We weren't close."

"It's fair to assume that Giles was expecting a visitor the night he died, and that it was someone he did not wish his wife to know about. Whether or not he expected this person to murder him is another matter altogether. Nevertheless, it explains why Giles waited until the one day his wife was in London before agreeing to host this person at his home."

Spector had finished his drink. I summoned the barmaid and ordered another.

"I always tend to think a businessman is born rather than made. I believe Giles Latimer pursued certain business interests long after his apparent retirement. Why not? After all, he needed something to keep his mind active on that desolate peak. I would also suggest that these business interests were something he worked hard to keep secret from his wife."

"You're trying to say that Giles was involved in something illegal."

"Perhaps not to begin with. Perhaps he initially only looked on it as a harmless pastime. But I think he soon saw the possibilities."

"What are you talking about?"

"The illegal import of contraband. Smuggling."

I looked at the curious old man sitting across the table from me. He was utterly serious.

He continued: "This was not a solo venture, of course—he had an accomplice. And when this accomplice visited him that fateful night on Widow's Perch, it was not to murder him, but to *warn* him."

"Then who is it?"

Spector chuckled. "Forgive me, I've a habit of letting my ideas run away from me. There are a number of potential candidates, but I feel that the most likely is a man called Wilbur Hemsby. Does the name mean anything to you?"

I shook my head.

"No matter. The morning of June sixth (the morning, I think, that Giles's remains were discovered at the foot of the cliff?) papers reported that a body was found in the offices of the Red Star Shipping Company in Canary Wharf. The body was Wilbur Hemsby. The poor man had shot himself. His illegal operation was compromised; a police informant had infiltrated his little gang. Wilbur knew he was out of luck, so he took the easy way out."

"But I don't see how you link this to Giles…"

"Though Hemsby did not mention in his suicide note exactly who his accomplices were, he *did* discuss certain 'partners.'" Infer from that what you will. But two deaths by violence, in the space of a few hours… while hardly watertight, I believe there is certainly scope for further inquiry.

"I think Wilbur Hemsby went to Widow's Perch to warn Giles that their venture was fatally compromised. During their conversation, I am in no doubt that he smoked a sequence of increasingly distraught cigarettes. I am also in no doubt that when he departed from Widow's Perch by cable car, your cousin Giles was still very much alive."

The fresh round of drinks arrived, but I was listening too intently to Spector's tale to notice the brimming beer glass at my elbow.

"Giles summoned the cable car back to Widow's Perch once Hemsby was gone. Then, his mind racing, he wandered the halls in anguish. Then, seeing no conceivable way out of this mess, he approached the precipice and stepped over the edge."

"This is all conjecture, of course," I said, "I mean, what proof have you got that Giles even *met* this Wilbur Hemsby?"

"Oh, none whatsoever. In fact, it is equally likely that the two men had never met in their lives. Wilbur Hemsby was a ship captain while Giles Latimer was a wealthy financier. In fact, I believe that once Hemsby's vessel the *Marmaris* is scuttled there will be little enough evidence that the poor man even existed."

"The *Marmaris*? What language is that, Greek?"

Spector gave a barely perceptible little smile. "Turkish."

"All right. Let us suppose what you say is true. Giles was a suicide. You've solved the mystery. *Except* of course, for the little matter of Margot's death."

"One thing at a time. Let us take, to begin with, the peculiar assassination attempt which she described to you. The mysterious figure who appeared in the doorway of the drawing room and fired a single gunshot which grazed her left arm.

"Margot told you that she did not know who had murdered her husband. Since we are now operating under the postulation that her husband was not murdered at all, but whose death was the result of suicide, we need to ask ourselves exactly what Margot *did* know.

"Did she know, for instance that her husband had in place a generous life insurance policy? A policy which would pay out in the event of murder, but *not* in the event of suicide?"

My mouth dry, I took a hefty glug of beer. "So she faked the murder attempt? To make it look as though someone had killed Giles, when the truth is, no one did?"

Spector sipped the curious green concoction. "You present me with a problem and I provide a solution. Whether that solution is accurate is a matter for your own conscience. All I say is that it would be a comparatively simple affair for Margot to inflict that wound upon herself, then concoct an appearance by a phantom gunman. To disguise a suicide as murder in order to ensure she obtained what she perceived as her marital dues."

I finished my beer in a few frantic swallows, slamming the glass down on the table in triumph. "But this is where your theory falls down—somebody *did* kill Margot."

Spector downed the remainder of his curious green fluid, emitting a satisfied sigh. "You're correct, Gerald. This is where my theory falls down."

But the smile did not leave his face. I could not take it a moment longer. "Well?"

"Ask yourself this—what is the one customary feature of suicide, present in a vast cross-section of cases, but apparently absent in this case?"

"A suicide note," I answered.

"Just so. If Margot found the suicide note, she would have almost certainly destroyed it. But now we must speculate as to exactly what the note contained. Not just a confession, but an *incrimination*."

He was watching me closely, trying to gauge my reaction, and the almost clockwork ticking of my brain.

"Margot Latimer stepped onto a cable car, which began its descent within a matter of seconds. She was alone, and as far as we know she carried nothing flammable about her person. Now we know that there had been no genuine murder attempt, there was no conceivable reason to fear for her life. So she must have had another reason to leave Widow's Perch in such a hurry. I wonder what it may have been?

"You saw a woman step into a death-box of steel and glass. Suspended in mid-air by wires, she burst into flame. There was no visible spark, nor any inflammable substance present in that car. Correct?"

I nodded.

"*Incorrect.* I happen to believe that there was both a spark, and an inflammable substance. We know that Margot was a smoker, but there was no evidence of any cigarette packet or lighter about her person when she died. So we must think harder. How would you describe the weather that day?"

"Summery."

"The sun was high?"

"And hot. It reflected on the glass as the cable car moved."

Spector leapt on this. "Is that right?" he demanded.

"Yes, why?"

Spector rubbed his chin. "Let's take another step backward. Margot's sister, Stevie—I believe she may have said something important."

"All I remember about Stevie that day is her telling me Margot's plan to strip Widow's Perch and relocate to the continent."

"When Margot announced her intention to leave, what was Stevie's immediate response?"

"She said "What about your luggage?""

"And all your little trinkets," correct? Or is that a misquote?"

"No, that's what she said."

"And just what trinkets was she referring to?"

"Jewellery, I suppose. What, you think it was one of these trinkets that killed her? Like a cigarette lighter, or something rigged with an explosive?"

"Nothing so elaborate. If I am correct, this was a trinket which performed the very function for which it was crafted. It took a few seconds, but that was enough to kill Margot Latimer."

"Let me get this straight. Someone laid a trap for her?"

"A death-trap, yes. It relied upon a single unfailing personality trait of hers: avarice. She could not wait to leave Widow's Perch, could she? And at the time you naturally thought this was because she feared for her life. But now we know you were mistaken. So what prompted her sudden departure? Let's say she was not running.

"Let's say that Giles left behind him a suicide note, which Margot discovered and later destroyed. And that in that note, Giles named a silent partner, someone who had taken part in his illicit dealings. Someone you had previously thought above reproach. Someone like Silas Critchlow?"

Spector waited for my response, but I had none to give.

He persisted: "This knowledge gave Margot the upper hand over poor old Silas. And that was a position he could not permit. It was within her interest to perpetuate the idea that Giles had been murdered. But she also saw an uncommon opportunity for blackmail.

"Silas and Margot reached an uneasy accord. They agreed to persist with the idea that an unknown quantity had killed Giles, and that this same person was now out to kill Margot. This would permit Margot to claim her insurance policy, thus buying Silas a little breathing space.

"You say it was Silas who summoned you and Stevie to Widow's Perch? At first glance this seems an unusual move. But when we consider it carefully, we see a classic example of reverse psychology at work. Silas invited you to the house at Widow's Perch in order to distance himself from the crime he was about to commit. He worked things out with Margot very carefully—provided her with carefully written instructions and strict orders *not* to open them until she was on the cable car. Perhaps he told her the instructions would lead her toward claiming the money with which he would pay her off. Perhaps she expected a bank account number? This explains Margot's restlessness and itch to depart as soon as possible.

"But—and this is the important part—he made two things very clear to her: first of all that she *must* board the cable car alone. Second of all, that she *must* open the letter once she was safely moving back downhill.

"To her credit, she followed these instructions to the letter. This is where the trinket of hers comes into play. We have tiptoed around it with talk of lighters and cigarette cases. But does it seem beyond the realm of possibility that Margot may have carried on her person a *magnifying glass*? A stylish, ornately crafted reading lens is a more than acceptable and fashionable substitute for a pair of spectacles. Silas was well aware of this, as, I suspect, was Stevie (though she may claim to have forgotten it).

"You tell me that no inflammable substance was traced within the cable car. What if I were to tell you that Margot doused herself in the substance which ignited with a single spark?"

"But how?"

"When you first saw Margot, what was she doing?"

"She... she was in the bedroom..."

"Doing what?"

"Spraying herself... with perfume."

Spector grinned. "I think you are beginning to understand. Silas doctored the perfume bottle with a substance, something easily obtainable like white spirit. When Margot applied it liberally to her wrists and to her throat, she sealed her fate. The dress she wore was made of rayon, which is itself very quick to burn—*in the right conditions.*

"When she boarded the cable car, I believe she quickly and eagerly produced the envelope containing her instructions. The typical behaviour on such a sunny day, and with a document printed in what you have described as Silas's cramped, knotted handwriting, and on such cheap paper, would be to angle the document toward the sunlight to make it easier to read. We may now put two and two together. The sunlight, magnified through a glass lens may cause paper to burn. If the *paper*, too, is coated with the flammable substance, a sudden spark is assured. The fluid on Margot's wrists and throat, as well as the flimsy rayon, caused her to burn like a firebomb. Of course, the fire incinerated any trace of the document Silas had prepared for her. It is easy to imagine Margot, in her death throes, flinging the magnifying glass through the shattered window of the cable car, never to be retrieved."

He folded his arms in satisfaction. "And there you have it," he said, "Spontaneous combustion, explained."

"It's... unbelievable!"

"Well, of course, I didn't say it was *true*. I merely present you with a possible explanation. If you have another, I'm happy to hear it."

We parted after a final round of drinks. I was a little unsteady on my feet as I clambered into the back of a cab, but Spector seemed none the worse as he waved me off from the kerb, leaning against his silver-tipped cane. My head was swimming.

As we headed toward the beaming lights of the West End, I tried to picture amiable old Silas as a heroin smuggler and a murderer. I could not do it. Spector was inordinately clever though, no question about that. Perhaps too clever. We all know that a little imagination can be a dangerous thing.

The revelation a few days later that the elderly solicitor Silas Critchlow had been arrested at his Bermondsey home on undisclosed charges gave me a similar jolt. The newspaper print was small and I found myself angling the page toward the window. I read the story over breakfast, the letters blurring together in the glow of the morning sun.

The Sleeper of Coldwreath

Know then, unnumber'd Spirits round thee fly,
The light Militia of the lower sky.
—Alexander Pope, *The Rape of the Lock*

The bell rang at a quarter to midnight. The maid, Clotilde, opened the door to admit the querulous figure of Mr. Elliot Weblyn. He stepped through into the parlour, where the man who called himself Joseph Spector was waiting for him.

"Sit down Elliot, please. Fetch us some tea will you, Clotilde?" Spector instructed. The young maid left the room as Mr. Weblyn was tucking himself into an armchair. When she returned he was finally getting around to explaining the singular sequence of events which had led him to pay this unexpected visit to the crooked house in the corner of Jubilee Court.

Elliot Weblyn was treasurer of the Greenwich Psychical Research Collective, a band of London misfits with too much time and money on their hands. He'd been compiling an immense tome, *Ghosts of the British Isles*, since the dawn of living memory. His host—the occultist, spiritualist and erstwhile conjuror Joseph Spector—would no doubt be called upon to write the foreword.

Weblyn was a pink blancmange in a pinstripe suit. His ruddy, jowled face and bulbous red nose told quite a tale, and his piggish little eyes held a mixture of intellectual curiosity and buffoonish wonderment. Curiously, he wore a large black top hat which gave him the appearance of a faded gentleman from a bygone era. Which, to be honest, is what he was. He came from the generation of upper class for whom eccentricities such as butterfly collecting or ghost hunting became a life's work rather than an occasional flight of fancy.

Clotilde poured the tea. "Thank you," said Spector, "now leave us."

Of course, she did not leave. Clotilde stepped out into the little anteroom and perched herself on the wooden stool behind the door, that she might hear every word.

"Well," said Spector, "I think you'd better explain yourself."

"I'm sorry, Joseph, I hadn't planned on turning up here in high dudgeon like this, especially so late at night."

"No matter. I seldom sleep."

"I've come straight from my club; I just received the news."
Spector inclined his head. "Go on."
"Do you know Coldwreath?"
Spector did not answer right away. "Coldwreath?" he repeated.
"I wouldn't be surprised if you hadn't heard of it, old chap. The name meant nothing to me, and I used to consider myself fairly *au fait* with the preternatural highways and byways of Britain."
"Then please... enlighten me."
"Very well. I'll give you the whole sordid saga. It started back in the nineties. A chap named Peberdy, who called himself 'Doctor,' though as far as I can tell he held no official qualification. The whole thing was a cocktail of mysticism and blasphemy, easily dismissed as the purest bunkum. But something occurred which nobody has yet managed to explain. Something which haunts the house known as Coldwreath to this day. Peberdy's particular field of interest was the spiritual capabilities of somnambulism. Sleep, dreams, and hypnosis were his stock-in-trade. Forty years ago, 1893, he conducted an experiment at Coldwreath which has proved the progenitor of all these myths.

"Peberdy came from a wealthy background, and operated in the upper echelons of London society. One day he butted heads with a financier named Lester Brownlow. Brownlow called him out on his mystical practices and challenged him to prove his power. This, as it transpired, was a grave mistake.

"Peberdy invited Brownlow to Coldwreath, along with a few guests. He claimed that when a subject was hypnotised he was completely within the doctor's power, and would perform any action, no matter what it might be. Brownlow of course laughed all this off and invited Peberdy by all means to put him under. Then, in the drawing room of Coldwreath, one chilly winter night, with at least eight witnesses of the utmost credibility, Peberdy placed Lester Brownlow in a trance. By all accounts, Brownlow slumped in his chair, his eyes half-lidded, his mouth open. It was reported that his face assumed the vacant aspect of a 'zombi,' such as one finds in the West Indies.

"Ladies and gentlemen," said Peberdy to his enraptured audience, "the sleep state is a gateway to a higher realm of consciousness. I will now induce our friend Mr. Brownlow to perform an action which none of you had ever thought possible. I shall send him through the gateway, beyond the wall of sleep." Under escort, Brownlow was taken to a bedroom on the first floor landing of Coldwreath.

"To prove that Mr. Brownlow's actions are entirely voluntary, and that it is his *will* which is within my power, Mr. Brownlow will close and lock the door to this room. We shall remain outside." They watched as Lester Brownlow ambled into the bedroom and closed the heavy wooden door. They listened as he twisted the key in the lock on the inside. Peberdy smiled, and there was evil in his smile. "Now we shall wait."

"Less than half an hour passed before the incident occurred. Peberdy and all his guests were seated in the downstairs parlour when they were jolted by a sudden and desperate scream. A man's scream. A scream of agony and despair. But you must understand why this scream was so terrifying, Spector—because it came from *within the parlour*. The very room in which they were seated. It seemed to come from all around them. The scream receded out through the door and along the corridor. They followed it. It led them a merry trail through the house and then, when they reached the still-locked door of Lester Brownlow's bedroom, it abruptly ceased. Only the echo remained.

"Peberdy looked at them all, his face alive with devious pleasure. "It is done," he said. They tried the handle. The door was still locked (on the inside) and utterly immoveable. It took the weight of three men to break it down. When they got inside—you do not need me to tell you quite what they found. The room was empty. The bed made. No trace of Lester Brownlow remained. It was as if no living soul had been in the room at all. Well, you can imagine the outcry. Accusations of devilry and witchcraft. Quite the tornado of gossip surrounded our friend Dr. Peberdy. Lester Brownlow had vanished from the face of the earth.

"This was when the ghost stories began to circulate. Sightings of a man's figure in the environs of Coldwreath. A number of visitors saw it—a kind of apparition with half-lidded eyes, as though in a trance. A phantom sleepwalker, wandering between the worlds."

"And what happened to Peberdy?" Spector inquired.

"He died not long after. Pneumonia. The place was left to his daughters. And the secret of the sleeper remains unresolved."

"The sightings persist?"

"In earnest. If anything, their frequency has increased in the last ten years."

"Who lives there now?"

"Mrs. Nix—Peberdy's youngest daughter. And her housekeeper, Miss Streek. Quite a gruesome pair, they are. And that's what I wanted to talk to you about. I just received word at my club, a message from

Mrs. Nix. She is a fiercely private individual, but she has just consented for me to visit her out at Coldwreath and…"

"Say no more," said Spector, half-smiling, "I think I can guess what comes next."

"Then you'll come out there with me?"

"My dear fellow, wild horses could not keep me from it."

"We shan't be alone. A young fellow who is working towards a doctorate in the parapsychological sciences will be joining us. His name is Francis Tulp. Don't you see what this means, Spector? At last I shall have the upper hand over that damnable Charles Tollyfield."

Spector sighed. "It is a dire state of affairs when the pursuit of knowledge is reduced to a competition."

"Tollyfield is a fool and a bon viveur; he doesn't share my passion for the supernatural. And yet he claims he's producing a book to rival my own. I know he's bluffing, simply trying to rattle me, and urge me to bring my own book out into the open before it is ready. But a story like this is just what I need to round out my narrative. And a testimony regarding its authenticity from London's most respected occultist will be the icing on the cake. You'll come, won't you?"

"You don't expect me to listen to a story like that and then decline the opportunity to visit the locale? When are you going?"

"Tomorrow afternoon. I'm taking the jalopy. You're more than welcome to join me."

"Will there be room for Clotilde?"

"The more the merrier," said Weblyn with a gregarious sweep of his outstretched arms. Not long after that he left, all but skipping down the garden path.

"Well what do you make of that, Clotilde?" Spector asked as the maid cleared away the tea tray. It was almost one o' clock. "Coldwreath. Of course I'm familiar with the story, but I was interested to hear Weblyn repeat it. Miss Streek and Mrs. Nix." He settled back thoughtfully in his seat and watched the fire.

*

Weblyn's fabled "jalopy," a Morris Cowley, rolled to a regal halt outside Spector's house at three o' clock the following afternoon. Spector and Clotilde were waiting, luggage packed, and went out to greet their eccentric chauffeur. A little over an hour later they arrived at Coldwreath, a vast and intimidating old place which looked all the more ominous in the fading winter light.

"There she is," said Weblyn over the chug of the engine.

"Remarkable place," said Spector. Clotilde did not say a word.

Spector rapped on the door with the handle of his cane. While they waited, Clotilde set down the cases and seated herself on them. Spector gave her a look and she quickly stood. The door was soon answered by a startled-looking woman, her hair a russet plume. She was bundling a bottle green cardigan around her wiry frame, as if for protection.

"Mr. Spector, Mr. Weblyn," she said. "Welcome to Coldwreath. I am Elizabeth Streek." She presented a hand which Spector daintily shook.

"Joseph Spector. This is my servant, Clotilde."

The maid offered the briefest of curtseys.

"Well, you are welcome. Your colleague, Mr. Tulp, is waiting for you inside. Come through."

She led the three of them through into the gaping hallway. The rear wall was framed by a dual staircase. Above them, an unlit chandelier.

No sooner had they stepped across the threshold than they were blinded by a flare of white light. Clotilde dug her knuckles into her eyes, rubbing furiously.

"Hell!" roared a young man's voice. Clotilde blinked away the last vestiges of the flash and made out the silhouette of the fellow. Spector, unflappable as ever, stood surveying this stranger coldly.

'Dashed sorry about that," said the young man, "you must have set off one of my little traps."

'Please be more careful. You've blinded poor Clotilde."

'Crikey, are you all right?"

The maid looked at this silly young ass and did not answer. Her wide, pink-rimmed eyes said more than she could.

'The name's Francis Tulp," he announced.

'Joseph Spector. Am I to take it, Mr. Tulp, that you are here in the capacity of spirit photographer?"

'That's me," the young fellow beamed, "official debunker."

Spector seemed to thaw slightly. "Then we have something in common. I, too, was invited to probe the Sleeper of Coldwreath."

'Wonderful story, isn't it? And just wait till you see the house! Full of nooks and crannies…"

'Well," Miss Streek announced, "I'm glad the introductions are out of the way. All except the mistress of course—Mrs. Nix is upstairs."

"In bed, I take it."

"Indeed. She snatches what sleep she can in the daylight hours. As you know, our nights have been somewhat… disturbed of late."

"Yes, the famous Sleeper of Coldwreath. Tell me, what has been your experience thus far?" Spector asked.

She paused, her brow furrowed. "Come through to the salon. I'll make you some tea."

Clotilde hovered in the corner of the salon as Spector, Weblyn, Tulp, and Miss Streek settled themselves on the moth-chewed seating in this wide and charmless room.

"I have been companion to Mrs. Nix for most of my adult life," Miss Streek explained. "Coldwreath has always been in her family, and for many years it was her sister, Miss Peberdy, who lived here alone. But when Mr. Nix died, Mrs. Nix returned to live with her sister. For a while, the two ladies lived here in harmony. Then, regrettably, Miss Peberdy herself passed on. And so now Mrs. Nix finds herself the sole owner of Coldwreath. These stories and superstitions have eaten away at her. She is alone, bedbound, with only her needlework to occupy her mind. Her health is failing. She is not long for this world."

"I'm most sorry to hear that. Will we be able to meet with her soon?"

"I'll go and check on her."

Spector watched as Miss Streek marched from the room. While they awaited their audience with the lady of the house, Francis Tulp engaged Joseph Spector in a lively discussion of spirit photography. Tulp was a painfully earnest young man with a prematurely receded hairline, skin the texture of candle wax, and a pencil moustache. He wore a three-piece suit in olive green, with a gold watch fob protruding from his pocket. When he spoke, his voice was soft yet rapid, as if the words spilled from his mouth before he could contain them. When he talked of the spirit cameras, he seemed alive with childlike enthusiasm, all flapping hands and gesticulations.

"Take a look at these, Mr. Spector," he said, proffering a number of photographs. "Clerkin Down," he explained, "last summer. See the actual, physical proof of the fabled "white lady." I defy any sceptics to challenge my evidence." The photographs were clear depictions of a corridor in the famous Georgian residence, marred by a faint white shape which may have been a wisp of smoke.

Spector skimmed the images. "Very pretty," he said, "and I cannot fault your dedication."

"One must exercise devotion to one's research. Personal sacrifice and the profoundest dedication to the pursuit of truth."

"Indeed," said Spector after a brief, albeit awkward silence.

"…So I've set up a number of cameras around the place—you'll see them hooked up to the ceiling, and in the lazy Susan over there."

"With what purpose?"

"The slightest movement—the *slightest* movement—and the cameras will set off. The place will be alive with flashes and we'll have our photographic evidence."

"How many cameras in all?"

"Thirty-four. Fifteen down here, the rest up the stairs and along the landing. Like I say, the *slightest* movement and we'll have our evidence."

Spector seemed satisfied. "Wonderful."

Elliot Weblyn had been quiet during this exchange, but to show he had been paying attention he, too, said: "Wonderful."

At that moment, their conversation was interrupted by a shrill moan which seemed to permeate the room.

"What's that?" Weblyn wanted to know.

"Just the flue," said Miss Streek, reappearing like a spectre in the doorway. "You know pigeons nest in there."

"It's eerie," added Weblyn with a melodramatic little shudder.

"Personally I can think of nothing less eerie than a pigeon," said Spector curtly, "but then I am not as auspicious a member of the Collective as you, my dear Weblyn."

"Oh, come now, Spector. You know there's something amiss in the place. Can't you feel it?"

"All I feel is a chill," the old man added grumpily.

"Photography," asserted young Mr. Tulp, "is the key. Spirits are like chemicals. Their presence in the air can cause strange reactions which affect film and photographic plates. It is the only conclusive way to obtain evidence of the paranormal."

"May I ask," Spector said politely, "how many successful experiments you have managed to complete?"

"All my experiments are successful," said Tulp, "because they prove what I set out to prove. If a house is haunted, I will show it. If not, then… not."

"And do you have high hopes this time around?" asked Weblyn.

"Confidentially," said the young man, "I do."

Miss Streek led the three men up the stairs to the bedroom of their hostess. She lay in bed, examining her guests with an uninterested eye. At her side was a vacant wheelchair draped in a tartan blanket. As Spector had expected, she was wan and cadaverous, and looked to be the closest thing to the undead that they would encounter that night.

"I'd like to thank you for your hospitality," said Weblyn. "Your house is a marvel."

"My colleague is right," Spector added, "and needless to say we are interested in the stories of the sleeper. Mr. Weblyn is convinced there is some unnatural force at work. I am more sanguine."

"My grandfather was a scientist," proclaimed the old lady in the bed, "not a conjuror. This somnambulism business was not a trick, it was a vital scientific discovery."

"So you yourself do not succumb to the superstitions of the sleeper, the walker between worlds?"

"I abhor them. To be frank, Mr. Weblyn and his entire profession make me nauseous. Nevertheless I can see the value in it: confronting a fool with his own folly."

"Frankly, madam," said Weblyn, growing pink in the face, "I think you are wrong. And I believe our experiments this evening will prove it."

The old woman gave a little twist of the lip which was almost recognisable as a smile. "Then I am happy to indulge your vagaries. I have reached an age where the few pleasures in my life stem from scrutinising the foibles of other people. Coldwreath is at your disposal."

With that, they left her. Spector found the woman most inscrutable—was she a believer, or not? On his way out of the room, his eye was caught by a framed painting hung on the inside of the door. It was a grotesque and bloody image of the crucifixion. He glanced back at their ailing hostess, but she was already drifting off to sleep.

*

Dinner was pleasant, if meagre. The sparsity of the repast was more than made up for by the lively discussions of the assembled guests. Miss Streek delivered the meal up to Mrs. Nix and then she herself dined with the gentlemen downstairs. Clotilde ate in her room above the garage.

Francis Tulp was explaining what he had planned for the evening. "It's a fool-proof set-up," he said with unrestrained pride. "The camera at the top of the landing, directed down the stairs, is triggered by a footpad in the stair carpet. The camera pointing northwards along the corridor outside Mrs. Nix's room is triggered by a second footpad under the rug at the end of the corridor. The south-facing camera at the opposite end of the corridor is triggered by a third footpad. So you see there is no area of the upper floor which is not covered by a camera. The slightest movement—even the merest pressure—and the footpad will be triggered. We will have our evidence."

"I am tempted, Mr. Tulp, to engage you in a hearty debate concerning the corporeality and non-corporeality of ghosts," Spector smiled, "but don't worry, I'm not going to do that. Instead I applaud your enthusiasm and attention to detail."

And so the evening progressed.

*

Eventually, Spector made his excuses and retired to bed. He read for a while—Wilfred Huggins, *Secrets of the Street Conjurer*—and drifted off into a doze before midnight.

His room was at the rear of the house, round the corner from that of Mrs. Nix. It was cosy, if a little spartan in its decoration, lit by a single candle at his bedside. Joseph Spector was by habit a light sleeper, but he might have gone through the whole night undisturbed, were it not for the scream which came from the corridor at three o'clock that morning.

Bundling himself in a dressing gown, Spector shuffled out of his room to find Francis Tulp, Clotilde, and Miss Streek already congregated outside Mrs. Nix's room. They were soon joined by Elliot Weblyn, who looked even more pink-faced than usual, and whose uncombed hair erupted messily from his cranium in a great grey plume. "What is it?" he demanded. "What's happened?"

"The cameras went off," said Tulp. "They... I think they caught something."

"There was a scream," said Spector. "Was it you, Miss Streek?"

"No, I... I believe it came from in here." She was indicating the locked door.

Spector pounded the door three times with the palm of his hand. No answer. "Mrs. Nix!" he called, "Mrs. Nix, are you all right?"

Again, no response. "Have you a key?" Tulp asked Miss Streek.

"Yes, but it won't do any good. Mrs. Nix always bolts her door on the inside."

"Well," said Weblyn, "there's nothing for it. We'll have to break it down."

It took perhaps ten minutes. Spector and Weblyn were both past their prime, and Francis Tulp was scarcely out of adolescence. But eventually, they heard the bolt give way with a crunch, and the door swung inward.

The five of them stepped into the bedroom, one after the other. Miss Streek screamed. Spector's whole body jerked as though he'd been slapped in the face. Clotilde stood between them, watching.

A vast four-poster bed was the centrepiece of this sparsely decorated little room. Apart from a small antique bureau, a wardrobe and a little stool, it was the sole piece of furniture. The walls and floors were bare. Spector noticed each of these details later, after the initial shock of discovery. You see, the bed, and the room, were empty.

Miss Streek dashed to the bed and began immediately diving beneath its folds, searching for her mistress. "Oh Mrs. Nix," she cried. Clotilde glanced to her left and saw Spector looking at her. He did not say a word.

"She's gone, Mr. Spector," said Miss Streek, all but weeping. "How can this have happened?"

"A worthy question indeed," said Spector. He headed straight for the square window along the eastern wall. He ran his chalk-like fingers all the way around it. "It's latched from the inside," he said, "but it makes no difference either way. This window clearly hasn't been opened in years."

"Even in the summer she makes me keep it closed. She's susceptible to the chill. Mr. Spector, what shall I do?"

"My advice is to go downstairs and telephone the local constabulary. Inform them of what has happened."

Nodding, quivering and wringing her hands, Miss Streek left the room.,

"Right." Spector sprang to life the instant she was out of sight. "Let's get to work, Clotilde. Mr. Weblyn, Mr. Tulp, I would advise you to leave the room. Clotilde and I have dealt with this kind of thing before." He sniffed the air. "Do you detect a strange scent? A certain chemical tang? Hmm." He shrugged, then flung open the wardrobe. It was lined with clothes. Next he dropped to his haunches and peered under the bed, at the vacant gap between the frame and the floor. "I must say I'm not disappointed. I came here expecting yet another musty old ghost story. Remarkable!"

Clotilde wandered over the bureau and slid open the top drawer. It was packed with papers. "Now, now, Clotilde," said Spector with mock severity, "it's rude to pry. Simply not cricket." He came and joined her, gracelessly riffling the papers. "All seems fairly innocuous," he murmured, "heating bills, food bills…"

Then he commenced to slither along the walls, panel by panel, his ear to the wood and his palms spread as he checked for some alcove or secret mechanism invisible to the naked eye. Finding nothing, he stepped out onto the landing and marched back and forth. His spectators could not tell if he was looking for something, or simply stretching his muscles and waiting for inspiration. He returned to the bedroom, approached the bed itself, and began to sniff the bedclothes. He only stopped when he heard Miss Streek returning upstairs. He stood quickly upright and almost banged his head on the steel handle which hung down over the bed. Spector had examined this first, and found it to be entirely innocuous. He surmised its purpose was to aid Mrs. Nix in heaving herself from the bed to the wheelchair.

"Did you make the call?" he asked Miss Streek.

"The police are on their way. Oh, what can have happened to her?"

"Try not to upset yourself, Miss Streek. I have some experience in this regard."

"Her chair," said Miss Streek, on the brink of tears, "her chair is still here."

This was true. The wheelchair lay eerily empty in the corner of the room, draped as before in a tartan blanket.

Tulp stood in the doorway, visibly shaken. "My God, what is it?" said Weblyn.

"The cameras…"

"Ah! Yes," said Spector, "did they capture something?"

"Nothing," stammered Tulp. "Nothing at all. They only flashed when you stepped in front of them, Weblyn."

"So how, I wonder, did she exit?"

"She was taken," hissed Weblyn.

"Gentlemen, please," Miss Streek protested, "there is a much greater concern than that. Where is she *now*? There's no way she could have left the room under her own steam. The muscles in her legs were completely atrophied."

They commenced a search of the house. Needless to say, they found no trace of Mrs. Nix in any of the upstairs rooms. Nor did their pursuit through the downstairs rooms yield so much as a vestige of her presence.

Spector drew Clotilde to one side. "This is very bad. Very, very bad. We've got to find the old girl. Come on, let's make a circuit of the gardens."

The pair stepped out through the French windows from the dining room onto the lawn. Spector took the left -hand side, Clotilde took the right. The snow-covered grass looked pure and smooth, utterly devoid of human mark. Tulp followed with his camera. Elliot Weblyn and Miss Streek trailed behind.

"Look!" yelped Francis Tulp. He indicated the pond at the far end of the lawn, surrounded by rockery. Beneath the frozen grey surface of the water a shape was discernible.

"Don't go any closer!" snapped Spector.

"It's Mrs. Nix!" shrieked Miss Streek.

And it was. Beneath the frozen surface of the water—needless to say, quite dead—and still in her daisy-pocked nightgown, lay the troubled shape of Mrs. Nix. She now wore a dressing gown—the sight of it added somehow to the pathos of the discovery.

"*No closer!*" Spector repeated. They all stood, rooted to the spot.

"But there are no…" began Miss Streek.

"Quite right," said Spector.

In a perfect circumference around the frozen pond, there were no footprints of any kind.

*

"Cause of death?" Inspector Flint demanded.

"Looks to be drowning, sir," said Sergeant Hook.

"Time of death?"

"Hard to say, what with the ice damage. Doctor reckons sometime in the night."

"Helpful as always," sighed Flint. "All right then, what does Spector have to say on the subject?"

"He seems preoccupied with the window in that room."

It was now nine in the morning, the sky was dimly khaki-coloured, and Coldwreath was overrun with police, helmed by the redoubtable Inspector Flint. When Flint first saw Joseph Spector on his arrival at Coldwreath, he was surprised to find the old man standing on tiptoe, fiddling gracelessly with the frames of the oriel window in the late Mrs. Nix's room. "Find anything yet?"

Spector jumped. "Inspector Flint! I had a feeling we might be calling on your services. What do you make of this little mess then, eh?"

"The Sleeper of Coldwreath strikes again. You know, if it was up to me I'd outlaw ghost stories altogether. They always have a way of coming back to bite you."

"There's reason in your argument. But I think a world without ghost stories would be a lesser one indeed. I fear our mental acuities would grow slack from ill use."

"So an old woman vanishes from a locked room. Any thoughts?"

"Oh, plenty," said the occultist. "Nothing repeatable, I'm afraid. But I do find it helps to frame the problem in purely literal terms. The door, we know, was bolted on the inside. The cameras rigged up by Mr. Tulp had not flashed once in the whole night. Mrs. Nix was almost entirely immobile, and yet her wheelchair remains here for all to see."

"So… what then? Some kind of secret passage? Somebody came in, snatched the old lady ,and ditched her in the pond?"

"This, while improbable, seems at the moment to be our best option. And yet I find myself drawn to this window. I know it's completely impenetrable. Bolted shut on the inside. But there's no other conceivable method I can think of by which poor Mrs. Nix may have been deposited in that pond without leaving any trace in the surrounding snow."

"Aha," Flint approached the glass, "So you reckon she was dropped into the water from on high? Makes a strange kind of sense, I suppose. But hold on—surely the pond is out of range of the window?"

"Alas, yes. My convenient theory is flouted on two fronts. The window, impenetrable. And the pond, out of reach of this window."

"Out of *this* window, you say. You reckon she may have been dropped from another window, further along? That still means she must have got out of the room somehow."

"Yes," said Spector absently, scrutinising the iron bolt, "I suppose it must do, really. Tell me, was anything found about Mrs. Nix's person? Anything in the pockets of her dressing gown?"

"Only a box of common or garden matches in the pocket. Just the sort that you or I might carry."

Spector led Flint out onto the landing. "We must approach this crime as if it were a purely conventional murder. Means and motive are our prime concerns. Means: how was the murder committed? Once we know this, we may move onto the question of *who* could have committed the murder. Motive: Who wanted Mrs. Nix dead?"

"Money," interposed Flint.

"That would be the customary solution. But I think you'll find that Mrs. Nix was perhaps not as flush with cash as we've been led to believe. Case in point: the dilapidation of Coldwreath. The place is falling apart."

"That's a little tenuous, Spector. You're forgetting that she was a bedbound old woman, and a notorious skinflint. It doesn't follow that she was penniless."

"Perhaps not. *This* however tells a different story." Spector held up the letter he'd found in the corner cabinet of the bedroom. It was a simple enough document, a letter from the lady's bank requesting an appointment.

Flint scanned the document. "How so?"

"Consider the conduct of your average bank manager. Would he *request* an appointment with his wealthiest client? I think you'll find it's not the done thing. Clients of wealth approach their bank managers, not the other way around. Don't let the saccharine tone fool you. Mrs. Nix would only have received a letter such as this if her finances were in a dire state indeed."

"But what if someone *thought* she was wealthy?"

"Who? She was a recluse. Her only visitors were ghost enthusiasts in thrall to the Sleeper of Coldwreath. Did she leave a will?"

"No."

"So where does the house go?"

"It's a bit of a tangled web. We're still trying to pull apart all the strands."

"I should be interested to see what the outcome of that is, though I doubt it has much bearing on her death. No, I'm more concerned with the house itself. As I'm sure you can imagine, I've searched it thoroughly."

"And?"

"Listen." Spector knelt, the bones in his knees cracking like chipwood. With his knuckle, he rapped on the panels of the wall. It produced a dull sound. "Nothing. This sounds as we would expect a wall to sound. But listen again." Now he stood, and tapped a panel further up the wall, almost at head-height. This time, he produced a hollow, echoing report. "You hear that? It's something hollow within the wall."

"What—a secret room?"

"Nothing of the kind! No, follow me…" He led the Inspector along the corridor, still tapping the wall and producing that hollow sound. "You see? It goes all the way along here, at the same height and consistency. I believe this wall conceals some kind of pipe."

"A pipe! Now I've heard everything. You're saying the poor old girl was fired at the pond from an insulated pipe?"

Spector gave a gallows chuckle. "The only window within range of the pond is the bedroom at the far end of the corridor. The bedroom which last night was occupied by Francis Tulp. *If* Mrs. Nix suffered defenestration at the hands of an unknown assailant, it *must* have been from that window. You see, all the other windows on this floor would be out of range, unless the poor old girl was fired from a cannon."

He turned to Miss Streek, who was just coming up the stairs. "Is there anything directly above us?"

"The attic room," she replied instantly, "but it only has one window, and that looks out on the front rather than the rear."

Spector nodded. "I should like to see this attic room."

They ascended and found, much as Spector had expected, that the attic room was not a viable option. It was a large square room in the gaping attic space, with the vast cavernous roof space above, but as Miss Streek described, there was only one window and this faced out onto the driveway at the front of the house. The only aspect of that gaping grey space of rotting beams and dust-clogged air was a curious trail along the ground. For a moment it looked troublingly as though something had been dragged along the floor. Then he realised the marks in the dust could just as easily have been made by shuffling feet. "Miss Streek, has anyone been up here recently?"

"Not for years," she said.

"Hmm," was Spector's only response.

Sunlight through the attic window illumined a square patch of floorboard. Spector scrutinised this with undue interest. "Flint, you see that?" He pointed. The old man dropped to his knees and all but pressed his crooked nose to the ground. "These grooves in the wood. It's almost as if they have been drilled out for some reason. Like they house something." He looked up at the high, curved ceiling. "In fact…" He stood, inspired. "Help me search. There must be a lever here somewhere in this attic."

They made a circuit of the attic, running their palms along the walls and floors. It was Clotilde who found it. It was a switch in the floor, concealed by a patch of carpet. She heard it click. Then, slowly, like some spiral clockwork mechanism, an iron staircase descended from a concealed hatch in the roof. Its metal struts clicked into place in those grooves in the floor. "Our mistake, you see," said Spector, "was in assuming that Mrs. Nix was taken *down* the stairs." Slowly, testing the steadiness of the spiral staircase with each trepidatious step, he began his ascent.

*

"To obtain a solution to this problem, let me divide the riddle into three parts." They were all gathered in the draughty salon, where the ghostly moan of the pigeon had troubled Elliot Weblyn the previous afternoon. Spector stood by the fireplace, holding sway with his habitual conjuror's flair. "The first part: how was Mrs. Nix extracted from the room? The second part: how was she taken down the corridor without triggering the cameras? The third and final part: how was she deposited in the pond, without the killer leaving so much as a footprint in the snow? Answer these three questions, and we have solved the conundrum."

"All very well," said Flint, "but I'm more concerned with *who's* the guilty party?"

"Good point, Inspector. This case is one of sweeping and dramatic gestures, but the answer, as always, is in the details. I am talking specifically," said Spector, "about dressing gowns. In particular, about the one belonging to Mrs. Nix. When we went in for our interview with her, I saw it draped over the foot of the bed. But when she was found in the pond, she was *wearing* it. Now, it is conceivable that she grew cold as the evening drew on and so she put on her dressing gown. But I happen to believe it tells us something else. Namely, that when she left that room, she did it *willingly*."

"So she went out under her own steam?" said Tulp. "Just how did she manage that?"

Spector turned to Weblyn, as though the young man had not spoken. "I must ask you something. When you came out of your room, and proceeded along the corridor to Mrs. Nix's, were the curtains on the landing open or closed?"

"Now let me see…" Weblyn havered. "They were closed. I know that for a fact, as there was no light in the passageway and I almost tripped on the rug."

"Excellent!" Spector exploded. "Then I am pleased to see that Mr. Tulp's costly experiment has not been entirely in vain. Observe the photographic evidence." Spector presented the single photograph which had been taken when Weblyn triggered the automatic camera. It showed the unoccupied corridor, the shapes of the doors barely discernible in the murk. And, quite clear to see, the floor-length curtains were closed.

"What's your point, Spector?" said Flint.

"My point, Inspector, is that *after* we conducted our search of the room, and came out again into the passage, I know for a fact that these curtains were *open*."

"And that tells us…?"

"It tells us, ladies and gentlemen, how Mrs. Nix met her death." Spector smiled. He had his audience right where he wanted them. "But before we solve the present conundrum, there is a spirit we must lay to rest. Namely, the Sleeper of Coldwreath. I am going to tell you now how Mrs. Nix's father, the illustrious Dr. Peberdy, induced a financier named Lester Brownlow to vanish from a locked room.

"First, it is important to consider the character of Lester Brownlow himself. My researches have shown me that immediately *after* Mr. Brownlow's disappearance, certain financial irregularities in his business came to light in the Fleet Street press. He was revealed to be, not to put too fine a point on it, an embezzler. It was only the "supernatural" circumstances surrounding his disappearance which kept this fact from entering into the public consciousness. Once we know this, it makes the motive for Dr. Peberdy's little magic trick all the more plain. The two men seemed eager to establish their profound dislike for one another right from the off. It was one of the first facts, Mr. Weblyn, that you were so keen to impart to me. But there was a method in their antipathy. It was designed to conceal the fact that they were in collusion. Because, you see, Lester Brownlow had a very good reason to disappear—and he paid Dr. Peberdy to help him."

"So the whole thing was a con," said Flint. "Of course I remember hearing about it. Just an old spooky story, I thought."

"And you were right, Inspector. The whole thing was a horror show, played out to an audience of unwitting stooges. The trance, the somnambulism. Really it was a cynical ruse to enable Lester Brownlow to escape from justice. We've no way of knowing what happened to him, but I would hazard a guess that he paid Peberdy off handsomely with his ill-gotten gains and then fled the country during the ensuing furore. But now, we must consider the locked room. Interestingly, Peberdy instructed Brownlow to lock himself in the room, before he and his guests retreated once more to the salon. It was only when they heard the eerie shriek that they returned to the room and found it still locked on the inside. Breaking down the door, they then found Brownlow had vanished.

"So how was the trick worked? I'm afraid the answer will irritate you. The locked room is pure bunkum, and I am partially responsible. It was a classic case of failing to see the wood for the trees. You see, in focusing so heartily on the bolt (which was, I promise you, impenetrable) I drew the attention away from the true means by which Lester Brownlow exited the room. He locked the door on the inside. But he was able to open it again *without disturbing the lock.*

"Consider the hinges which hold the door in place. To what, exactly, are the hinges affixed? It's a rhetorical question, Flint, there's no need to answer. The hinges are affixed to the doorframe, which, as far as we can tell is made of sturdy wood. But how is the *frame* affixed to the wall? Conventionally it would be nailed into place or sealed with some kind of adhesive. But what if the *doorframe* too was held in place by a concealed hinge, invisible to the naked eye? That it was possible for the whole *frame*—complete with the door, still locked in place—to swing out far enough to permit someone to exit? Then for the door and frame to swing back and click neatly into place, the door still locked in its frame? It's a concealed mechanism, and it took me a little while to work out how it might be employed. There is a gimmicked floorboard; you depress it with your foot and it releases a catch which releases the doorframe—complete with the door—from its moorings. A door within a door. You can push it open and slip out into the corridor, then push it back until it clicks once more into place. And all the while the bolt remains in place.

"This was an invention of Dr. Peberdy's, I believe. A neat little illusion, and the only conceivable way by which Lester Brownlow might have vanished."

"Nice trick," said Tulp, "but what about Mrs. Nix?"

"Please understand, the floorboard gimmick was used to enable Lester Brownlow to escape from the room and effect his disappearance all those years ago. But I do not believe it was used by Mrs. Nix last night. Though I've no doubt she was aware of the clever device her father had installed, I don't believe it still functions. I have located the trick floorboard, but on pressing it the doorframe failed to yield. I think over the years it must have gone faulty somehow. And so it was useless to Mrs. Nix."

"So what are you saying?" demanded Miss Streek. "That Mrs. Nix arranged her own disappearance?"

"That's exactly what I'm saying. But she did not use the same method as Lester Brownlow. But she did it herself, and she did it entirely alone."

"But she couldn't walk!"

"No!" Spector exclaimed, jabbing the air with a declamatory finger. "No, she could not. But we have been so fixated on the wheelchair and the lack of footprints in the snow that we have failed to consider the fact that she did not *need* to walk. That, in fact, she had devised an altogether more effective means of conveyance. She owned crutches, did she not?"

There was a silence as Miss Streek considered this. "Well, yes. But she seldom if ever used them."

"Where were they kept?"

"In the wardrobe."

"None were found when the police searched the bedroom, Miss Streek. How do you explain that?"

The woman looked at him curiously. She did not answer.

"The truth is that you were well aware that Mrs. Nix *could* have left that room under her own steam, weren't you? You knew she was perfectly capable of moving without the wheelchair. And yet you failed to say anything. Why? I think that—even though you did not necessarily know how the trick with the locked room was to be worked—you had intuited enough from your mistress's behaviour to work out what she was planning. But when we found her in the pond, dead, you were genuinely shocked weren't you? You had no idea that the circumstances were going to escalate this far."

"That's a horrible thing to say!"

"But true, I'm afraid. So how did she do it? Well, it took a bit of ingenuity. But I've a feeling she was a rather indomitable lady. The key is noting the framed picture of Christ which was nailed to the inside of the door. A grotesque if ever I saw one. But the useful feature is the nail. She was fond of needlework, and we found a number of threads among her effects. So it was comparatively simple for her to take a length of thread, loop it around the hasp of the bolt, up and around the nail, and then out through the keyhole. When she was out in the corridor, she was able to pull the thread and thus pull the bolt into place. Perhaps the thread itself was coated with some flammable substance? I noted a chemical smell in the air when we investigated the room. Either way, the only explanation is that she then struck a match and ignited the thread, burning it away to nothing. And so there was no trace of the trick she used to get out of the room. She was out, and upright, thanks to those elusive crutches of hers."

Miss Streek began to crumble. "Mr. Spector, you've come as close to the truth as anybody. I might as well tell you the whole thing. You're right, I knew well enough that Mrs. Nix didn't need the chair. But I didn't say anything straight away because... well, I was trying to protect her. You see, she had let something slip to me a few nights before you all arrived. I was putting her to bed when she happened to mention that she might soon have found a solution to her money problems. Then, when she vanished like that, I realised what she was doing. Somehow she was replicating her father's trick in order to cash in on the Sleeper of Coldwreath story."

"But when we found her dead, why didn't you tell us?"

"I was in shock. I couldn't think. And I did not know if you would believe me—after all, those crutches vanished too, didn't they? You never managed to find them."

"Oh, I found them. But please, we're getting ahead of ourselves.

So far we have established how Mrs. Nix exited the room. We have placed her in the corridor. Where to from there?

"Now let me see. The business of the curtains. Mrs. Nix could have made it to the window seat without triggering the camera; as we know, the pad for the camera was concealed beneath the rug at the far end of the corridor. So, she seated herself in the window, pulling the curtains closed in front of her and concealing herself from view. She could then easily attract Mr. Tulp's attention with a cry or shout of some sort. Tulp came barrelling out into the corridor, discharging the camera en route to the locked bedroom door.

"Whilst we were congregating at the door and working out how to gain admittance, Mrs. Nix could easily make her way towards the door which leads to the attic room. Then, slowly (after all, she had plenty of time), Mrs. Nix headed for the attic. From there, she headed up, to the secret roof garden."

"But why?" demanded Francis Tulp, who had been quiet for some time. "What's the point of all this?"

"Patience, my young friend. All the strange and eerie mechanisms in this house were devised by Tobias Peberdy for the precise purpose of enhancing the haunted reputation of Coldwreath. He wanted people to take the stories seriously. I am now quite sure that he passed on the secrets to his daughters. And, with financial ruination looming, Mrs. Nix decided to put her legacy to use. She was going to create a haunting."

"But who was going to *pay* her for this?" said Weblyn, now incensed. "After all, *my* interest is purely in the advancement of science...."

"She had a benefactor," said Spector. "You forget, my dear Weblyn, that there are other members of the Collective who lack your integrity. And who also lack, if I may say so, your gullibility. Certain rivals with considerable money at their disposal, and the malevolent desire to see *you* made a fool of."

"So you're saying... all of this was for *my* benefit? They were trying to dupe me?"

Spector nodded slowly. "I'm afraid so. I think you'll find the root of this lies in your rivalry with Charles Tollyfield."

"Tollyfield! He'll do anything to sabotage my book."

"Anything. And, as we have seen, this is quite an elaborate scheme."

"But it was such a big secret, how did a dope like Tollyfield find out about Coldwreath?"

"The same way you yourself did."

"Finish the story, Mr. Spector," said Tulp. "Tell us what happened to her."

"She got up to the roof. Now what, I asked myself, could an old (albeit sturdy) lady want on the roof of this creaky old house? When I got up there myself, I found the answer. The problem of the "wandering voice" was one I was struggling to fathom. But when we found the network of internal pipes in the walls, I had an inkling. I recalled the sound of the pigeon which we heard in this very salon, even though the chimney flue had long been sealed up. Then I thought of the "whispering chapel" in St. Paul's—you know the one? Where the sound waves of people's voices are carried from certain spots by the curvature of the walls. It was then that I realised the purpose of these pipes. They were another innovation of Peberdy's, and their only purpose was to carry *sound*. The "speaking tube" would have to be very carefully concealed. Really, there was only one place which would serve the purpose. That was the secret roof garden, and that's why Mrs. Nix made a beeline for it when she left the bedroom. You remember the ghostly cries of Lester Brownlow, which frightened the guests in this very room some forty years ago? Well, Mrs. Nix intended to replicate them, and further convince Mr. Weblyn of the veracity of the Sleeper story. Then, once you were fully committed to include the tale in your book, my dear Elliot, she would reappear and prove the whole story a nonsense. And your face would be liberally festooned with egg. To a man like Charles Tollyfield, the whole thing was little more than a jolly prank. To a desperate woman like Mrs. Nix, it was the promise of financial salvation. But neither of the masterminds could have predicted how their scheme would end. You recall the gale that night? And you recall the long, flapping dressing gown which Mrs. Nix wore when she was found? The roof garden is penned in by an iron fence at about waist height. This woman who had always been so forthright and powerful found for the first time the true extent of her physical frailty. It was too much for her. And like smoke, she was carried away on the breeze. All that was left of her on the roof was a pair of metal crutches."

"So the whole thing was an accident?"

"Or the macabre design of some malevolent entity within this house. It all depends on your perception."

"No murder, then?" said Flint.

"Alas, no," said Spector. "Just an unfortunate turn of events. A needless death. And for all the ghosts of this house which have now been laid to rest, I am afraid to say another has taken their place."

*

Spector and Clotilde were the last to leave Coldwreath. The vagaries of Mrs. Nix's estate were so messy and difficult to untangle that Miss Streek would remain in residence for a while at least. Spector wondered how the domestic would cope with her new role as mistress of the house.

He was thinking about that when he heard her cry.

"Dear God!" she shrieked. Spector and Clotilde bolted from the salon out into the hallway.

She stood at the foot of the staircase, her hands over her mouth in abject terror, her shoulders heaving up and down with each ragged breath.

"What is it?" Spector demanded.

"Look..." She pointed up the stairs.

Spector saw what had startled her. At the top of the stairs, still draped in the dead woman's blanket, stood the wheelchair. It looked like it was waiting for them.

"Something in this house, I tell you," said Miss Streek.

"Don't upset yourself, madam," Spector said.

"She's still here, I know she is..." With that, she disappeared through to the kitchen.

Spector looked at Clotilde and saw that she too was studying the wheelchair with a worried crease in her brow. "Clotilde, in a house which—as we now know—is subject to the peculiarities of air currents, I think an explanation for this phenomenon should be readily attainable."

Clotilde crossed herself. "Clotilde!" the old man admonished. "Don't tell me *you're* subscribing to this puerile superstition, too?"

Clotilde, her gaze still rooted to that great lumbering wheelchair, did not reply.

The Footless Phantom

Vision is the Art of seeing Things invisible.
—Jonathan Swift, *Thoughts on various subjects, Moral and Diverting ("Further thoughts on various subjects")*, 1745

Nobody knows why Joseph Spector came to Greeley in the bitter January of 1932. Maybe they don't want to know. Maybe the wind simply blew him in.

Greeley is an old mining village in the Cotswolds of western England. It consists of a ramshackle church from which a few dwindling streets spiral outward like ripples on placid water. The place has little history of note, though it has existed on that same spot for some five hundred years. Nobody famous has ever visited there, nor anybody infamous. At least, until Joseph Spector arrived.

Spector was a retired music hall conjuror, and like a lot of people in show business he liked to propagate an air of mystery, starting with his age. Not even his closest confidants could tell you his real date of birth. He might have been fifty; he might have been eighty. He travelled alone frequently, for no purpose save the pleasure of motion. But this was his first visit to Greeley—strange that it should coincide so neatly with the villagers' brush with the "footless phantom."

Winter was still in the air, though the nights were finally beginning to draw out once more. The sun that day set at five p.m. rather than four. It was pitch-black by the time Spector got there; he looked to have arrived on foot. He wore a black velvet cloak over a three-piece pinstripe, and a homburg perched on his head. He walked with a cane, a slick black number with a silver handle. He looked every inch the conjuror.

He arrived at the Horseshoe Inn with a single suitcase just as the snow began to fall. Nobody knew it then, but these first wisps of white stuff were the onset of a snowstorm that was to blanket the entire village by the following morning. The Horseshoe Inn was one of those old English pubs where it is difficult to tell if it is musty or merely "authentic." These days, Spector spent much of his life in such places.

It was a Friday evening so naturally the place was packed out with locals. Once they had got over the initial shock of a stranger in their midst, their chatter was amiable. Spector approached the bar, where a rubicund fellow in shirtsleeves pulled pint after pint of murky ale. "A pint of that please," said Spector, studying his tired and creased face in the great gilt-framed mirror on the rear wall. "And I don't suppose you can offer me a room for the night?"

"I can at that, sir. We have a room upstairs just for travellers such as yourself. And my rates are perfectly reasonable."

"Wonderful," said Spector after his first sip of ale. It was difficult to tell if he was referring to the news, or to the viscous booze now coursing down his gullet.

"My name is Arden," said the landlord, who had a whisper of white hair combed over his great dome-like head, and looked a hardy sort built for winters such as this.

"Joseph Spector," said Spector as the two men shook hands over the bar.

"Pleasure, sir. Now if you'll just wait here a moment, my daughter will take you up to your room. Sally! Sally!"

The landlord loomed up on tiptoe, trying to pick out his daughter from the crowd. Eventually she emerged with a tray of empties. She was a pretty young thing, perhaps twenty, with voluminous blonde hair. She studied Spector with a faintly mistrustful eye.

"Sally, take Mr. Spector upstairs. He's our new paying guest."

"Certainly," she said, depositing the tray on the counter. "Right this way, sir."

She led Spector through a door behind the bar and up a narrow, creaking staircase to the first floor. "Here we are, sir," she said, stopping at a varnished, unnumbered door. "I hope it will be satisfactory." Her spiel was unnecessarily clipped. No doubt it had been drilled into her by her father from a young age.

"We can do you a breakfast if you wish, sir. Just let me know," she told him as she unlocked the door. The room was spartan to say the least, it reminded Spector of the prison cells he had encountered in his time. The walls were dank matched by the murky sky beyond the single window. There were no carpets or ornaments. Just a bed, a moth-bitten chair, and a bowl for him to wash in.

"This will do nicely," said Spector, depositing his case on the bed. "I don't suppose I could trouble you for a meal of some kind? I've travelled an awful long way."

Sally gave a scarcely perceptible sigh and then launched into the next round of her spiel. "We can offer you sandwiches and cold meat, sir, nothing hot I'm afraid, but if that suits let me know and I'll prepare it for you now."

"That would be fine. Thank you."

"And will you be eating up here or downstairs?"

"Downstairs, I think. I'd like to get acquainted with the locals."

Sally seemed almost to roll her eyes at this as she left the room, closing the door behind her. Spector sat down on the bed for a moment to catch his breath. He peered out of the window and noticed for the first time how thick the snowfall had become, and how the road beyond the glass was now smothered in white.

*

A few minutes later Spector was back downstairs with a second pint of ale in his hand. He sat on a barstool and produced with a flourish from his sleeve a deck of cards, which he began to manipulate with various riffles and elaborate cuts. He attracted quite an audience and, inevitably, came the demand for a trick.

"Very well," said Spector, fanning out the deck. "Pick a card."

The man who had spoken, a young fellow bundled up in an overcoat and sporting a flat cap, reached out with a fingerless-gloved hand and took a card.

"Good. Now place it on top of the deck."

The fellow did so.

"Now—shuffle." Spector handed the young man the cards and watched as he began to shuffle them clumsily. "Lovely. Now hand them back." The fellow did so. "And will it amaze you, ladies and gentlemen, if I can not only name this gentleman's card, but also produce it, and *all with the power of my mind?*"

There were cheers, a few drunken jeers and general good humour. Spector gave an enigmatic smile. "Your card is the ace of clubs."

"He's right!" the fellow said.

"And now," Spector continued, "to produce it. Are you all happy, ladies and gentlemen, that I have not gimmicked these cards in any way? You have seen, for example, that all the cards are different and yet from their backs they seem identical? I have had no unfair advantage?" There were general mumblings of assent. "Marvellous. Then will it amaze you to find that the card in question has magically transmogrified and *left the deck altogether?*"

He reached out with a single swift motion and gripped the brim of the young man's cap. Whisking it away, he revealed the card, face-up, inside the cap. There followed cheers and applause, and a free beer from Mr. Arden in exchange for another trick.

The evening passed pleasantly, and soon Spector found himself engaged in conversation with a well-dressed elderly man who introduced himself as Doctor Moorway. "I take care of all the aches and pains of this motley bunch," he said, with an expansive gesture which seemed to encompass the whole village.

"Then you're privy to their darkest secrets, aren't you, Doctor?"

Moorway smiled. "You could say that. But tell me, what brings you to Greeley? I know we're a bit off the beaten track."

"Just passing through," said Spector. "A hoary and unsatisfactory answer, but I'm afraid it's the only one I have to give."

"You're good with those cards," said Moorway. "And you have a certain look about you. Have you performed on the stage by any chance?"

"Oh, once upon a time. Every now and then I like to flex my illusory muscles in exchange for a free drink or two."

"Well, you're onto a winner with Arden. Old Lionel's a soft-touch when it comes to strangers."

"He seems a most gregarious host."

"He is. Can't say the same for that daughter of his. I doubt she'll stick around long."

"Mr. Arden is a widower?"

"Yes. Lost his wife eight years ago now. Just him and Sally these days."

"And you, Doctor Moorway? Are you married?"

Moorway gave an embarrassed little chuckle. "No, no. We seem to be a village of bachelors, don't we? It's a wonder we've produced any offspring at all!"

Spector produced from his trouser pocket a coin which he began to flip. As he did, he cast his gaze around the bar. The fellow with the cap, the one who had been part of the card trick, was engaged in a low, heated conversation with another man of about the same age. *This* man was taller and altogether more commanding a presence. Good-looking, too. Spector gathered from their frequent glances toward Sally Arden that both men were looking to woo the landlord's daughter.

"He's a troublemaker, that one," said Dr. Moorway.

"Mm?"

"Danny Snape. Young fellow with the cap. I'd watch out for him if I was you."

"I was just thinking that myself. He seems to be up to some sort of mischief with that other fellow."

"Other fellow? Oh, you mean Tim Underdale. No, I shouldn't think so. Tim's rather sweet on Sally, God help him. Personally I think she'd eat him for breakfast. But all the same, it seems Danny Snape has been making certain overtures of his own. I doubt either of them has much of a chance."

"A love triangle," said Spector. "My, you do have some stories in these little English villages."

That was when Underdale, buoyed by some comment of Snape's, took a swing for him. Snape took a step back and the punch hit empty air. Underdale overbalanced and stumbled against the bar. Snape laughed.

"Dear, dear," said Dr. Moorway. "These boys do get in some scrapes."

"Now then!" bellowed Arden. "I'll have none of that in my pub."

"Tim!" cried Sally. She took Underdale by the arm and swept him out of the bar. Snape was still laughing, surrounded by cronies. After a discreet moment or two, Spector slipped away to follow Sally and her beau outside. For all his veneer of propriety, he was just an old snoop.

Outside, the snow was still falling thickly. Sally and Tim made a beeline for what looked to be a small workshed, away from prying eyes. Or so they thought. They ducked inside, out of the cold, but were within view of a small square window, caked with grime and dust. Spector crept up and listened.

"What the hell are you playing at, Tim?" Sally whispered.

"You didn't hear him, Sal, you didn't hear what he was saying…"

"I don't care. It doesn't matter to me. You know he's nothing to me. Nothing at all." And she kissed him.

"Will you marry me?" said Tim.

"Don't be stupid." She kissed him again. Then she slipped out of the workshed and headed back into the inn.

Spector waited a moment. He saw through the dirty glass as Tim Underdale struck a match and ignited a cigarette. The young man stood pensively for a moment, his face hauntingly lit by the orange glow. He looked so melancholy, it reminded Spector of his own love-lorn youth. The lighting of the cigarette gave Spector a better view of the workshed, too, which was lined with all manner of bric-a-brac. Fishing rods, tools, saws, paint buckets, a sewing machine, a coiled hosepipe with handle, a pair of milk cans, wooden barrels… and poor Tim Underdale, just another misused and unwanted object.

Tim stayed a moment, smoking his cigarette and staring at the blank wall of the shed. Spector debated whether or not to disturb him, and then took his chance and rapped on the wooden door.

"Who's there? Who's that?" Tim called out.

Spector opened the door and stepped inside. "Mr. Underdale, my name is Joseph Spector. I'm a stranger in the village but I couldn't help but notice you seemed to be in some distress. I wondered if I could help."

"I see. Well, you can't. But thanks anyway."

"Can I buy you a drink at least?"

Underdale thought about this for a moment. "Why not?"

They headed back inside, and Tim was clearly making a conscious effort *not* to look at Danny Snape. Snape, for his part, seemed to be making eyes at Sally again from across the bar. It was only on his second glance that Spector realised the local gigolo was apparently eyeing his own reflection in the gilt-edged mirror on the back wall.

"I gather Mr. Snape has something of a reputation?" said Spector discreetly.

"Yeah, well… there's someone like that in every village, isn't there?" Tim was doing his best to be non-committal.

"I suppose you're right."

"People make excuses for him because he never had a dad. Or I should say, because he lost his dad. It was the cave-in."

"Cave-in?"

"At the mine. Twenty years ago now, I was only a lad when it happened. Remember it well though. Awful, it was. I don't think the village ever recovered."

"Goodness, I had no idea."

"Of course, it's no excuse. A disaster like that, everybody lost someone. This is a small village."

"Forgive my ignorance, but I didn't know this was a mining village."

"It isn't. Least, not any more. Used to do all right, but that cave-in finished it off. The mine's derelict now."

"Tragic," said Spector thoughtfully. He looked over at Snape, who was now chatting to the doctor. The doctor looked singularly unimpressed by whatever he was being told.

That was when one of the drinkers took an unwieldy step back and bumped against the bar, knocking over two glasses of beer and sending them spilling out across a number of other patrons. General consternation. The culprit, a rotund fellow whose hat was set jauntily askew on his head, turned around slowly, slurring apologies.

"Right," said Arden, "come along Rafferty, time for beddy-byes."

"That's Miles Rafferty," said Underdale, "gamekeeper out at Dillane House. We all know he likes a drink. He's harmless though."

Spector nodded, smiling and taking all this in.

Things began to quiet down soon after that. Underdale headed for home, as did Danny Snape. Soon Spector found himself seated at a small corner table with the doctor once more. The doctor had put away several pints, and was inclined to gossip, so Spector took the opportunity to ask him about the mine.

"Who told you about that?"

"Tim Underdale mentioned it."

"Is that right? Well, I'd advise you not to speak about it to Lionel Arden. The poor fellow has never got over it."

"Arden? Why not?"

"Because he worked the mine in those days. He was the winder. A tragedy, it was; faulty headstocks sent a cage full of men down to their deaths. But nobody *blamed* Arden. Of course it wasn't his fault, and he was as horrified as the rest of us. But the mine was closed after that. It had been on its last legs anyway. A lot of the workers moved on. There are plenty of other mines in the region. And we're the ones that stayed."

This cast the village in a new light for Spector, living in the shadow of a great tragedy. The villagers these days were the survivors, the ones who had clung onto their homes in spite of everything. He thought differently of Lionel Arden, too: a man who had endured a great tragedy, who had through no fault of his own, taken part in the deaths of an unspecified number of men. Now his friendly bluster seemed all the more poignant. It was a mask.

On that maudlin note, the doctor decided to call it a night. The place was emptying out now, and Sally was beginning to wipe down the tables and get ready for closing time. Arden rang the bell for last orders.

Spector said good night to his hosts and made his way slowly and creakily up the staircase. When he got to his room, he scarcely had the energy to undress. He fell into bed and dropped instantly to sleep.

*

When Spector woke, the sky was still dark, though his watch told him it was close to eight a.m. Lazily he heaved himself from the bed, washed with ice-cold water from the bowl and then dressed. Breakfast was a subdued affair; he ate alone in the kitchen at the rear of the inn. Contrary to his expectations the meal was hot and hearty, and filled him most agreeably.

Sally bustled in and out of the kitchen, but Spector noticed that she seemed intent on peeping out of the window every now and then, as though waiting for something.

"Is everything all right, Miss Arden? You seem a little distracted."

"Sorry, Mr. Spector. There was some hullaballoo this morning while you were still in bed. Danny Snape has disappeared."

"Disappeared?"

"Yes. He never got home. They're all out looking for him. My father's with them."

Spector looked out the window at the ground layered thickly with snow. At the merciless white sky. "Has anybody called the police?"

"No police," she said. "Snow brought the phone line down. The nearest police are twenty miles away."

"I see. So we're cut off."

She looked at him strangely. "I suppose we are."

After breakfast, it did not take Spector long to pick up the trail of the search party. The cluster of footprints led him around the village and out to the north, toward a dark nest of trees which a faded sign identified as Greeley Wood. He pressed on.

He had not got too far when a shape loomed between the trees, a sort of oblong silhouette. As he approached, Spector realised it was a rusty old Austin van, and that it was surrounded by people.

"Mr. Spector!" a voice called. Drawing nearer, Spector saw Lionel Arden looking particularly pink-cheeked. "Look what we found."

"Whose is it?"

"Why, it's Danny Snape's."

"Any sign of Mr. Snape himself?"

"Yes, actually," Arden said. "When we got here, the driver side's door was open and there's a set of footprints leading off into the wood. Near the Crag."

"The Crag?"

"It's a local landmark. You'll know what I mean when you see it."

They pressed on, following the single line of footprints deeper into the wood.

"There!" somebody cried. A few of the men broke into a run. It was a sort of heap lying in the snow. Spector recognised it straight away.

Danny Snape lay prone on the white ice-caked ground, the back of his skull caved in, a mess of pulp and blood. His body was frozen solid, the dead hands reaching out with grasping claws. He lay at the foot of a sheer granite cliff-face; Spector glanced up at the Crag, which was perhaps 150 feet in height. This great wall of stone was the terminus of the wood.

"Well," said Dr. Moorway, "we've found him at least. And to think, Arden, *you'd* have had us dragging the river."

He had plainly been dead for some hours.

"What was he doing out here?" Spector wanted to know.

"Most likely poaching," said Moorway. "He was notorious for it."

"Yes," said Arden, "but that's why I thought he couldn't *possibly* be out here. Last night was no night for poaching. Even the game know better than to venture out on nights like that."

Gingerly, the doctor approached the body. "Looks like a single blow to the back of the head is what did for him."

"Something fell on him, maybe? A chunk of ice?" Arden suggested.

"No, no." Moorway was quick to cut him off. "If a chunk of ice fell and hit him, then where is it? There's been no great thaw, the snow's still thick on the ground. A chunk of ice should be too."

"Well," Underdale chipped in, "maybe it's not the way it looks. *Maybe* what happened is that he was up on the Crag and he fell."

"On the Crag? But the van is down here. And so are the footprints. Besides, if he had fallen I think there would be a great deal of other visible injuries. Broken limbs. Bruises. Not just that single wound to the back of the head. And *if* in the unlikely event he *had* fallen, why should he be lying on his front and not on his back, where the injury is? Of course, that would be ignoring the evidence of the van and the footprints. No, no, he was hit by something. Some..."

"Blunt instrument," Spector supplied. This silenced the searchers. They did not like the way it sounded; the suggestion of violence.

"Well, yes," Moorway went on, slightly cowed. "It looks that way."

"This is a strange scenario indeed," Spector continued, taking the reins from the doctor. "I would agree that Mr. Snape looks to have been bludgeoned." Another ugly word. Sideways glances, now, from the onlookers. "But the crime appears to have occurred in such a way that no one could possibly have committed it. If the weapon was dropped from on top of the Crag, then where is it? And if the weapon was swung by a human hand, then how did the culprit approach and depart without leaving a single footprint?"

Brooding on the prospect of a weightless, invisible assassin, Spector drew the doctor to one side. "These woods are on Dillane land, is that right?"

"Yes. The house is just over in that direction." He pointed.

"And you said Miles Rafferty was the gamekeeper, correct?"

"Yes, he has a little cottage in the grounds of the house."

"Then we should hear his version of events."

Rafferty's cottage was as stark and puritanical as any other property in the village. Its thatch was threadbare and its walls caked with half-peeled paint. Spector rapped on the door and, after a moment, Rafferty appeared on the doorstep, still in his nightshirt and looking singularly worse for wear.

"Mr. Rafferty. Sorry to disturb you, but there's been some trouble out in Greeley Wood."

"Trouble?" the gamekeeper echoed.

"It's Danny Snape. He's been found dead."

"Dead?" The hangover must have been particularly virulent. Rafferty blinked away the glare of the winter sun on the snow.

"He looks to have been murdered, sir. That's why we've come to speak to you."

Miles Rafferty's bleary, pink-rimmed eyes blinked at Spector. "What's that supposed to mean?"

"Well, I understand Mr. Snape had something of a reputation for poaching."

"I caught him on Mrs. Dillane's land once or twice, that's true."

"Was there an altercation?"

Rafferty sighed. "All right, yes. We had a scuffle. It was his own doing, he shouldn't have been there in the first place. But he kept coming back. He was a tricky devil."

"Did you see him in the wood at all last night?"

"Mister, I didn't see *anything* last night. Don't know if you know, but I had a tot or two too much to drink. Knocked me right out. I barely got through the door at home before I keeled over into bed and didn't wake up until five minutes ago."

They left Rafferty soon after that. The fellow was in a bad state indeed, and he would not be of much use to them until his head was clearer. All the same, Spector had little cause to doubt his claim that he had not surfaced at all during the night.

"Who is Mrs. Dillane?" he asked the doctor.

"Lynette Dillane. A very wealthy, respected lady."

"Does she live out at the house alone?"

"She used to. Can't any more, since she had a stroke a couple of summers back. Now she's got a nurse living with her, one Miss Caroline Chivers."

"I'd like to speak with them. Do you think that will be possible?" The doctor shrugged. "We can try."

About half a mile from the spot where Danny Snape lay dead at the foot of the Crag, the Dillane house loomed cold and grey as a tomb. Its halls gaped like cavernous hollow throats, with great shadowed eaves arcing overhead. Once, the place might have had some glamour. But by the harsh white snowy daylight, it looked like nothing so much as a decrepit church, deconsecrated and forgotten.

Nurse Chivers answered the door. She was square-faced and singularly unfriendly. "Mrs. Dillane won't be any use to you," she said. "She can't speak."

"I'm very sorry to hear that. But will it be possible to see her, all the same?"

The nurse sighed and pivoted on her heel, leading the two men a sonorous clip-clopping passage down the hall and into the lounge. Mrs. Lynette Dillane was indeed a pitiful specimen in her wheelchair beside the blazing fireplace. She was swathed in blankets against the chill, and her entire body was curled into the shape of a question mark. Her eyes darted toward the two men as they entered.

"Two visitors, Mrs. Dillane," Nurse Chivers announced flatly.

"Mrs. Dillane," Spector extemporised, "I just wanted to visit and pay my respects. I'm a stranger in town and heard tell of your wonderful home.…"

*

"I couldn't break the news to that poor woman that a man was murdered on her land," Spector explained to the doctor once they were out of that room. "It's obvious she had nothing to do with it." Which, for what it was worth, was true. The woman was completely immobile and incapable of speech. A tragic sight. "But," he continued, "that nurse of hers may yet be of some use."

Nurse Chivers appeared from an alcove along the hallway, where Spector surmised she had been lurking so that she might hear their conversation.

"Ah, Nurse Chivers, we were just talking about you."

"Yes? May I be of assistance?"

"I'm sorry to be the one to tell you this, but a man named Danny Snape was found dead this morning in Greeley Wood."

"Goodness." She spoke the word entirely impassively.

"Did you know him?"

"No. I knew *of* him, certainly. The fellow had a reputation. I understand he recently returned from two years' hard labour."

"Really? Nobody's mentioned that previously." Spector looked at Dr. Moorway, who shrugged.

"No. Well. Some people are not as attentive to current events as I am."

Spector's eyes narrowed perceptibly. "I hear he was a poacher."

"He was. Mr. Rafferty, the gamekeeper, frequently clashed with him."

"So there was enmity between them?"

"I should say so."

"Miss Chivers, were you aware of any disturbance at all in the night? Any sound, or any movement in the trees?"

"Gentlemen," she said with an air of finality, "I scarcely have time to scrutinise the local foliage. I assure you that Mrs. Dillane herself is more than enough to keep me occupied."

"So you saw nothing?"

"Nothing. Now good-bye." And she opened the front door for them.

*

"There are so many things which don't make sense," Spector mused as he and the doctor headed back into the village on foot.

"I know. I mean, it's obvious someone did Snape in. For a single blow like that to do such damage, it must have been inflicted with real savagery."

"But we still have the enigma of the missing footprints."

"Indeed. For a moment I *did* wonder if perhaps he had fallen from the Crag and the footprints gimmicked somehow. But why? For what reason? And of course, the head injury was totally inconsistent with a fall from a height like that. There seemed to be no broken bones or even much bruising to speak of."

They were approaching the inn now. It was quiet and barren-looking by daylight. Spector caught a glimpse of Sally peeking out at them from an upstairs window, before she quickly withdrew from view.

"Tell me about the Crag, Doctor."

"Not much to tell. You've got the sheer cliff face which cuts off Greeley Wood somewhat abruptly. But the Crag itself slopes outward toward the road on the other side."

"Hmm. So you might say the Crag acts as a dividing line between the wood and the rest of civilisation."

Moorway gave a dry, gallows chuckle. "You might, at that."

They entered the bar, which was empty, and perched on a couple of stools.

"Tell me this, Doctor: did Snape have anything notable on his person, in his pockets for instance?"

"Nothing in particular. No cryptic note or photograph or anything like that. Nothing so tangible as a clue."

"Please tell me."

"Very well. He had his personal belongings. A little bit of money. A handkerchief. A spare pair of gloves…"

"Really? A spare pair?"

"Well, he wore the fingerless gloves. But he had a pair of full gloves in his pocket."

Spector did not speak for a moment. His mouth hung open in a faintly ungainly manner. "I beg your pardon?"

Moorway looked a little bemused. "Two pairs of gloves…"

"Dr. Moorway, this changes everything." Something had clicked into place. A smile spread across Spector's creased old face.

"Does it?"

"Of course. Two pairs of gloves…" The old man was shaking his head in wonderment. "To think all it took was a spare pair of gloves, and now it all makes sense."

"Mr. Spector? You've cracked it?"

"I have. And really, it's the only way for it to make any sense. Why should he be wearing *fingerless* gloves, when he had a pair of full gloves in his pocket?"

"Well, I suppose he was doing something which required a degree of dexterity in his fingers."

"Quite. But what? What was there for him to do out in Greeley Wood? Certainly not poaching. He had no poaching paraphernalia in his van, did he?"

"No, you're right. He didn't. The whole thing is most odd."

"It certainly is. It's constructed like a puzzle, calculated to confuse the onlooker."

"But you've cracked it?"

"Yes. I rather think I have."

"All right. Go on."

Spector cleared his throat. He was used to delivering these disquisitions to an audience of more than one. "Very well. Nurse Chivers first gave me an inkling. You remember she said Snape had recently completed two years' hard labour?"

"Yes."

"Well, the maximum penalty for poaching is one year. We can infer from this fact that Snape was actually jailed for a different crime altogether, most likely theft, or burglary or some such.

"When he was here at the inn last night, I noticed he had taken a fancy to that mirror behind the bar. No doubt he thought it was of some value. That's why he came back to the inn in the dead of night to steal it.

"That's why he wore the fingerless gloves, you see: for the delicate work of picking the lock. He couldn't do it with the full-fingered gloves on. But Sally Arden, as we know, is a particularly astute young lady. She heard him entering the inn. And with a weapon of some kind, perhaps a poker, she snuck up on him and caught him a savage blow to the back of the head. She only meant to incapacitate him. Unfortunately, she killed him.

"Of course the poor girl panicked. She ran upstairs to wake her father. The plan was all his, I'll wager. You see, you yourself told me that he once worked as the winder in the Greeley mine. His job was to operate the hoist which raised and lowered a metal cage into and out of the mine. And that was the principle he used when he came up with his plan.

"Let's not forget, Danny had parked up in his van outside the inn. He had the keys on him, so it would be comparatively little effort for Sally to drive the van out to Greeley Wood and park it up where it was eventually discovered. But an important detail to note is that when she did this, she was wearing the dead man's boots. She took them from his corpse and put them on herself. Why? Well, to make the footprints of course.

"Meanwhile, Lionel Arden loaded the corpse into his own car, which he drove a circuitous route out to the Crag. Using an ingenious invention of his own, he was able to heave the corpse to the top of the Crag. He needed only a few items which were readily available in his workshed. Namely, the reels of fishing wire and the hosepipe. Or rather, not the hosepipe itself but the hand-crank which is used to ravel and unravel the hosepipe. Picture this: he ties the reels to the corpse at the bottom of the Crag. Then he carries the crank up to the summit, where he begins to reel it in again, dragging the corpse up the hillside to the very top. It's a manual job, and would take considerable physical effort, but he's a stout fellow and I'm sure he could manage it.

"So, we have Sally at the foot of that sheer cliff face on the other side. Her father is at the top with the corpse and the makeshift hoist. Why does he not simply drop the corpse over the side, you ask? Because he is too clever for that. There is another layer to his plan. Instead, he begins to lower the corpse down the sheer cliff face. Sally is there to ensure it lands neatly in the snow, with the single trail of footprints leading from the van to the body directly, supposedly denoting the path Snape himself took with his own two feet. With the body in place, Sally removes the dead man's boots and replaces them on Danny Snape's poor frozen feet. Then she gives her father the all-clear signal and is hoisted to safety. They drive back to the inn, and the whole affair has taken less than an hour."

"It's… rather fantastical," said Dr. Moorway. "I mean, I'm not saying I don't believe it. But why was it so important to have a single trail of footprints leading to the body? Surely that would only raise questions? And why couldn't he just throw the corpse from the Crag?"

"Ah, yes. You see, Arden anticipated that the body would be found by Miles Rafferty. He thought the gamekeeper would stumble across it while on his rounds, therefore leaving a second trail of footprints to the corpse. In short, his idea was to make it seem as though only Miles Rafferty could have killed Snape. A rather sneaky trick, but he did it to protect his daughter, so I suppose that nullifies the dubious morals of the whole thing.

"You'll remember, of course, that Arden was the one who tried to lead the search party *away* from Greeley Wood, toward the river. It compromised the entire plan when the search party found the body together. Because you see, each man knew the other could not have done it. If Rafferty had found the body while he was out alone, things would have looked decidedly murky for him. It would have been his word against… well, anyone's."

"Very clever. Brilliant, in fact."

"Yes," said Lionel Arden, appearing from a back room. "Very good, that."

"I should be going," said Dr. Moorway, looking flushed.

"Yes," said Spector, "perhaps you should."

"I, um, well…" he looked awkwardly from man to man. "Yes. Good-bye." And Moorway scuttled out of the bar, out into the chilly daylight.

Spector favoured the landlord with a sad little smile.

"So you've cracked the case, have you?" said Lionel Arden.

"I wouldn't go that far. Though I do have certain ideas."

"Well, let me say something to you, Mr. Spector. This is a small village. And when a young fellow like Danny Snape goes around making a nuisance of himself, sometimes these things just happen."

Spector nodded. "There's a status quo to be maintained."

"Right. And I know what'll happen if this gets dug into too deeply. It'll end with people getting punished who don't deserve it. You see?"

"Perfectly."

"And I want to prevent that. I *have* to prevent that. It's my job. You see?"

"I see, Mr. Arden."

"So how's about it, Mr. Spector? Do you think we can reach an agreement?"

Cryptically, Spector replied: "I think we already have."

He settled his bill and left a generous tip, which the landlord pocketed warily. The two men did not shake hands. Instead, Spector began his lonely traipse through the snow. He walked slowly, steadily, with the crunch of the snow beneath his feet. Arden's eyes were on him, burning into his back all the way along the road, until he finally turned a corner and disappeared altogether from view.

What Happened
to Mathwig

If I were not such a gentleman, I would not have agreed to kill
Chester Mathwig. Claire said *she* would do it—that as his wife she
felt it was her place—but I wouldn't hear of it. Murder, I told her,
is the man's job.

We'd been talking about it for months. A part of me always knew
poor Chester would have to die. But with the real, tangible prospect
of his murder in sight, I began to grow afraid.

When I met Claire for afternoon tea in the Lyon's Corner House,
she slipped a parcel to me under the table. "Everything's in place,"
she told me softly. Back at my car I unwrapped the parcel. There in
my lap, snug in its nest of brown paper and string, lay a revolver. Its
serial number had been filed off.

Chester Mathwig spent most evenings at Robson's in Latimer
Row. Robson's is a gentleman's club of which he was a long-standing
member, and it's a brief walk from there to the Mathwig residence.
A pleasant enough stroll when the weather's good—it takes you
along a short, isolated stretch of riverside towards Tower Bridge.
On summer nights, Chester often made the return journey alone.
Then would be the ideal time for an ambush.

So, on the night of July fifteenth 1938, I pulled up my car at the
riverside. It was just after eleven and not quite dark—the sky had
a lambent orange glow and the river churned and burbled. A chill
breeze tingled down the back of my neck. I sat with the revolver in
my lap, waiting for Chester.

A chain of streetlamps lit the way beside the water, so I could
see when Chester approached. I had met him before only once or
twice, but his appearance was distinctive enough that I was not fearful of a misidentification. He was a squat little man in his mid-fifties,
with a bushy, Dickensian beard. He was also an old-fashioned fellow who often wore a top hat and carried a pearl-handled cane. I
sat, gun in hand, and waited.

Soon I heard the distinctive patter of Chester's patent leather
shoes and the clack of his cane. He came into view beneath a street
lamp. First I saw the shape of him; stocky in a three-piece suit. Then
I saw his face: the streetlamps reflected in his spectacles, so his eyes

seemed like two glowing orbs. The top hat perched at a rakish angle on his head. He looked to be smiling.

I let him draw nearer. Slowly, I eased myself out of the car. I was concealed in shadow; invisible to anyone on the other side of the road. In my hand the gun was heavy and cold. He edged closer and closer. When he crossed beneath the streetlamp directly opposite me, I stepped out from the shadows.

"Mathwig," I called out. My voice did not sound like my own. He paused and turned in my direction. I raised the revolver.

*

I first met Claire Mathwig in purely professional circumstances. She came into my Harley Street office one bleak October day and began to tell me her dreams. I have practised psychiatry for over twenty years, but never in all that time have I encountered a woman like Claire.

She confessed her darkest dreams to me and, like a good therapist, I offered my interpretation. She was young, beautiful, with eyes that crackled with fiery intelligence. The moment I met her I knew I was damned.

She told me she was married to a much older man, an industrialist named Chester Mathwig. I vaguely knew Mathwig; he was a friend of a friend. But, like most men in suits, one is much like another and I could not recall the circumstances of our meeting. She showed me his photograph, which she kept in a locket round her neck. This, she explained, was a purely token gesture.

Theirs was a marriage of convenience. Claire was the youngest of an important business dynasty and Mathwig no doubt hoped to facilitate certain transactions along the line. "Happens all the time," she explained. "It's the way business is done in the modern world."

I tried to help her—really I did. I advised her to leave him. To leave the country. Anything. But all along, the outcome was inevitable. We began our affair in February.

I would often invite her out to my cottage in the country, where I lived alone. But there always lingered a shadow over our happiness.

"He'd never give me a divorce," she said. "It would be too risky. He's a man who likes to deal in certainties. Sure things. He likes to be in control."

"Well," I told her, "he has to learn that control isn't everything."

To begin with, I was not serious. It was just something to say. But soon I realised that I had begun to *believe* my own bluster. Things came to a head a couple of weeks ago at my cottage.

"I have had an idea," she said. She took me by the hand, sat me down beside her on the sofa, and looked me in the eyes. Then, slowly, she told me what we should do.

*

The revolver flared in my hand. The first bullet caught Chester just below the collarbone: it flung him back against the iron railing. I squeezed the trigger again. This bullet punctured Mathwig's throat. The third and final shot caught him just below the right temple. It knocked the hat from his head and sent him tumbling backwards, over the railing and into the water.

I did not stay to see what happened next. I ducked into my car, fired up the engine and roared away. You must understand—all this unfolded in front of me like a dream. As I drove through the London night, the revolver still smoking on the seat beside me, I did not seriously consider that Chester Mathwig was really dead. Not *really*.

Claire and I had made an agreement when we first set out to do this—we would wait at least a week before communicating with each other once her husband was dead. The next day I went in to work as usual. Patient after patient. Reiterating the same pat diagnoses. But through it all, at the back of my mind, I thought of Claire. And of poor deceived Chester, tumbling dead into the Thames.

But please understand—I did not for a moment regret what I had done. I knew it was for the best. In the garden of my cottage, I took the revolver, emptied it of its three unspent bullets, then with a hammer I cracked it into three pieces: the handle, the bullet-chamber and the barrel. These three pieces I took with me to work later in the week and, during my lunch hour, I took a walk along the Thames and dropped each piece into the water a few hundred yards apart.

It did not bother me that no one had found the body. I presumed the current had carried him away, and that he would soon wash up somewhere miles from London. And when they found him, there was nothing to connect him to me. I had only met the man a couple of times; we were vague acquaintances at best. As the spouse, Claire would be the one to fall under suspicion. But I remembered her last words to me when we parted the day before the murder: "Trust me."

The week was agony, but it passed. I kept my eyes glued to the paper each morning, riffling through for some reference to a body washed up in the Thames. But each morning there was nothing. Finally, when eight whole days had passed, I relented. I picked up the phone and dialled.

"Claire?"

"Claire's not here," said a voice. "Who's this?"

It was a man. And though I had only heard the voice a few times before, I recognised it instantly. I hung up the phone. I seized my coat and ran out to my car. I barrelled across London to the Mathwig home. Then, parking up across the street, I sat for a moment, my gloved hands tight around the wheel. Steeling myself, I climbed out of the car and crossed the street. I climbed the three steps to the front door and pressed the bell.

"We've met before, I think?" said Chester Mathwig, stepping aside to admit me to his home. "The psychiatrist, yes?"

I couldn't speak. I stood in the hallway, gazing dumbly at the face of the man I had killed. My brain seemed to short-circuit. The event replayed in front of me again and again: the three bullets, the blood, the splash of a corpse hitting the water... no. This latter detail was an invention. I had heard no splash. Nothing to indicate the corpse had landed in the Thames. Or even that there was a corpse. But the final bullet hit him in the skull....

"I wanted to speak with your wife," I managed to get out.

"She's not here. For the life of me, I couldn't tell you where she's got to. Friend of hers, are you? Like a drink?"

He took me into the lounge and began to pour a scotch. I took it gratefully and downed it in one.

"My," said Mathwig. "There's a healthy thirst."

I needed to speak to Claire. Claire could explain all this. "I'm sorry," I said, "I have to go."

"But you've just got here! Another drink? One for the road?"

I shook my head, uttered some excuse and stumbled out into the street. I did not go to work that day. From a call box I advised my secretary to cancel all appointments for the next few days. I was ill, I informed her.

As I drove home, I cursed myself for not having taken greater care that night. There were so many details I had missed. Could I be certain that the man I killed was Chester Mathwig? But he matched Mathwig's description perfectly, down to the eyeglasses and the walking cane. And besides, I scanned the paper every morning; nobody else had been reported dead, injured or even missing.

When I got home, I paced through the halls of my cottage for a while. I was waiting for something, but could not tell you what. Some clue.

There came a knock at the door. I looked at the clock on the mantelpiece: it was close to three in the afternoon. The sun streaked through the windows, illumined the dust motes in the air. I took a deep breath. Then I stepped out to answer the door.

The man on the doorstep was a stranger. He was middle-aged and bald; an unimpressive specimen.

"Where is she?" he said.

"Who?" I said.

"Claire."

"I… I don't know."

He looked me up and down. "Something's happened to her," he said, his tone softening.

"Who are you?"

He removed his hat. "My name is Erasmus Cole. I'm a friend of hers."

I studied this man. "How do you know Claire? And how did you find out where I live?"

"I followed you from London," he confessed. "I saw you coming out of the Mathwig house. What were you doing there?"

"Looking for Claire. But she wasn't around." I stepped back from the doorway. "Come in, Mr. Cole."

"No. No, there isn't time. I need to find Claire.…"

"You still haven't told me how the two of you met."

He looked at me like a startled animal. "Haven't you guessed? We're lovers."

Slowly, I nodded. "And when did you last hear from her?"

"I have to go," said Cole. "I can see I've made a mistake. I'm sorry to have bothered you."

He spun on his heel and dashed back to his waiting car. I watched as he roared away from the cottage. That was when I decided to go to Spector.

*

Joseph Spector was the only other living soul I would trust with this story. Spector is not his real name of course—he used it when he trod the boards as a music hall conjuror many years ago. Now he was retired, it had stuck. These days, he plied his trade as a spiritualist medium, but he'd not lost the art of mesmerism and magic. He is the closest I have ever come to encountering a genius. And what's more, he is discreet.

I drove back into London the following morning, to Spector's house in Jubilee Court. It was a funny, ramshackle old house. By daylight entirely benign, but at night—when its upstairs windows were lit—it came to resemble a hollow skull.

I rapped on the door. To my surprise it was Spector himself who answered. He looked unwell. There was always something faintly cadaverous about him. His hollow cheeks looked sallow and unhealthy. His watery blue eyes were half-lidded and sleepy. But when he saw me, he smiled.

"Old friend," he said, "come in."

I followed him through to the drawing room. "My maid is ill," he explained. "I fear I too am succumbing to the sickness. Hot, sweet tea, honey and fluids—they're the answer."

He sat me down by the fire which, in spite of the summer warmth, was lit.

"Now. What can I do for you, my friend?"

I began to tell him my story. He listened astutely, and in silence. When he was entirely up to date, he sat for a moment. In his old age, he liked to let ideas ferment.

"You've been a fool," he said.

"Spector, I didn't come here for a lesson in morals. I want you to tell me just what the hell's going on here."

He sighed. "Because of our prior friendship, I won't report this to my friend Superintendent Flint. But I would urge you to confess as soon as possible. It will be better for you in the long run. You may not even hang."

"But Spector, I don't even know if there's anything to confess to! There's been some trickery and I need you to explain it. Someone's played me for a fool."

"Yes," he said, "on that we can agree. Now, let me get something straight. You and Claire have been lovers for the past few months. Have you any idea how long she and this Erasmus Cole have been an item?"

"No."

"I see. And Chester Mathwig—how did he seem when you met him? Was there anything in his behaviour that alarmed you?"

"I was too confused to notice."

"And ever since the incident eight nights ago, you've not heard from Claire Mathwig?"

"Not a word."

"You've not seen her?"

"No."

"And did Chester Mathwig say anything—anything at all—that could give us a clue to her whereabouts?"

I shook my head.

"Very well. Leave now, please. I need to think. And besides, I wouldn't want you to pick up this bout of flu. I'll be in touch. You can see yourself out, I think?"

*

I wandered for a while. London was stifled by the summer heat, so I headed for the river. And soon enough I found myself at the site of the shooting. Even by daylight it felt isolated, like an island in the middle of the city.

Slowly, I traced the dead man's steps backwards toward Robson's. Rounding a corner, I found myself in bustling Latimer Row and there, ahead of me, stood the club.

I slipped the doorman a pound note and stepped inside. In the foyer I approached a beady-eyed old porter behind the front desk. The sort of cove who could get you the rarest wine vintage at only an hour's notice.

"Were you on duty eight nights ago?"

He studied me as a professor might study some algebraic equation. "I am on duty every night, sir. It is my vocation. But let me see… eight nights ago, that would be Monday. Yes, sir, I believe I was here at this very desk for most of the evening."

"Did you see Chester Mathwig?"

His eyes narrowed. "Are you a friend of Mr. Mathwig's, sir?"

"Yes. Old friends."

I placed a pound note on the desk in front of him. He considered it for a moment. "Then yes, I do believe Mr. Mathwig was in attendance on the night in question. Quite a surprise, too, to see him on a Monday. He spent a number of hours here with his friend Mr. Cole."

"Did you see Mathwig leave?"

"Half-ten on the dot, sir."

"And which way did he go?"

"His usual route. Down by the river."

I chewed this over for a few moments. The porter waited patiently. "Has he been in since then?"

"Now that you mention it, no. I haven't seen Mr. Mathwig since last Monday."

"What about your other regulars? Any unexplained absences?"

"I don't believe so. I would have to consult our logbook to make sure.…"

I slapped another pound note on the desk. "Do it now. I'll wait."

He disappeared into the back room and returned with a weighty logbook. I watched as he leafed through the densely inscribed pages. "No, sir. No irregular absences."

"You're sure?"

"Quite sure."

I left the club with my head spinning. So distracted that I almost missed the sound from a nearby shadowed doorway of a woman whispering my name. I approached and saw the outline of a figure.

She wore a lightweight mauve jacket and a matching cloche hat. She looked like a woman about to undertake a journey.

"Claire!" I said.

She smiled. "It's good to see you again, darling."

"Where have you been?"

"Lying low."

"Claire—it's all gone wrong. The man I killed—it wasn't Chester."

"What are you talking about? Of course it was."

"No. No it wasn't. I went to your house and he's there, he's alive and well...."

"You shouldn't have done that, darling," she said.

"Well then, who did I kill? Claire, I need to know."

"There isn't time now. Tell me tonight on the train."

"Train?"

"The nine o' clock to Southampton. We sail for New York tomorrow lunchtime."

"But... but Claire..."

"We can still salvage something from this. We can still be together."

"Who is Erasmus Cole? At least tell me that."

Claire sighed. "Meet me at St. Pancras at eight-thirty. Platform four. I'll tell you everything."

"Claire!" I called after her. I started to follow, but she was gone.

*

I got to the station an hour early. Settling myself on a bench at the end of platform four, I smoked my way through a pack of Woodbines. I had brought nothing with me. I was content to leave it all behind.

My crime—if it *was* a crime—felt like a fragment of some warped delusion. I told myself that everything would change now. The hour ticked by slowly, but finally it passed.

My only regret was having brought Spector into the whole mess. That was a mistake. But it could be righted—I was leaving the whole debacle behind me. And whether Chester was alive or dead, Claire would be with me.

A second hour passed. I bought myself a fresh packet of cigarettes and set about demolishing it. Innumerable trains hissed to a halt and then heaved away again. Crowds bustled by.

I had begun to sweat. My hand shook as I raised the cigarette to my lips. Then, as the steam from the latest departure cleared, a figure approached me. I looked up hopefully. I felt a jolt in my chest when I saw Joseph Spector.

He was leaning on his silver-tipped cane and blowing his nose. Without a word, he slumped down on the bench beside me.

"What are you doing here?" I said.

"I couldn't bear to watch you any longer."

I sighed, and watched the smoke plume out in front of me. "You've been following me."

He nodded.

"For how long?"

"Since you left my house."

"And what did you see?"

"Enough. She's not coming, you know."

I stubbed out my cigarette on the surface of the bench. "I know."

"They set a trap and you walked right into it. But the truth is, were I in your shoes, I would most likely have done the same thing."

"So you know how it happened?"

"Oh, I know all right. I had my suspicions when you first outlined the problem to me. But this afternoon I had it confirmed by a letter from Erasmus Cole."

"I knew he'd be involved somehow."

"Mr. Cole is sadly not going to be involved in anything any more. He was found in his flat two hours ago, hanging by the neck. A messy suicide—it seems his neck did not snap, and he was left to swing help-lessly as the life choked out of him. But he left a note."

I tried to light another cigarette, but the match scraped ineffec-tually against the matchbox and did not produce a spark. "And what about Claire?"

Spector leaned back in his seat. "*That* has been the question all along, hasn't it?"

"Just tell me," I said.

"Very well. Your mistake when you spoke with Erasmus Cole on your doorstep was to assume that you and he were talking about *the same woman*."

"What the hell do you mean?"

"Do you recognise her?" From the folds of his coat Spector produced a photograph. I studied it a moment: it showed a stout woman in a floral dress. She was round-faced and did not smile. Her hair was fair and she was pocked with freckles.

I shook my head. "Who is she?"

Spector sighed. "This photograph was found in the wallet of Erasmus Cole. You fell for a woman who induced you to murder her husband, correct? But what if the woman you fell for was *not* Claire Mathwig?"

I studied him.

"Had you ever met Claire before she stepped into your office last October?"

I shook my head.

"Then there is nothing, nothing whatsoever, to fundamentally prove that the woman who seduced you was Chester Mathwig's wife? Don't say anything. Just think. Because I would now like to put to you that the woman who told you she was Claire Mathwig was not.

"Chester and Claire were an unhappy couple. We know that Claire began an affair with Erasmus Cole. But if what if Chester also had a mistress, and *this* was the woman who seduced you over a number of months, with the ultimate aim of inciting you to commit a murder?

"What if Claire and Erasmus Cole had already cooked up a plot to eliminate Chester? And what if Chester stumbled across the plot? Perhaps he read one of her letters, or listened in on a telephone conversation? The natural reaction for a man like Mathwig would be to turn their own scheme against them.

"Claire's aim was to firmly establish that Chester Mathwig was at Robson's that night. Then to stage a robbery gone wrong—to kill Chester and dump his body in the Thames, framing some faceless thief.

"In the meantime, Chester sent his lover off to seduce you, the willing dupe, and induce you to kill 'Chester' on the appointed night. Little did you know that you were in fact killing Claire's impostor."

"But who was it?"

"It was Claire herself—the real Claire. The woman in the photograph. She dressed in her husband's clothes, spectacles, hat, a false beard, and she entered Robson's that night for a rendezvous with Erasmus Cole. The porters know Chester by sight, and admitted her in her disguise without a second glance. So she spent the evening in the gentleman's club, conversing with Erasmus as her husband. She then left alone, not realising she was walking directly into the path of a gunman who thought he was killing Chester.

"Claire knew Chester did not normally visit Robson's on a Monday, but hoped this minor inconsistency would be outweighed by the authenticity of the disguise. Of course, if called upon to speak then the whole game would be up. But Claire was lucky. This part of her plan went off without a hitch. She intended to head for home, making sure the staff and patrons at the club saw 'Chester' leave on his customary route."

"So... I killed Claire Mathwig?"

Slowly, Spector nodded. "She was to go home, to prepare for the murder. This part of the plan was purely so that witnesses could attest to the fact that Chester was in the club that night. So she was not the last one to see him alive. As simple as that."

I became aware of a figure looming behind me. I turned.

"I'm sorry to do this to you, Jacob," said Spector. "This is my friend, Superintendent Flint."

Flint stepped round to face me. He was short, moustachioed and wore a pork-pie hat. "There we are sir, nice and quiet," he said, like a doctor administering a painful jab.

"Now just hold on," I said, "you don't expect me to believe this do you? That I killed a woman in *her husband's clothing*? It's ridiculous. You mean to say that sloshing around somewhere in the Thames is the body of a woman in a man's three-piece suit? With a false beard stuck to her chin?"

"You didn't see the evening edition yet, did you, Jacob?" Spector held out the newspaper. It was folded back on the third or fourth page. I did not take it from him, but I read the headline:

"A MOST UNLIKELY DISCOVERY."

I looked at Spector, then at Superintendent Flint. I studied these thoughtful, morose men and heard myself begin to laugh.

Invisible Death

Snow is falling outside, and I am thinking about the Samodiva. It seems strange now, but there was once a time when I had never even heard the word. Since then, the Samodiva has infected the course of my life in many ways.

The story was told to me in 1935. War was still a few years off but England was in the grip of a fierce winter. My fiancée Ruby Soames (as she was then) had invited me out to stay with her family over the Christmas period. It was a comparatively small house, but set in a wide expanse of snow-dappled land. As we drove up the gravel drive, I saw Ruby's mother and father waiting for us, framed in the glowing doorway like a couple of phantoms.

Ruby's mother was a quiet and insipid woman. She was stout and dignified, with a sweet little voice. She always wore black, and today favoured us with a funereal dress that reached her ankles and culminated at her neck in a rippling ruff. With her white skin and sunken eyes, she looked like nothing so much as one of those Victorian *memento mori* photographs. Mrs. Soames gave us a faint smile as Ruby and I climbed from the car, our breath snatched from us by a biting wind.

Ruby's father was more garrulous in his greeting. He stepped forward and gripped my hand in a tight shake: "How are you, my boy?"

"Well, thank you, Colonel."

He wore a fabulous silk smoking jacket embroidered with an oriental dragon. His breath smelt of hot brandy. They each hugged Ruby tightly then ushered us into the house, where the rooms were well-lit, and fires blazed in comfort and warmth. We settled in the parlour and enjoyed a brandy as we told them tales of London and made plans for our festive visit.

We had not been there long when the front door was flung open and a young man tumbled into the house. This was Bill, Ruby's cousin. He beamed when he saw us and snatched us both to him in a great enveloping hug.

Though he was handsome and clean-shaven, with black Brylcreemed hair, Bill was bundled up in a furry overcoat at least two sizes too large, and resembled some Appalachian bear trapper.

He joined us in a brandy and told us of his latest exploits. Bill fancied himself an adventurer and had just got back from the Australian outback. This, Ruby told me, was the influence of his uncle.

While these days Colonel Soames's life was largely sedentary, I knew that he had been quite the daredevil in his time. Recently, the memoirs of his time in Europe during the Balkans Campaign had been published. I made sure to compliment him on the volume's success as we ambled through to the dining room.

"Tip of the iceberg, you know," said the Colonel. "There are things I saw that are so horrible and fantastic they could never see print."

We sat down to dine and as the soup dishes were placed in front of us by two housemaids, Colonel Soames began to tell us the story of the Samodiva. He looked from Bill to Ruby to myself, but never once did he lock eyes with his wife as he spoke.

"We were stationed in Albania in the winter of 1915. Like yourself, Michael, I am a medical man, and I was operating a field hospital out of an abandoned church. You've never fought in a war, Michael, nor you, Bill, and I pray that you never do. But it can do funny things to a soldier's mind. The Slavs have their own ghoulish folklore just like any other region, but it began to exert an insidious effect on the soldiers. It seemed to infect them like a sickness.

"We had established a sort of 'common room' at the rear of the church, in the vestry, and there the healing soldiers would congregate. I would go in there to talk with them sometimes, and to drink with them.

"One of the soldiers I encountered was a chap called Anderson. He was missing his right hand. We'd bandaged him up and doped him, but for a while I was afraid infection had set in. He was starting to get delirious. It was touch and go. By November of 1916 we'd been there for close to a year. It felt like the end of the world. Anderson's recovery was long and there was no chance of us getting out anytime soon.

"There was a civilian settlement nearby. Anderson used to socialise with them. They took him in as one of their own. And once, we were drinking together in the vestry and he started to tell me a story about the Samodiva.

"I'd never heard the word, but Anderson was full of it.

"They told me about it in the village," he said. "At first I didn't believe them. I thought it was just silly talk. But last night I saw it."

"Take it easy, Anderson," I said. "You've had too much to drink."

"It came to the church gates. It wanted to follow me in but it couldn't. You see," he leaned toward me, "it can't walk on consecrated ground."

"Well, as you can imagine I didn't think too much of it. But the next time I spoke to him, he said, "It came a little closer last night." There was terror in his eyes.

"It can't get in, Anderson," I said, trying to placate him. "The consecrated ground, remember?"

"I was wrong," he whispered. "I must have been wrong."

"But that night, something happened. I saw the creature for myself.

"It was a white shape, much like our most trite conception of a ghost. Anderson stood in the doorway of the church, watching it move toward him. Its feet did not touch the ground. I opened my mouth to speak, but I was struck dumb. I saw its bright white face. It extended its white-robed arms and enveloped him in a dark embrace.

"Within seconds, I snapped from my reverie and dashed over to Anderson. He dropped to the ground like a stone. The Samodiva loomed over him. It was tall and white and inhuman. And this is the sight that will haunt me forever. It still crops up in my darkest dreams. You see: *it looked at me.*"

You could have heard a pin drop in that room. The very lights dimmed around us.

"That's enough," said Mrs. Soames.

The Colonel seemed to snap awake. "Of course. Apologies, all. Hardly fit subject matter for the dinner table."

"But what happened to Anderson?" asked Bill.

"He, ah, he died. I am sorry I mentioned it. I seem to have soured the mood."

A silence.

"Well," Ruby chipped in, "you must have mentioned it for a reason."

Another lengthy pause. Then, Soames said something that has stuck with me ever since. "It's just that lately I have started to feel that same dread as I felt the night Anderson died. As if the Samodiva might have remembered my face. As if it might be coming for me."

*

Morning came—a Sunday—and I confess I had not much slept. The house creaked and moaned in the rattling wind and my lonely little room on the top floor looked out on a vast empty expanse of snow-caked earth. The light was insufficient to read, and besides I did not think my concentration was up to it. So I lay there, my eyes wide, staring at the blank ceiling and picturing Colonel Soames face to face with the Samodiva.

I almost missed breakfast; the family were avid churchgoers and were preparing for the morning's service. All, that is, except Soames. He ate little and gazed vacantly at nothing. I was unsurprised when Ruby quietly informed me that he would not be joining us today.

When I spoke to him he responded with the conventional bluster, but in the cold light of day it seemed somehow hollow. "Case of nerves, that's all," he said. "I just need to take a few hours and catch my breath."

"My husband is going to spend the morning at his painting," said Mrs. Soames. "He gets the melancholy sometimes. All he needs is a little quiet contemplation."

Mrs. Soames wore her usual black. That morning I mentioned it to Ruby: "Why does your mother dress like that all the time?"

Ruby gave a sad little smile, but did not answer.

Cousin Bill, too, was oddly subdued, but his appetite was hearty and he was the first among us to don his coat and linger at the front door waiting for the off. While the rest of us scrambled into our winter-wear, Colonel Soames approached his daughter and gave her a damp little peck on the cheek. Then he shook Bill's hand firmly and gave his wife a kiss, at which she almost seemed to shy away. Finally he gave me a warm handshake and when I looked into his eyes I could not escape the feeling that this was a gesture of farewell.

While Bill warmed up the car to take us into the village, Mrs. Soames perched on a little stool in the hallway with all the dignity of a crown princess. She wore a curious pair of spectacles, faintly tinted, so her intractable gaze was masked from view.

Colonel Soames began to mount the stairs and Ruby, unexpectedly, followed him. Halfway up, she turned to me: "Come on!"

I followed. We trailed behind her father as he unlocked the door of the little upstairs room which served as his studio. Then she sprang.

"Daddy!" she called.

He jumped and turned to face us. "What is it, Ruby? I thought you were leaving."

"We just wanted to give you something. A little gift we picked up in London. I was saving it for later, but since you're down in the dumps you might as well have it now."

It was a little trinket we snagged in a pawn shop in Bond Street, but Ruby had fallen in love with it. The old man's face lit up as she produced from her handbag the small velvet box. He plucked it open and studied the object inside.

"And this is from both of you?" he said. We nodded. "It's absolutely marvellous," he went on, placing the object on the flat of his palm. It was an old fob watch, an antique, that Ruby was convinced her father would adore.

"Come in, come in," he said, ushering us into the dank little wood-panelled room. His easel was already set up, with a half-finished still life in place. Various paint pots and jars brimmed with multi-coloured fluids and a row of brushes was lined on a trestle table like a surgeon's instruments. Over in the far corner, covered by a beige tarpaulin, his other paintings lay propped against the wall. The Colonel placed the watch on the large oak sideboard beside a bronze candlestick and began to struggle into his paint-spattered dungarees.

"Thank you both. I know I'm just a superstitious old fool."

"Our pleasure, sir," I said.

"Now get along, both of you, or you'll have my wife to answer to."

We made to go, but before we reached the top of the stairs Ruby turned back and gave her father a hug. She whispered something to him I could not hear. He retreated with that same smile on his face.

Mrs. Soames was still waiting in the hall. "Car trouble," she said.

I went out to assist and found Bill in the driveway with the bonnet up and his head buried in the engine compartment.

"Nothing to fret about," he informed me in his gung-ho fashion, "just a loose gasket."

Bill dashed back into the house like an eager schoolboy. I watched him bound past his aunt and up the stairs—two at a time—to hammer on the door of his uncle's studio. From my vantage point I could not see the door but I heard it creak open.

"Yes?" said the old man's voice.

"We need the spanner, Colonel, do you have it in there?"

"One moment." The sound of footsteps from the studio. Then the old man's voice again: "Here, take it."

The door slammed and the lock clicked before Bill could even thank his uncle. Bill returned looking faintly nonplussed. "The old man uses it to adjust the easel," he explained.

Within five minutes the engine was chugging and the four of us were climbing into the car. As we drove away from the house, there was no doubt in my mind that Colonel Soames was safe and secure in his studio.

*

The events of our return from church at half-past twelve now unfold in front of me on an endless loop, like some infinite cinema reel, or spinning zoetrope. The sun was low and orange in the sky. It already seemed like twilight. After a number of hours in an ice-caked church, we rushed into the house to get warm. Ruby and her mother immediately headed for the blazing fireplace in the lounge, while Bill poured out four glasses of brandy.

"Go and see if Father's all right will you?" Ruby instructed me.

I took my time going up the stairs. When I rapped on the door I was unsurprised that the old man did not answer straight away. Probably hard at work, or lost in some artistic reverie. But then I knocked again. No answer this time either.

I tried the door handle but it held firm. I dropped to one knee and screwed up my eye at the keyhole, but could see nothing. The key, I concluded, must be in the lock on the other side.

Just as I was getting ready to barge the door open with my shoulder, Bill came up the stairs behind me. "What is it?"

"I can't get any answer out of the old man," I said softly.

Then Ruby joined us, her arms wrapped round her shoulders and a shiver in her voice: "What's going on up here?"

"The old man's locked himself in and fallen asleep or something."

Ruby tried the handle for herself and found the door stuck firm. "Daddy," she called through the wood. No answer.

It took the three of us a good fifteen minutes to break open the door. When we gained entry to the room, what we saw inside is now burned into my memory. That hideous tableau of death. The floor, drenched in blood. The old man himself, seated in a small wooden chair by the window, cold and dead. His half-lidded eyes were fixed on something beyond the glass. On his face was an expression of icy dread.

The events of the crime itself have been recorded and studied in minute detail by criminologists and theorists over the years, but it is perhaps worth outlining them again purely for myself. Colonel Soames had been dead perhaps half an hour when we found him, though the medical examiner estimated from the amount of blood that he had been stabbed in the stomach perhaps an hour before that. Since we had been out of the house for over three hours, this left the family in the clear.

The room was locked on the inside; the Colonel's were the only fingerprints on the key. The window too was bolted from within. There was no visible weapon, no secret door by which an assailant could have gained entrance. Colonel Soames had been stabbed in a hermetically sealed room.

We were all questioned and re-questioned. Ruby was hysterical, her mother stoic. Only Bill surprised us in his response: I caught him in the kitchen an hour after the discovery dabbing at his eyes with a tea-towel. He had been crying genuine tears for his dead uncle.

And what of the room itself? Its contents were catalogued and re-catalogued, but no weapon was ever found. The easel, and its never-to-be completed still life of a fruit bowl, had been knocked over, as though in a struggle. The bowl itself, piled with green apples, stood on a high wooden stool near the window. The trestle table of paint pots and brushes of varying length had also been knocked over. Several jars had been smashed. Interestingly, the beige tarpaulin had been wrenched from the completed paintings in the corner and now lay in a ball in the middle of the floor. Beneath it, investigators found a blackened patch on the bare boards, as though they had been scorched somehow. The walls were bare and white, and cold winter sun sent chilly rays through the glass.

I sit now in my own study, watching the snow fall beyond the window. Much has changed in the twenty intervening years. Ruby is now my wife, and sleeps upstairs. She is older; plumper; her hair is greying. Mrs. Soames died perhaps a year after her husband. It was pneumonia rather than a broken heart that saw her off.

And today—this morning—I received through the post an answer to the riddle. I now know that when Colonel Soames told us his story the night before he died, and predicted that his own personal Samodiva would soon catch up with him, he was speaking the truth. I do not know what to do. There is no one to whom I can confide my fears, so I am setting them down in ink. The pieces have always been there, just waiting for me to slot them together. And today it came to me.

*

It wasn't until some years after the Colonel's death that I got my first inkling.

In 1942, Cousin Bill was killed. I've mentioned his lust for adventure, so it was no surprise when he expressed a desire to join the RAF. He was to be a pilot.

It was such a stupid and senseless death. Bill lost in a ball of flame. It felt like the end of everything; I do not know quite how Ruby survived the loss.

When the war was over, we travelled for a while. Through battle-scarred Europe to Africa, where I worked as a surgeon. When we got back to England in 1949, we found a country much changed. It was an end of innocence. But somewhere in the back of my mind, lingering like an errant shadow which should not move but does, I had never quite got rid of the Samodiva.

At a surgeon's conference in the spring of 1950, I bumped into a former associate of mine called Barney. He had risen to a high-up clerical post in the British Medical Association, and was privy to all the latest gossip.

Taking me by the elbow, he drew me aside. "Have you heard about Hutchings?"

"What about him?" I said, startled, sloshing my cuff with champagne from a brimming glass.

"Arraigned two days ago."

"No! What charge?"

"Bribery. Apparently he was taking kickbacks in order to falsify medical records."

I took a swig of champagne.

"The reason I'm telling you this," Barney went on, "is that I wouldn't want Ruby to find out."

"Find out what?"

"Find out, old chum, that if not for Hutchings then her cousin Bill might still be alive today."

"How so?"

"Bill evidently paid Hutchings to fudge his medical records, so they'd have him in the Air Force. Everybody knows you can't have a colour-blind pilot!"

*

I thought back to that weekend—to the furtive glances amongst the family. To the story the major had told. I remember the chilly dread in his eyes when he said he felt the Samodiva was coming for him at last. I remember the way he looked at Ruby and myself on the morning of his death, when he said that final good-bye.

And of course, poor colour-blind Bill, who darted up the stairs to retrieve a wrench. Bill only described in the vaguest terms what he saw in that room: his uncle, he said, was a little curt and strode directly to the wrench in the corner. He seized it and handed it to Bill.

"It was almost as if," I remember Bill saying, "he couldn't wait for me to leave."

That caused considerable intrigue among the investigators. Was the Colonel waiting for someone? No one was ever identified, and of course the snow around the house betrayed no unidentified footprints.

I thought back to that dinner party of the previous evening, and the behaviour of each guest. Ruby was as lively as ever—perhaps more boisterous than usual. The Colonel was in campfire storytelling mode—all sepulchral tones and arched eyebrows. Bill was the adventurer—just a boy at heart really. Mrs. Soames was deathly quiet. But the major never quite met her eye.

Perhaps it is easy to construe significance from the most benign circumstances, but I can look back now and see a silent conversation taking place between husband and wife at that dinner table. A conversation that was dark and deep, like some burbling underground river. What could be read from that connubial silence? He did not look at his wife as he spoke because his eyes were fixed on Ruby.

*

Recently, I attended a lecture at the British Library. The speech was dull enough, but as I was leaving I happened to pass the section labelled 'OCCULT. " I had never noticed this before, and took a few minutes to wander among the stacks.

I was looking for nothing in particular, but when I spotted one title it felt as if Providence had led me to it. *Slavic Folklore: A Compendium of Demons and Ghosts*. I picked up the book from the shelf and flipped to the index. There, sure enough, was the word I had been half looking for all along: *Samodiva*. The entry was brief, but it was enough to set my imagination in motion.

The Samodiva, it read, *is a fabled fairy or wood-nymph of Indo-European origin. It commonly takes a female, humanoid form, with an affinity for fire.*

The last three words were the key. I replaced the book on the shelf. I was thinking of the blackened boards on the floor of the murder room. And the way Colonel Soames spoke on the morning of his death, as though he knew something was coming for him.

But I could not leave it there. I needed to know more. Subsequently, I tracked down a more comprehensive overview—a tome bound in yak-skin—from an occult book shop in Camden. This book was titled *Gremlins of Carpathia* and it had this to say of the Samodiva:

The Samodiva is less a fleshly creature, and more a manifestation from within. An extrapolation of man's weaknesses and his desires, visited upon him and transmuted into horror.

Of course I said nothing of my endeavours to Ruby. But ideas were forming, and when she was out of the house one day I made certain arrangements, the object of which will soon become clear.

Today—that is, November thirtieth 1955—a parcel arrived. It contained a pair of spectacles, slightly tinted, much like the ones Ruby's mother wore that fateful day. I was careful to examine them when Ruby was elsewhere, I do not know what I would have done if she found out.

Slipping the spectacles on, I found myself disorientated. The room around me took on the hue of overexposed photographic negatives. Colours blared like sirens.

Colour-blindness is a hereditary complaint. It is passed down through the genes. Thus, both Mrs. Soames and her nephew were apparently afflicted. To my knowledge, Ruby is not. But these spectacles—with corrective lenses—gave me an idea of the effect of the condition upon everyday perceptions. They also gave me the only viable solution to the Colonel's death.

It was a conclusion no one had seriously considered at the time: that when Bill visited the studio to retrieve the wrench, the fatal wound had already been struck. That it was struck in my presence, by the woman who is now my wife.

With a hatpin or some such unobtrusive implement she clutched her father in an embrace and punctured it deep into his guts. *Before my eyes.* The narrowness of the blade belied the depth of the wound. The shock meant he did not necessarily feel the instant pain. But he knew he had been struck.

When Bill visited the room, it is likely the Colonel's wound had only just begun to bleed. But why, if this was the case, did Cousin Bill not react? When I found out Bill was colour blind, that provided me with my answer. To his eye the crimson blood would be indistinguishable from the green paint with which the Colonel's apron was already smeared. And so perhaps he noticed a certain abruptness in the Colonel's demeanour, or the odd twinge in his movements. But he could not have known that he was speaking with a walking dead man.

With the door safely locked behind him, Colonel Soames had quite a task on his hands. Acutely trained in survival techniques, his first instinct would be to stanch the flow of blood. This is how the blackened patch on the floor came into being—he removed the tarpaulin from the completed canvases and, from the underside of one such canvas, wrenched away the copper wire designed to append the picture to the wall. This, he looped and heated over the candle before—can only imagine the agony—holding it close to the wound in an attempt to cauterise it. This may have been sufficient to close up the wound temporarily, and stanch the heavy flow of blood.

But then things went wrong. He must have grown woozy, and spilt the contents of a jar with a careless arm. The content was turpentine.

This, with the flame of the candle, explains the blackened patch in the centre of the floor. In his panic, the Colonel seized the tarpaulin and used it to suffocate the flames. But this action was enough to wrench open the wound. A wound that had been sealed shut, then wrenched open again: that is the explanation for the time discrepancy of the coroner's report. How the amount of blood the Colonel lost could indicate that he had been stabbed two hours *later*.

The fire completely burned away the fragments of jar and the loop of copper wire, so no trace of them was ever found. All that remained of the fire itself was the black patch on the floor and the lingering smell of chemical fumes in the air. Colonel Soames collapsed soon after that, the blood loss was too great for him. But he struggled to the chair, his imminent mortality dawning on him. He sat and looked out at the snow. And that was where he died.

A patricide is a terrible crime to consider. But I am afraid the motive is more troubling still. I remember the Colonel, so certain that the Samodiva was coming for him. But my failing then was that I did not fully understand the *nature* of the Samodiva. It is an embodiment of man's wickedest desires, come back to torment him, and to seek vengeance. I think back to that ill-fated dinner party, and the story the old man told us. He could not meet his wife's eyes—because his gaze was fixed on his daughter.

So you have heard my story. And my theory, such as it is. I will go upstairs now, to Ruby. I shall lean over and kiss her sleeping face, before stretching out fully clothed on the bed. I think I shall lie there, silent and still as the dead, staring up at the blank white ceiling, waiting for morning.

The Three-Minute Miracle

The swift hour flies on double wings.
—Seneca the Younger, *Hippolytus*, 1141

"Two houses, both alike in dignity," said Joseph Spector.

The two houses he was talking about were Clerkin Down in Ely and Longmeadows in Market Harborough. Both immense, and Gothic in aspect; both set in expanses of broad, bland, greenest England. Separated by fifty miles.

Spector was a retired music hall conjuror, and was given to Shakespearean vagaries when he ran out of ideas. He lived in a squat little place in Jubilee Court, Putney; in musty rooms surrounded by weird and occult arcana, with only his mute housemaid, Clotilde for company. He was an avowed urbanite with little patience for the green-belt upper class. But all the same he had a particular reason for taking an interest in Clerkin Down and Longmeadows. The previous night— scarcely nine hours ago in fact—a woman was shot dead in the library at Clerkin Down. But the murderer was at Longmeadows. Fifty miles between killer and victim! Quite an aim that gunman must have had.

Inspector George Flint, who had been called in to work on the case, sat in an armchair across from his eccentric elderly host and chewed on his unlit pipe, as he tended to do to show how hard he was thinking.

"Well, Flint," said Spector, "speculatively speaking, how much time would Mr. Mellors have had to travel between Clerkin and Longmeadows in order to commit murder?"

"Three minutes," answered Flint. He had been puzzling over the problem since three o'clock in the morning, and was now considerably morose. Even a cup of Spector's unholy black coffee had not sufficiently revived him.

"Three minutes from Market Harborough to Ely," Spector repeated. "Some sort of record, I'll wager."

"The whole thing's impossible, Spector," said Flint. "That's why I thought of you."

The question was not who but how. For there was truly only one person who would have wanted Anthea Wheeldon dead. Mrs. Wheeldon was a philanthropist and patron of various London hospitals, as well as a benefactor of a multitude of charitable concerns. She had recently turned fifty—was growing old gracefully—and, though a widow, had retained that same romantic spirit which had endeared her to her late husband.

Typically when a person whom nobody could want dead dies by violence, there soon emerges a veritable rogues' gallery of plausible assassins. It turns out the victim was a smuggler or a swindler or some other variety of miscreant. But not so Mrs. Wheeldon. Indeed, she was an altruist to her very core. Only an altruist would have taken in and cared for her late brother's orphaned child, especially a boy as troubled as Alec Mellors. Alec went to the best schools, and had all the advantages that would have been given to Anthea's own son, had she produced a child.

Mrs. Wheeldon did everything right. It was not her fault that things went so badly for Alec. The boy nurtured a bad seed within him. He was always aggressive and surly, and his behaviour only worsened as he grew older. He was louche and a drunkard, and his undergraduate studies did nothing to relieve him of the baser aspects of his personality. Indeed, they enhanced them considerably. Such a shame for his poor aunt, who had tried so hard. The boy grew up incurably mendacious; he had a plentiful allowance but always wanted more.

The first hint that something was truly amiss came when Colonel Miles Welch, an old friend of Anthea's, paid her a visit out at Clerkin Down. This was back in January of 1934, a full six months before the murder. Welch was a rare soft-spoken military man; an adept strategist. As he walked into the study, he scanned his surroundings as though looking for unseen enemies. Perhaps he was. Perhaps he thought some assailant might be lurking beneath the wainscoting, or in the drinks cabinet.

He was of course moustachioed, and looked better suited to the cover of a boys' adventure magazine than a mere domestic library setting. He eased his angular frame into an armchair and said, "Anthea, I'm afraid that boy of yours has gone too far this time."

Anthea, who was accustomed to Welch's clipped mode of address, was nonetheless startled by the reference to Alec. "What's happened? Surely nothing that can't be remedied?"

"Blackmail, that's what. Pour me a whisky, would you?"

Anthea did so, still unsure whether the whole thing might turn out to be some kind of gag. But Welch was not the type to tease.

"What's that you're trying to say, Colonel? That Alec has been black-mailing you?"

"*Trying* to. He's got a nice little scheme going, with photographs supposedly showing myself, with a certain lady."

"And he approached you for money?"

"Five hundred pounds, the cheeky blighter! I sent him off with a flea in his ear and a kick in the pants. I have of course no doubt that the fellow in the photographs is himself, disguised."

Anthea Wheeldon had begun to shake, and sloshed whisky onto the counter top. "My God," she said. "Well, I never."

"Look, if this were anybody else I should press charges immediately. But since he's your nephew, I'm willing to look the other way on this occasion, as a favour. But I shudder to think how many similar schemes he's come up with."

"Alec has always been greedy," said Anthea with a melancholy lilt to her musical voice. "He always wanted more and more."

"Well, what are you going to do about it? Talk to the boy?"

A leaden pause, then: "Nothing, Colonel. Alec Mellors is not a boy any more. He is a man. You must do as you see fit."

So Welch did. He reported the incident to police—complete with the reproductions of the photographs which Alec had supplied. Alec Mellors was duly arrested and charged with blackmail. All the while he protested his innocence; that was not surprising. What did surprise Colonel Welch was how cold-blooded Anthea had been that night. He had expected some form of discreet apologia. In a way it was admirable that she had stopped mollycoddling the boy, but in another way it was quite disturbing.

Welch's accusation opened the floodgates. Soon men from all walks of life were queuing up to report that Alec Mellors had in some manner or another inveigled monies out of them, either by intimidation or trickery. It did not look good for the fellow. The woman in the blackmail photographs was never identified, which added a frisson of mystery to the scandal.

Mellors managed to worm his way out on bail, but Anthea made it quite clear that he was no longer welcome at Clerkin Down. So he holed himself up at Longmeadows, fifty miles away. (Longmeadows was the home of one of his old school chums, Richard Snee.) This stalemate between aunt and nephew might have remained until the trial, were it not for one factor.

Two nights ago (that is, two nights before the shooting, before she became a murder victim) Anthea arranged an appointment with her solicitor, a fellow called Norris. It was no secret that she was looking to change her will. Instead of going to Alec, her vast and almost incalculable fortune would be split amongst a selection of worthy charities.

The appointment with the solicitor was made for two days hence; that is, nine hours ago. Just before the murder occurred.

So you see, really there was only one man who could have wanted poor Mrs. Wheeldon dead. And that man was Alec Mellors. Were it not for the fact of his unassailable alibi fifty miles away, he would have been under lock and key that very moment. But he had an independent witness to state that he was at Longmeadows some three minutes before the murder occurred. He was in the drawing room there, by turns dozing and reading and smoking cigars.

"But there's more to it," said Inspector Flint, who had done his level best to tell the story to Spector in as few words as possible.

"I thought there might be," said Spector, lighting a long black cigarillo and pluming smoke into the gloom.

*

"There's only one way to go about it. He must be extricated from the will. It's the only answer."

Colonel Welch was unsure why Anthea had chosen him of all people to confide in. He was flattered of course; for truthfully he had been a little in love with her for most of his life. But he conceded to himself that there must be a more practical explanation. Perhaps it was because he, Welch, had been the one to bring Alec's skulduggery to her attention, thereby making him complicit.

"If you say so. I was perfectly prepared to let bygones be bygones, but if you're sure."

"Oh, I'm sure. To think what his father would say. It's so *shaming*, Miles."

Colonel Welch had to allow that it was indeed shaming, this whole mess. Disinheriting Alec Mellors was really the only thinkable solution. "But I wouldn't trust him as far as I could throw him. I'd keep my eyes peeled if I were you, old girl. He might try to knobble you."

"Violence against me, you mean? Yes, I had thought of that. So far you and my solicitor are the only two people I have told of my intentions, but I've no doubt the story will have spread far and wide before too long. Alec may well find out. He may try to stop me."

That was when Colonel Welch made the selfless offer that would prove a catalyst in The Case of the Three-Minute Miracle.

"Let me help," he said. "Keep an eye on the place. Make sure nothing untoward happens."

"Oh, I couldn't ask you to do that."

"Like hell you couldn't. After all the favours you've done me over the years? That money when I was on my uppers? You're a good egg, Anthea, and I'll not let that little rat do you any harm."

Anthea smiled, and it was a sad smile, as though she knew it was already too late.

But she consented to Colonel Welch's plan. And so Welch began his nightly vigils at Clerkin Down. Rather than impose himself on Mrs. Wheeldon's household, he decided these should be outdoor affairs. He set up a makeshift camp in the trees so that he was in perfect view of the frontage of the house, with its great wide library windows. It was for him an adventure, a reminder of glory days long past, and he would not have missed it for the world.

He soon realised, of course, that watching Anthea was only half the battle. That to ensure no trickery transpired, he would need eyes on Alec Mellors, too.

He therefore put in a call to an associate of his, an old warhorse named Captain Peter Lear. They had served together at the Somme and had come out of that wretched mess alive, so why not this one?

Captain Lear was a few years older than Welch, and had been discharged following a particularly nasty bout of shell shock. But he was a stout fellow, a solid dependable character who would do anything within his power to help his friends. And that was how Captain Lear came to be outside Longmeadows the night of the murder. That was how he happened to be watching Alec Mellors through the drawing room window, so that he could attest beyond all doubt that the young criminal had *not* travelled fifty miles that night to gun down his aunt in cold blood.

At that same moment, Colonel Welch was in the grounds of Clerkin Down, peering through the library window at Anthea, who was awaiting the arrival of the solicitor. Norris had been delayed by car trouble, had called to say that he would be an hour late. So Anthea had stayed up. She had sat in her library and read books, just as her nephew was doing at Longmeadows at the exact same moment.

Colonel Welch watched through sleep-deprived eyes, camped out beneath the trees. It was a dry evening, fortunately, and though late, the sky was not yet dark. Welch observed the library door ease open and a man step through. A little presumptuous of the solicitor to enter without knocking, surely?

Anthea had not even noticed the man arrive. But then recognition dawned. Welch saw that it was Alec Mellors stepping into the library, and that he had a gun in his hand. The colonel was about to cry out, to warn poor Anthea, but Mellors simply aimed the gun and fired three times. The gun was silenced; there were three bright white flashes but no sound beyond the glass. Anthea twisted in her seat, her face contorted with agony, then spilled head first onto the floor and out of view. Welch was already sprinting full-pelt across the grass toward the windows, but Alec Mellors simply turned on his heel and left the room.

Colonel Welch tried the handle and found the window locked on the inside. Eventually, he broke the glass with his fist and undid the latch. Inside he found Anthea Wheeldon supine on the carpet in a slowly spreading pool of blood. She was already dead.

*

Joseph Spector considered the account as Inspector Flint had delivered it. "What time did the shooting occur?"

The answer was 9:17. It was pure instinct—Welch glanced at his watch the moment the shot was fired. So he could say with absolute surety that Anthea was shot dead at 9:17 p.m.

"We've no reason to doubt him, Spector."

"And what was the latest recorded time that Alec Mellors was observed at Longmeadows?"

"Peter Lear stated that Mellors left the drawing room at 9:14 p.m. He took note of the time."

Spector nodded, then added glibly: "How was he to know that Mellors was actually going to sprint fifty miles to kill his aunt?"

"Look, I know the whole situation is ridiculous, but I can't get either man to budge. They're both adamant that the fellow they were looking at was Alec Mellors. And honestly, I've no reason to doubt either of them."

"So you don't think there was some trickery with doubles, or anything like that?"

"No need to take my word for it, Spector. You can ask the men themselves."

Colonel Welch and Captain Lear had come out to London and were staying at the Grosvenor to assist with Scotland Yard's inquiries. That evening, around six, the two men met for dinner in the hotel dining room, where they found Inspector Flint waiting for them with his peculiar associate.

"Who's this fellow?" demanded Lear. He was older than Spector had anticipated. His hair was salt-mine grey and his face looked sunken and ruddy as an overripe plum. His otherwise smooth forehead was racked in the middle by a cratered hollow, a messy scar. He spoke with the bluffness of a military man, but there was an air of tangible disquiet about him.

Introductions were made and the four men sat at a table by the window. Colonel Welch was as Spector had anticipated. A handsome adventurer; he had no reason to doubt his word. Peter Lear was a different matter altogether.

"You have a good set of eyes, Mr. Lear?"

"*Captain* Lear," Lear corrected. "And yes I do, as it happens. I know the whole business is impossible, and that you're thinking one of us must be wrong. Now I've no reason to think Welch here has made a blunder, but I can tell you for damn sure that I haven't either."

He seemed convincing enough. Spector produced a coin. "What's this?" said Lear. "Magic tricks?"

Spector smiled, and in his other hand produced a cigarillo. With the coin flat in his palm, he tapped it with the end of the cigarillo, and it vanished. "You'll have to do better than that," Lear continued. "It's in your other palm."

Spector grinned at this and made the coin reappear. Next he closed his palm around it and opened his other hand to show the coin had apparently leapt invisibly.

"Two coins," Lear said.

Spector did a few more tricks, and Lear saw through them all.

"I take my hat off to you, Captain. You do indeed have a good eye."

"This is a man who took down a Boche at five hundred yards with only a service revolver and a single bullet," said Welch.

"Mightily impressive," said Spector. He had performed the tricks a fraction slower than normal, although typically even then their mechanics would not be perceptible to the naked eye. "But please, do tell me how you came to be involved in this affair, Captain Lear."

The two old soldiers glanced at each other. "We hadn't seen one another in some fifteen years," Lear explained. "But a few months ago we met by chance at Aloysius Monk's in Harley Street. Monk is an excellent physician. Welch here goes to him because of the, uh, you know…" He made a vague gesture with his hand.

"Mustard gas," Welch supplied. "I got a hefty dose of it out in France, and the effects have left me somewhat debilitated."

"Yes, well. Quite a thing, bumping into each other after all those years. And in the same surgery, no less!"

"It always amazes me what a role coincidence has to play in our affairs," said Spector. "In many ways my entire profession is built on it."

"And that's why I thought of Lear when this Mellors business came about. During the war, Lear was a formidable ally. Count on him to sniff out enemy hidey-holes. The man had the keenest eye of any soldier I served with."

Captain Lear inclined his head.

And so talk turned to the events at Clerkin Down. "My only thought," asserted Welch, "was that there might have been some business with doubles. I'm thinking of the blackmail photographs Mellors was bandying around. There was trickery there for certain, and I had assumed they showed Mellors wearing a disguise. But it mightn't have been. It might have been a double. Or an actor or something."

"Do you think you would have been fooled by a disguise?" The two men looked at each other. The answer was evidently no.

Spector cracked his knuckles. "Let's broaden our assessment of those three minutes between 9:14, when Mr. Mellors left the drawing room at Longmeadows, and 9:17, when he arrived at the library of Clerkin Down. Colonel Welch, you had been at your station outside Clerkin Down the previous two evenings, is that right?"

"Quite right. I'd set up a base camp by the front of the house. Clerkin Down backs onto the river, so unless he came by dinghy the blighter couldn't have got past me."

"And Captain Lear, you had been stationed at Longmeadows the two previous nights?"

"That's it. Same scheme as Welch here. Just a tot or two of whisky to keep me warm. I knew who I was looking at and I knew where he was at all times."

"Did you know the house? Had you been there before?"

"No, but my driver got me there and back in one piece. Then I sent him to the pub in the village. The idea was for Welch to call him on the telephone at the pub to let him know the lawyer had arrived safely. Or rather, to provide a code word. Norris's name was *never* used explicitly, I saw to that. Then he would drive back out to Longmeadows and give me the all-clear."

"How much did your driver know about what he was doing? Was he fully briefed?"

"I gave him as little information as possible. I believe in absolute discretion."

"Hmm. And was there anything different about the night of the murder? Anything that sticks in your mind as unusual? That's a question for both of you gentlemen."

With that, Colonel Welch produced a notebook densely packed with scribbles. Captain Lear did the same. "We kept detailed reports of our patrols," Welch explained, "for circumstances just such as this."

Welch went first. "Mrs. Wheeldon had a cook and a housemaid at Clerkin Down. Anthea told me the housemaid—her name is Greta—was going out to visit her mother, who's in hospital with appendicitis. She got back at around eight o'clock. I saw her arrive."

"I've checked up on that, by the way," put in Flint, "about the mother with appendicitis. It's true."

"And Greta returned home alone?"

"She did."

"Anybody else?"

"Nobody," Welch continued. "Anthea was waiting for her solicitor, Norris, but he didn't turn up until after the shooting. Delayed by car trouble, he said."

"You wouldn't have mistaken him for Alec Mellors though, would you?"

"Certainly not. Norris is a great fat fellow; have you met him?"

"I've yet to have the pleasure."

"Well, there's no mistaking him, you take it from me. Mellors is thin as a rake, sort of girlish."

"So as far as you are concerned, how many people were in the house when the shooting occurred?"

"Three, including Anthea. That is, Anthea plus the housemaid and the cook."

Spector turned to Lear. "And how about you, Captain?"

"I had my eye on Longmeadows from early evening. I was late arriving—spot of car trouble myself—but I was there in time to see Alec Mellors turn up. His drunken friend Snee was nowhere in sight."

The friend—not much had been said of him thus far. He was similar to Alec in build, but his skin was paler and his hair fair. They had been comrades since Oxford, partners in crime, so to speak.

"And when did you leave Longmeadows, Captain Lear?"

"When my driver arrived with the all-clear. As I say, he was at a pub not too far away, waiting for a call from Welch."

Spector arched an eyebrow. "So your driver received a call, supposedly from Colonel Welch?"

"Needless to say," Welch asserted, "I never made the call. The solicitor never arrived. But had he done so, and everything else gone according to plan, I should have headed for the house to make the call."

"But who was it your driver spoke to, Captain Lear? Someone he mistook for Colonel Welch? Someone impersonating him?"

"You had better ask the fellow himself," said Lear, "though I doubt you'll get much out of him. I tell him nothing, and he knows better than to ask questions."

*

While the others finished up their meal, Spector took Captain Lear's advice and sought out the manservant. His name was Bernard, and he was waiting with Lear's car, a minutely polished Bentley. "I have one or two questions, if you've the time."

The man was reluctant, but not unduly so. He remained polite but subdued. "I'll do what I can, sir."

"Captain Lear tells us that you drove him to Longmeadows, with instructions only to return when you had received word via telephone from Colonel Welch that the solicitor arrived safely at Clerkin Down. Is that so?"

"It is. I was at the village pub, waiting for a phone call."

"You came with the news at approximately quarter past nine, correct?"

"That's right. I had a call telling me the solicitor had arrived in one piece."

"What did the caller say?"

"It was a code word agreed with Captain Lear and Colonel Welch. He just said 'Sentinel.'"

"And that was the code word?"

"Right. I had no reason to doubt it was Colonel Welch. He, Captain Lear and myself were the only ones who knew the code word, you see."

"What happened then?"

"I drove back to Longmeadows and gave Captain Lear the all-clear. Then I drove him home. When we got back, Captain Lear put in a call to Colonel Welch but received no reply. Then he called Mrs. Wheeldon, and got through to a policeman. And then he found out what had really happened. It was a devilish trick, it was. I mean, how was I to know old Norris couldn't get there? Car trouble's not something you can predict."

"Did you see Alec Mellors when you were at Longmeadows?"

"No, sir. I followed Captain Lear's instructions to approach the house from the west face, so that I should not be seen by any of the occupants. I parked the car by the road, then headed through the brush until I located Captain Lear at the appointed area. Then I told him I had received word, and we both left the way I had come."

Spector nodded, thanked the man, and meandered slowly and ponderously away.

*

That night, Spector did not sleep. He thought about Welch and Lear. Two reliable witnesses. Welch was a long-time friend of the victim's, with a personal stake in her welfare. Lear had been a crack shot in his day with remarkable eyesight.

But the driver, Bernard, did not see Mellors at all. And that telephone call he received at the pub…

The following morning, after a brief reconnoitre at Kings Cross, Joseph Spector took a train out to Ely, to Clerkin Down. Inspector Flint took a train out to Market Harborough, to Longmeadows.

Clerkin Down was immense and ornate as a wedding cake. It was the last of James Wyatt's great domestic creations; a neo-Gothic masterpiece of startling symmetry. The place was now eerily tranquil, since the police had vacated and only the merest echoes of Anthea Wheeldon's presence remained.

Spector rang the bell and it was swiftly answered by the housemaid, Greta.

"Yes?"

"Good morning, my name is Spector…"

"Who is it, Greta?" demanded a voice from down the hall. Spector looked past the girl and saw a stout middle-aged woman whom he assumed was the cook.

"Don't know, Mrs. Blythe," said the girl.

"Well you'd better bring him in."

Spector was duly brought in and installed in the kitchen, where the cook plied him with hot watery tea and interrogated him as to his business there at that house of death.

"I'm working with the police," he said. "We're trying to find out what happened to your mistress."

"Well, I'll help if I can," Mrs. Blythe said, "But I don't know if I'll be of any use. The kitchen is my domain, and I don't go out of it if I can help it."

"And did you that evening?"

She shook her head. "No. I cooked the food, and Greta took it up for her. Then I was just doing bits and pieces down here, I can't remember what."

"So where were you when the shooting happened?"

"Down here, of course."

"And Greta?"

"I don't know. Upstairs somewhere. You'll have to ask her. The first I heard of it was when that Colonel came down here shouting the odds."

Spector finished his tea, thanked Mrs. Blythe and left the kitchen in search of Greta. He caught her in the drawing room, tidying books aimlessly. She was oval-faced and gamine, with smooth skin, almost doll-like.

"I'm sorry to trouble you, Greta, but I need to ask about that night."

She spoke slowly, and her half-lidded eyes seemed heavy with sleep. An impact of the shock, Spector surmised. "My mother," she said, "she's in hospital. Her appendix. I took the mistress her meal, then I went out to see Mum at the hospital."

"And when did you come back?"

"Around eight, I think?"

"Ah. And did you see anybody in the house, anybody at all, when you returned?"

She shook her head with ruminative slowness. "What happened then?"

"Well, when I heard the gunshots I headed to the library. I didn't know what they were then, of course. Then I heard breaking glass. And then Colonel Welch came out to meet me in the corridor."

"And there was nobody else? Nobody running out of the library into the corridor? Nobody armed with a pistol?"

Again she shook her head.

*

Longmeadows was a neo-Gothic pile in the vein of Pugin, though lacking his finesse. It was essentially a bricked-in cube, albeit one disguised as an auspicious country seat. In that respect, it suited Richard Snee.

Snee was a slight man, but intractable in his rebuttal of Inspector Flint's questions. The two men were in the drawing room; the very drawing room where Alec Mellors had been observed on the night of his aunt's murder.

"He was here all night," said Snee. "I'll swear to it in a court of law."

"It's not the whole night we're concerned with, Mr. Snee. It's 9:17 p.m."

"In that case, he was most assuredly here. We dined. I went to bed early, as I had an early start the following morning. Alec went into the drawing room to listen to music and read and smoke, or whatever it is he tends to do with his time."

Flint considered this a moment. "What did he listen to?"

Snee seemed flummoxed by the question. "He had the door closed, Inspector. So as not to disturb me."

"Then you couldn't hear?"

"No, I couldn't hear."

Flint strode around the grounds for a while. He found the spot where Captain Lear had set up his sentry post, but there was little else to see. He looked back at the house and established to his own satisfaction that, with the windows fully lit, there could be no mistaking the identity of whoever might be in the drawing room.

Flint left Longmeadows feeling profoundly dissatisfied.

He took a taxi out to a pub called the Peveril Arms, which was some twenty-five miles from Longmeadows. When he got there, Spector was waiting for him on a bench outside.

It was a pleasant patch of verdant countryside spliced by drystone walls and narrow meandering roads. "Afternoon," Flint called.

"Afternoon, Flint. Care to join me?"

Flint sat beside the old magician. They reposed for a moment, watching the livestock in a nearby field. "Do you know where we are?" said Spector. Flint turned to glance at the pub sign, but Spector continued: "We are precisely equidistant to Clerkin Down and Longmeadows."

"Is that so? Slap bang in the middle?"

"Mm. That way—" he pointed to the right "—is Longmeadows, straight down the road. And *that* way—" he pointed in the opposite direction—'is Clerkin Down."

"Twenty-five miles each way," said Flint.

"And *that* way," said Spector, pointing up a second road which spiked off from the main road in a T-junction, "is St. Judith's Mount. That's the village where Captain Lear lives."

"Closer than you think, isn't it?" said Flint.

"All paths converge on the Peveril Arms." Spector nodded.

"Almost makes you wonder…" Flint began, but trailed off.

"Wonder what? If Alec Mellors *could* have done the trip in three minutes?" Spector gave a hollow, deathly chuckle.

Flint turned and looked the old man straight in the eyes. "Something has gone on here, Spector. Something very iffy indeed."

Spector changed the subject. "How was Mr. Snee?"

"A little overeager to defend Mellors. He claims he went to bed early, but that he's nonetheless willing to swear that Mellors didn't leave the house at all that night."

"Why would he say something like that?"

Flint shrugged. "Your guess is as good as mine."

"I would imagine Mellors still has some dirt on his old friend. Something he's wielding over him, to guarantee compliance. I think we can discount his testimony entirely."

"I'm inclined to agree," said Flint between puffs on his pipe. "Now how did you get on at Clerkin Down?"

"Well. As well as might be anticipated. I met the cook; she told me she cooked a meal for Mrs. Wheeldon and that she ate it heartily."

"And where was she when the shooting occurred?"

"In the kitchen, she says."

"So she saw nothing?"

"Nothing. The maid admits going out to visit her mother, but claims she was back by eight, which ties in with Colonel Welch's testimony about seeing her arrive."

Flint moaned and rubbed at his forehead with a calloused palm. "I just don't know. What do you make of it, Spector? What do you make of the whole rotten mess?"

"Nothing at all," said Spector softly. "Unless…" but then he trailed off into silence, and his pale blue eyes misted over.

*

They took the train back to London together, but their conversation was stilted and rather fractious. Spector was uncharacteristically sullen. The two men parted ways at Kings Cross once more, with a promise to meet the following morning at The Black Pig in Putney, which was Spector's habitual alehouse. In fact it was one of the few places that would tolerate the odour of his tobacco.

Flint stood on the platform and watched his old comrade retreat into the encroaching darkness, and for the first time he was conscious of the old man's frailty; of his narrow, slumped shoulders, and his head hung low.

*

Spector was late for their appointment. He got there at around quarter-past eleven, having kept Inspector Flint waiting well over an hour. Flint had chewed at his fingernails until they almost bled, before eventually succumbing and ordering a half of stout.

Finally, Spector exploded into the snug with a flourish of his silk-lined cloak. "Flint!" he bellowed. "Good morning to you. And thanks for bearing with me whilst I tied up a few loose ends."

Flint was on his feet. "What do you mean 'loose ends?'" You mean you've put it all together?"

"That's exactly what I mean, old man." They sat, and Spector ordered an absinthe. "Same for you, Flint?"

"Thanks, but no. Now please, tell me what you've been up to."

Spector grinned. "I was seeing an associate of mine. An old friend in Harley Street."

"Harley Street?"

"You heard me correctly, Flint. Start drawing up the arrest warrant for Alec Mellors—we've got him. You might also wish to arrest Lear's driver, Bernard. And the housemaid, Greta."

"For what?"

"They're accomplices, or accessories, or whatever legal terminology you prefer. I realised the driver must have been in on it when he let slip a fragment of information that an innocent man could not have known. He mentioned the solicitor, Norris, and his car trouble. Captain Lear told us explicitly that he had not used Norris's name to the driver. So how did he find it out? This was, after all, scarcely common knowledge. The answer could only be that he was aware of it *before the fact*. He must therefore have been in on the trick.

"Once I got used to this idea then it became clearer to me how the trick *might* have been worked. It made little sense, though, until I paid a visit to Doctor Aloysius Monk of Harley Street. I remembered the name—who could forget it?—as someone who had been visited by both Colonel Welch and Captain Lear. I managed to inveigle out of him a piece of medical information which further supported the idea that was growing in my head. It was clever all right, and outright wicked."

"Very well," said Flint, "you had better tell me."

"I remembered that Welch and Lear had rekindled their friendship over a chance encounter at a Harley Street surgery, where Welch was being treated for the ongoing effect of the mustard gas poisoning he suffered in the trenches. Naively perhaps, I assumed that Captain

Lear's long-term injury which had seen him invalided out of service was similar. But it wasn't. There was of course that scar on his forehead, which I should have understood instantly.

"Peter Lear has a bullet in his brain. Typically, this does not affect his day-to-day life at all; it certainly has not altered his impeccable eyesight. But it *has* left him susceptible to a certain type of trickery. The bullet caused irreparable damage to the posterior cingulate cortex. I had no idea as to the function of that particular nugget of brain until I consulted Doctor Monk. It handles the sense of direction. Not spatial perception, such as recognising your surroundings, but determining routes *between* two familiar locations.

"He is bluff and stubborn, so of course he is in deep denial about the impact of the brain injury. But the fact is he could not have found his way to Longmeadows himself. He simply could not do it. He was reliant on the honesty and dependability of his driver.

"There was no doubt in my mind that Captain Lear was the weak link, but I could not determine how. His eyesight was flawless. But when he mentioned a problem with his car, an idea began to form. And then when I met you at the Peveril Arms, it all fell into place."

"But how would Mellors have found out about the bullet in the poor fellow's brain?"

"The same way I did. I should have thought it was simple for a man in his position. He still has a network of spies to fuel his blackmail enterprise. He knew Colonel Welch, he knew there were no flies on that particular gentleman. But he is adept at singling out a weak link and exploiting it. He could have found out that Lear was driven everywhere. He could even have had eyes in the Harley Street office, to find out the scope of the injuries and how they might be used to his advantage. But either way, it must have been clear to him that Captain Lear's injury would be key to establishing his alibi."

"I still don't understand, Spector. So Lear couldn't have got to Longmeadows on his own, so what?"

Spector beamed. "But don't you see? That changes everything! It means he was reliant on somebody else to transport him there. It means that we can trust what he saw, can take his descriptions literally, but the entire context in which he saw them is altered! All it would take is for Alec Mellors to pay the driver off and then he could carefully orchestrate exactly what Lear saw that evening. He was in complete control."

"But if he was at Longmeadows…"

"That's just it, Flint! He wasn't!"

Flint opened his mouth to say something, then closed it again.

Spector went on: "If you think about it, Alec Mellors is the only person who had visited both Clerkin Down and Longmeadows. So he was the only one in a position to observe the outstanding similarities in their Georgian and neo-Georgian architecture. The fact of it is, Flint, the houses are *not* identical, but their floor plans *are*. They are built from the same blueprint, so to speak. One is an authentic example of Georgian architecture, while the other is a meticulous imitation. But they are situated in identical patches of land, and their furnishings are similar. Not *the same*, but then I'm sure Mellors made a conscious effort to have Greta arrange the furniture in the Clerkin Down drawing room so that it resembled the one at Longmeadows. The walls of both are conspicuously bare, so it was just a matter of moving chairs and the odd coffee table. Setting the scene for a performance like no other, to deceive the keen eyes of Captain Lear.

"With Lear's driver on his side, Mellors was able to orchestrate the vantage points of both men so that they were at opposite sides of *the same house*. Welch was watching the study, where Mrs. Wheeldon was waiting for Norris. And Peter Lear *thought* he was watching the drawing room at Longmeadows. In fact it was the one at Clerkin Down. So when he saw Alec in that room, he was actually only in the room across the corridor from his intended victim."

"In that case why did it take three whole minutes for him to walk from one room to the next?"

"Picture him in the corridor between those two rooms, Flint. Between worlds, so to speak. In one he is merely a scoundrel. In the other, a murderer. And there he stands between them, in the midst of the ingenious trick he has devised. He is crippled by indecision. But he—how does dear Lady M. have it?—screws his courage to the sticking place." And in so doing, he damns himself."

"This raises more questions than it answers," said Flint, rubbing his forehead. "I mean, how did Mellors get into Clerkin Down without being seen by Welch?"

"Yes I puzzled over that for a while too. But then it dawned on me—the housemaid. There has been so much speculation over the identity of the mystery woman in the photographs Mellors tried to use to blackmail Colonel Welch. What if it was Greta? And what if Mellors recruited her into his murder plot? All he needed to do was convince her to vacate the house for a while and leave him with the key. He could disguise himself as her (don't forget he is slimly built and small, "girlish," Welch said) and from afar—with his face covered—he could be mistaken for her. I know she lied, too—she told me she heard gunfire, but Colonel Welch claims the gunman used a silencer. So, when Welch saw the housemaid enter the house, he actually saw Alec Mellors arriving to murder his aunt.

"Alec snuck in unnoticed by Mrs. Wheeldon or by Mrs. Blythe, the cook. Then he changed into his everyday clothes and presented himself in the drawing room, where he knew he would be observed by Peter Lear. He idled for a while to establish an alibi, then he got up, went out into the corridor, readied himself, entered the study (in full view of Colonel Welch), and committed murder. He used a silenced pistol so Lear wouldn't hear him on the other side of the house. Then, while Welch was breaking the study window to gain access, Alec Mellors simply exited via the front door. Greta must have been waiting somewhere outside, hidden, so that she could slip into the house when Alec slipped out. Then she could run through to the study and meet Colonel Welch, giving the impression she had been in the house the whole time.

"Lear meanwhile was at the beck and call of his driver. What proof do we have that the telephone call he supposedly received at the pub ever happened at all? Far more likely that Greta signalled to him that the deed was done, perhaps by flashing a torch, and that was when he headed round to deliver his 'all-clear' to Captain Lear."

With that, Spector's drink arrived. He toasted Flint in silence, and drank. Flint meanwhile looked to have descended into speechless apoplexy. His face had turned claret, and he seemed to be struggling to find the words.

*

Joseph Spector was not present when they hanged Alec Mellors; he would not have wished to be. But he felt a curious frisson as he sat alone in the snug of The Black Pig, a tingle down his scoliotic spine. And for an instant he was there, with the black hood over his head, and the noose gently looped about his neck. He blinked and it was over; daylight seeped back in.

Though an avowed sceptic, a marked debunker, Spector was paradoxically afflicted by these occasional bouts of *déjà vu*. He could not tell if they were unwarranted fits of antic imagination, or if they were genuine phenomena. But the day Alec Mellors died—that very instant, twelve noon—was the closest Spector ever came to being in two places at the same time. It was not an experience he cared to repeat. With a low sigh he lit a cigarillo and signalled the barmaid for more absinthe.

The Problem of the Velvet Mask

"Don't lower your mask until you have another mask prepared beneath—as terrible as you like—but a mask."
—Katherine Mansfield, letter to John Middleton Murry, July 1917

1.

The retired conjuror Joseph Spector shared his Putney home with a collection of mysteries and enigmas. It has been said that stepping into his study was like stepping into his carnivalesque mind. Just inside the door stood a squat little skeleton—ostensibly, the bones of "Tom Thumb." On the far wall was a square portrait of indisputable provenance, depicting none other than the great occultist Cagliostro. And on a shelf stood a genuine first-edition *Malleus Maleficarum*—"The Hammer of Witches"—Kramer and Sprenger's mad witchfinder's handbook, a text which set the template for countless witch hunts; the persecution and torture of innocents over hundreds of years.

But in many ways Spector's most interesting "exhibit" was his housemaid, Clotilde. She had no surname anyone was aware of, nor any living family. She was mute. She had a brittle, almost porcelain beauty; in some ways it echoed the diaphanous creases of Spector's own aged face. There was speculation that she might be his daughter, or even granddaughter—but this was just silliness. Nobody knew where she came from. She had been with Spector for as long as anyone could remember. This in itself was an interesting paradox, for she seemed to be only in her mid-twenties. Nobody ever asked him about her. She was simply there, and went about her duties with almost uncanny prescience, as though she and Spector shared a psychic bond. She was his familiar.

It was through Clotilde that Juliette Lapine managed to track the old man down. Somebody had mentioned that Spector had an uncanny knack for solving apparently insoluble problems, so she sought him out. But Juliette was not a Londoner—indeed, she was Parisian by birth—and was daunted by the nebulous, stygian byways of England's capital. She came across Clotilde in Putney market; did not meet her face to face, but her eye was caught by this eerily silent, doll-like young woman, so she asked one of the vendors about her.

"Oh, that's Clotilde," the old woman behind the stall explained, "We all know Clotilde. She looks after that old magician."

And all at once, the chase was on.

The night in question, about a week before Christmas 1933, Juliette Lapine strode through the icy mist of lamplit London, crunching the treacherous snow-caked streets past chestnut sellers and carol singers. She found the Spector place nestled in the corner of Jubilee Court, a squat little house which blazed like a jack o' lantern. When she reached the front door, her resolve almost deserted her. But she rang the bell and bundled her furs tighter around herself, shuddering a little.

Clotilde appeared at the door.

Juliette cleared her throat. "My name is Juliette Lapine. Is Mr. Spector at home? I need to speak with him. Please. It's life or death."

Clotilde had a slight smile on her face as she stepped aside to admit the young woman.

Spector was awake still; apparently he seldom slept. He sat in his study with some ancient grimoire propped open in front of him, smoking rancid-smelling cigarillos as he turned the pages. He looked up at Juliette with an appraising smile.

"Lapine? I've heard the name somewhere before..." he said. "Incidentally, don't worry about Clotilde. She's mute. Take a seat, won't you, Miss Lapine?"

Juliette did so.

"Now what brings you to Putney at this time of night? Gone eleven, isn't it?"

"I'm not here for myself," she explained, "but for my father. Someone is out to hurt him."

"Oh yes?"

"There's a man who wants to kill him. A man who wears a mask."

"Please," said Spector, "begin at the beginning."

"Very well. I live with my father, Lucien Lapine, the French diplomat. Perhaps you know his name from the newspapers? I grew up in Paris but was schooled in England, and we settled in Knightsbridge about a year ago. Also living with us is my younger brother Étienne, and my father's personal secretary Bourdin.

"There's a house across the street from ours which has been vacant for some time, and last week I spotted removal men delivering some furniture, so I assumed a new resident was finally moving in. I asked one or two of my friends who live in the street, but nobody knew anything about the new arrival. He finally put in an appearance on Friday. And I can tell you for a fact, Mr. Spector, that he's dangerous. He means us all harm.

"He arrived in a funeral car, like the grim reaper himself, the great hearse splicing the fog like the prow of a ship. He was all in black, with a wide-brimmed hat. But he wore a mask—a mask of black velvet which concealed his features, save for his beady eyes that twinkled like black diamonds."

"So the fellow moved into the house opposite?"

"Yes. Dauger is his name, Eustache Dauger. And it generated much talk in the street, as you can imagine."

"Naturally. But what gives you the idea the man is dangerous?"

"I could write the mask off as eccentricity. But there is something about the man—and the way my father reacted to him. As though he had been expecting him for many years."

"So your father was there when he arrived?"

"Yes, we were both returning from a stroll. Dauger and my father shared a… look. It was as though they recognised one another. But my father has refused to discuss the matter since."

"Eustache Dauger. An interesting choice of pseudonym," said Spector. "It was one of several aliases ascribed to the so-called 'Man in the Iron Mask,' the notorious historical prisoner whose real identity has never been established."

"Thank you, Mr. Spector," said Juliette, "I'm aware of the historical connotations. My father made sure I was well schooled in the arts of history, diplomacy and warfare." She spoke brusquely, fists clenched in her lap.

Spector smiled. "You want me to look into the matter, is that it?"

"Let's say I'm aware of your reputation for dealing with bizarre and inexplicable circumstances. I have money, if that's a concern."

"We can discuss the details later. I think I should like to see this Dauger character for myself."

"Perhaps this will interest you," added Juliette, producing a folded sheet of paper from her handbag. Spector took it and carefully unfolded it, as though it were some sacred parchment. In fact it was a pencil sketch of a man in black, who wore a wide-brimmed hat over a face that was completely covered by a mask.

"You drew this yourself?"

"From memory. My father wanted me to be a musician like my mother," she said with a little shrug, "but I draw."

Spector examined the picture. There was nothing about the man he could pin down. The mask was smooth and featureless. "How tall is he?"

"Tall. Perhaps six feet."

"Of course, that tells us nothing. A short man might wear lifts in his shoes."

"Does this mean you'll look into it? You'll protect my father?"

"It means I'm *curious*, Juliette. But what would you have me do? I'm just an old man, and your father can surely look after himself? From what you tell me, there's nothing to indicate conclusively that this man is a threat."

"My father has scarcely spoken a word since this Dauger put in his first appearance. He's terrified, but he doesn't want to show it."

"And what about your brother?"

"My brother is young and ready to take on the world. In other words, he is stupid. He is no use to me in the current situation."

"And you mentioned your mother…?"

"She died when I was young."

"Then who else lives in the house with you? Servants? A secretary, I think you said?"

"We have a woman who cooks, but she doesn't live with us. The only live-in staff is my father's secretary, Bourdin."

"Ah yes. What can you tell me about him?"

"He's an old family friend from a long way back. The closest my father has ever had to a confidant."

Spector thought about this for a silent moment. "So there are four of you in the house. And this Eustache Dauger—you believe he is a figure from your father's past?"

"It's a feeling, Monsieur Spector. But a powerful one."

Spector studied her for a little while. She was painfully aware of the probing nature of his gaze, and of the faintly sinister silhouette of Clotilde in the corner of the room.

"Very well," said the old man.

2.

The following morning, Spector began making his own discreet enquiries. Lucien Lapine was a name which triggered a vague memory. It did not take too much digging to unearth details of the man's illustrious career. His greatest claim to fame was his involvement some twenty-five years ago in the notorious "Duchesne Affair," which had racked French politics and caused a global scandal.

It was not the sort of story which typically interested Spector, but he remembered all the same that "Duchesne" had turned out to be a spy in the French corridors of power, and that Lapine had been responsible for unmasking him. Since then, Lapine had gone from strength to strength. He was now pushing sixty, and comfortably settled into his retirement, his glory days a long way behind him.

Spector arrived in Knightsbridge early. In fact, it was still dark. He wanted to get the measure of the place. He strode up and down Quentin Crescent, the street of genteel Victorian terraces where the Lapines lived. Their house was pleasant, but ultimately nondescript, save for a bamboo trellis up the western wall; the sole hint of exoticism. In the summer no doubt, it was threaded with flowers.

As Spector walked, his silver-topped cane clacked rhythmically on the cobbled pavement. He was there as the winter sun rose, bathing London in a feeble half-light. He kept a surreptitious eye on the Lapine place, but his main focus was the house across the way. Nobody went in or out. All the same, Spector was conscious of an ominous presence in the top window, watching him.

As the morning wore on, traffic increased. Spector managed to strike up a conversation with two ladies out for a stroll—they introduced themselves as the Weatherill sisters from the end of the street. His inquiries revealed that the house in question had indeed been rented by an unusual and mysterious individual. A man who— whenever he appeared by daylight—wore a black velvet mask. A man going by the name 'Eustache Dauger.'

So Juliette's story was true. The sisters reported that Dauger had a low, sonorous and sinister cadence to his voice. And his eyes were narrow and dark. But apart from that, he was an enigma. Like a vampire he seemed to shun daylight. His only servant was a chauffeur who drove the hearse—a young man who spoke a language which had not yet been identified. "Some strange foreign chatter," one of the Weatherill sisters observed unkindly, while Spector looked up at the house, at the pair of invisible eyes, blazing down with silent fury.

3.

"Flint, season's greetings!"

Spector strode into Inspector George Flint's office unannounced, as he often did. The old conjuror was a familiar face at Scotland Yard thanks to a febrile working relationship with Flint.

Flint looked up from a heap of papers, his moustache drooping.

"Spector. To what do I owe? Or wait a moment, don't tell me. A chap named 'Eustache Dauger."

Spector eased himself into a chair. "How did you know?"

"Oh, an educated guess. And the fact I've finally managed to evict an irate young man named Étienne Lapine from my office. He seems to think this Dauger has murder on his mind."

"Étienne Lapine? Juliette's brother?"

"Yes. And a bumptious twit he is. He's demanding police protection for his father."

"Have you managed to find out anything about Eustache Dauger?"

"Not a bean. Name's most likely an alias, but my hands are tied. Unfortunately there's no law against renting a house."

"Have you been out to visit the Lapines?"

"No. And I'm not going to, either. There are five days until Christmas, Spector. Have you any idea how busy this time of year is for Scotland Yard?"

"Of course, foolish of me. What about Lucien Lapine? Is there anything I ought to know?"

Flint sighed. "Why don't you ask him yourself? I've got better things to do with my time."

Spector bowed slightly, and withdrew.

He meandered for a while. He was half-tempted to present himself on Eustache Dauger's doorstep and simply ring the bell, but something told him to play a more discreet hand. Juliette had invited him over for dinner that evening so that he could meet the Lapine household. So he bided his time. By early afternoon, he was at The Black Pig, his favourite Putney watering hole. That was where Georges Sorel tracked him down.

Spector was in the snug, nursing a half of stout when a man approached him.

"Your name is Spector, yes? Like the ghost?" His conically brilliantined beard protruded from his chin like that of a pharaoh. His hair was boot-polish-black; too black, in other words, for a man his age. All in all, he looked like a diabolical circus ringmaster.

"Yes," said Spector, "like the ghost. Have we met?"

"I am Georges Sorel. Perhaps you have heard of me?"

Spector had. Sorel was a reporter. One of France's most esteemed, in fact.

"Am I right in thinking you are interested in a man named Eustache Dauger?"

Sorel smiled. "Not quite. I am here because of Lucien Lapine."

"And how may I help you?"

"I understand you have been hired by Juliette Lapine. Is that so?"

"It might be."

"Well, I do not know how much you know about Lucien Lapine, but I imagine you have heard of 'the Duchesne Affair'?"

"Yes. I know Lapine is a diplomat and that he was involved with tracking down a spy in the upper echelons of French intelligence."

"The Duchesne Affair," said Georges Sorel, "is a dark shadow in our country's recent history. Felix Duchesne was falsely accused— and I can prove it."

Spector considered this. "Is it a coincidence that your revelation comes hot on the heels of the sudden appearance of a masked stranger named Eustache Dauger?"

Sorel smiled. "I don't know. But it is quite a story, yes? Do not misunderstand me, I play my cards close to my chest. I know I look feeble, but last year I traversed the length of the Loire Valley by bicycle in pursuit of a lead. I am someone who is willing to go 'the whole hog,' as you say. All the same, I thought I might possibly find an ally in you."

Spector nodded. "Quite possibly. The Duchesne Affair was some twenty-five years ago, wasn't it?"

"Correct."

"And what happened to Felix Duchesne himself?"

"He was treated like a common traitor. He was sent to Devil's Island."

"Do you think it's possible he might be here in London?"

Now, the journalist gave a single, harsh laugh. "Fairy tales. Felix Duchesne succumbed to dengue fever less than two years after his conviction."

"How do you know that?"

"I have my sources. A monsignor who travelled out to Devil's Island once on a mission of mercy wrote an account of the death by fever of an 'accused spy.' The prisoner was never named, but from the description it's reasonable to assume it was Duchesne. Even more damning, a former convict named Sarnac gave me a personal account of Duchesne's death. The two men were friends, you see, during Duchesne's brief tenure on the island."

"But Duchesne was never officially declared dead...."

"It was hushed up. The French military wanted to sweep the mess under the carpet, as you say. So when Duchesne died, they suppressed the story. Any accounts were prevented from ever seeing the light of day. Until now, that is," he added, playfully drumming his fingers on the tabletop.

"This is most interesting," said Spector. "I presume the story you are cooking up features Lucien Lapine as one of the conspirators against Felix Duchesne?"

"The head conspirator. He does not know it, but my story will ruin his life."

"It begs the question, though: if Eustache Dauger is not Felix Duchesne, then who is he?"

Sorel shrugged. "It might be anyone. It might be me. It might even be you. Now tell me, will you be visiting the Lapines?"

"Yes. Tonight. Juliette invited me to dinner to try and find out about 'Eustache Dauger.'"

Sorel snorted. "Then I wish you luck, *Monsieur-le-fantome*. I will be staying at the Savoy, should you wish to contact me."

4.

When the cab deposited Spector in Quentin Crescent for the second time that day, three figures descended the stone steps from the Lapine porch to greet him. The first was Juliette, in an exquisite evening dress. She took his right hand in both of hers and gave it a squeeze; it was a gesture which conveyed a great deal to Spector, though her facial expression remained still and intractable.

Next came her brother. Étienne Lapine was boyishly handsome and smooth-chinned. He had slightly protuberant ears, but otherwise his features were well proportioned and his hair thick and black. He looked as though he were incapable of producing a smile; one of those agonisingly earnest young men who are quick to anger, the sort who die before their time for stupid reasons. He shook Spector's hand, but made it plain that he was tolerating the old conjuror's presence.

The last to appear was Lucien Lapine, and the messy business of the velvet mask almost ended before it had even begun. The heel of Lapine's slipper skidded on the icy step and he slid messily down to the ground. He dropped with a yell, and Juliette, Étienne, and Spector rushed to help him.

Lapine was plainly embarrassed, less so by the fall than by the effort it took to get him up again. It took all three of them to restore him to his feet, and even then he still seemed shaky.

"God, I'm so old," Lapine said as they headed up the steps and into the house. Spector commiserated. It did not dawn on the old conjuror until later that they might all have been saved a lot of misery and pain if Lapine had simply broken his neck and died right then. Then they would not have needed to pursue the Eustache Dauger angle any further.

Aside from that unfortunate misstep, Lapine was a picture of decorum and courtesy. He made Spector feel at home, and the two men sat in his study in the east wing before a blazing fire while Juliette and Étienne fussed around their father, threatening to call a doctor to give him a once-over.

"You shall do no such thing," Lapine finally said. "Now please, both of you, leave Monsieur Spector and me alone."

Grumbling among themselves, the children began to withdraw. "I have aspirin in my room," said Juliette from the doorway. "Will you take some?"

"Thank you, but no."

"I shall fetch it anyway."

When they were gone, Lapine gave a sigh. "You'll forgive me for saying so, but I wish my daughter had not seen fit to involve you in this."

Spector smiled. "Nevertheless, she has. She seems to believe that this 'Dauger' is some enemy out of the past. I understand that your son, too, has been to Scotland Yard."

Lapine sighed. "Foolish, both of them. Foolish." They heard footsteps directly overhead. "Oh, those damned aspirin," he said underneath his breath.

"Do you know who Eustache Dauger really is? It's fair to assume the name is an alias."

"No, I do not know. And to be honest, I do not care."

"Do you think it might be Felix Duchesne?"

"Duchesne," said Lapine, shaking his head. "Wherever I go, his name follows me. No, Felix Duchesne is dead. I think it more likely that this 'Dauger' is some associate of Duchesne's, out to avenge him."

"Really? After all this time? I didn't think spies bore grudges."

Lapine smiled. "I like you, Monsieur Spector. I see why my daughter hired you."

At that moment, the study door burst open and Étienne stampeded into the room once more. He had plainly been listening in the corridor, and could no longer restrain himself.

"Felix Duchesne was a coward and a traitor," he told Spector. "He was a spy who smuggled French military secrets to the Germans. He was lucky we did not put him up against a wall and shoot him dead."

Lapine coughed, evidently embarrassed by his son's fervour. "I knew Duchesne," he said. "We served together. He tried to make himself out a martyr, and curry favour with the popular press. It almost worked. He twisted them around his little finger. He had a way with words, you see. If you spoke to him for five minutes he could soon turn you round to his way of thinking. But in the end, he was nothing but a liar. And the truth condemned him."

At that moment, another man appeared in the doorway, a tall, imposing figure. "Dinner is served," he said.

"Ah," said Lapine, struggling to his feet. "Shall we?"

Lapine and his son left the study, but Spector tarried a moment with this third man.

"Bourdin, I presume?"

"Correct, sir." His voice had an engine-like throb, as though choked by coal smoke. He was tall and well-dressed, with a pencil moustache that must have been the envy of Étienne. He wore a black patch over his left eye; indeed, the whole left side of his face was threaded with an intricate network of scars. A man who had seen action, then.

"You're Monsieur Lapine's secretary, is that right?"

He leaned against the mantel. "More of a general factotum. Right-hand man, if you like. We go back a considerable way, he and I."

"Back to the Duchesne Affair?"

Bourdin smiled. "Correct."

"Did you *know* Duchesne?"

"Oh, I met him on a number of occasions."

"And may I ask, what is your opinion of the *Dauger* Affair?"

"I have no opinion."

"Have you seen the masked man?"

"Yes, I have. Everyone has. He made quite an entrance." Bourdin cracked open a silver cigarette case and offered one to Spector. Spector noticed the embossed legend: LES DIABLES BLEUS.

"Could you tell me a little about the security here?"

"Well, it's a home, not a fortress. But the doors and locks work, as far as I can tell. Oh, save for the window at the end of the gallery. The latch is broken, so I've had to repair it with sticking tape. The man is coming to fix it in the next few days." Bourdin ignited his cigarette in a flare of amber flame.

"You don't seem terribly concerned," Spector observed.

"Personally, I am trying to absent myself from what you call the 'Dauger Affair.' I believe we are too old for this cloak-and-dagger nonsense."

Spector grinned. "I'm inclined to agree. Nevertheless, there is a masked man prowling the vicinity. Have you any idea who he might be?"

Bourdin sighed, exhaling smoke. "If you want me to say it's Duchesne, I won't do it. Duchesne died on Devil's Island."

"Is that proven?"

Bourdin looked lazily about the room, as though a sudden ennui had swept over him. "I shall see you at dinner, Monsieur Spector." And he ambled out into the hall, leaving a trail of fragrant smoke behind him.

5.

Dinner was a sullen affair, but it gave Spector the opportunity to fathom the complex network of relationships between the Lapines and Bourdin.

While they settled down to coffee, Juliette exhaled noisily. "It's so warm in here."

Lapine laughed. "My daughter is a contrarian soul. In the summer, when the heat is unbearable, she has that little gas fire of hers blazing away. I ask you, a gas fire in that magnificent room! What a waste of a fireplace. But in the winter, when there is snow on the ground, she cannot stand the heat."

"It's the fire," Juliette explained. "It makes me feel queasy. If you'll excuse me, I think I'll retire a little early." And she got up to leave. "Good night," she said to Spector. The two syllables contained a lot of meaning.

"Well, have you solved it?" Étienne said once his sister was out of the room.

"Solved what?"

"You solve mysteries, don't you Spector? Isn't that what you do? Well, this Dauger business is quite a mystery."

"True enough," said Spector. It was his last word on the subject.

The evening dragged, and around forty-five minutes later Lapine said to Bourdin: "Go and check on her, would you? See she's all right up there."

Bourdin nodded silently and got up to go.

"Good God!" said Étienne. His voice came out in a yelp.

"What? What is it?"

"There!" The young man pointed at the window. "It's Dauger! Prowling around the house!" The four men clustered around the window and there, sure enough, was the receding silhouette of a man.

"Quick," said Spector, "let's get after him. Lapine, you go to the study and lock yourself in. Étienne, go with him. Bourdin, come with me."

So Spector and the lumbering, laconic Bourdin headed out into the night. "He went back to the house across the street," Bourdin said. Spector squinted in the darkness and—yes—there was the shape of a man.

"Dauger!" Spector called. The man briefly paused and looked over his shoulder, then broke into a run. "After him Bourdin!"

Bourdin thundered after the assailant, disappearing in the shadows of the building opposite. Spector headed back into the house and found Lapine and his two children in the study. Juliette wore a nightdress with a dressing gown wrapped around her. She was as pale as the snow beyond the window. "I came down when I heard the commotion," she explained.

Étienne had half-filled a tumbler with whisky, and knocked it back. Only Lapine himself seemed calm, seated behind his desk. "Mr. Spector," he said. "I hope you didn't catch a chill."

"Call the police, Monsieur Lapine," Spector instructed. "Ask for George Flint."

Lapine gave a sly, sardonic smile. "Foolishness," he said.

"Étienne, go upstairs with your sister. Leave your father and me alone."

They did so wordlessly. Spector placed his palms firmly on Lapine's desk. "There is something going on here, and I do not like it. I am going outside—will you please do me the courtesy of locking the study door and ensuring all the windows are locked, too?"

"Well… all right. For you, Spector. But I say again, the whole thing's foolishness." Lapine escorted Spector to the door, then closed it in his face. Spector waited until he heard the click of the key in the lock before departing.

Étienne met him in the corridor. "I put my sister to bed," he said.

"Good. Her room is directly above the study, is that right?"

"Correct."

"Then perhaps we should go up there. It might give us a better vantage point of the street below."

They made for the stairs, but before they could begin their ascent Spector froze. "Hush! Listen! Do you hear that?"

Étienne listened. "It sounds like a window rattling."

"Where is it coming from?"

"The gallery, I think."

Étienne led the way down the hall in the opposite direction, through into the gallery. That was when Spector remembered what Bourdin had told him about the broken window latch. Now the window in question was swinging back and forth, wide open, banging loudly against its frame. Spector peered out at the perfect snow. No footprints. Then he leaned out and pulled the window to. "Well, nobody has come in this way," Étienne observed.

"No," said Spector dubiously. "But all the same, I don't like this. Come on. I've changed my mind. Let's go back and sit with your father."

So Étienne and Spector returned to the study. Spector rattled the door handle and, to his satisfaction, found it locked. Then he rapped on the wood. "Lapine, it's us. Let us in."

Nothing. Spector glanced at Étienne, who looked worried.

Then came the gunshot, an earth-shattering sound, blaring like a flash of white lightning.

Spector pounded on the study door. "Lapine! Open up, for God's sake!" But the only reply was awful, deathly silence. Spector rattled the handle. He dropped to his knees and peeked through the keyhole. Nothing.

"Étienne, go to the telephone in the hall. Get Flint over here now. Then fetch your benign sister from upstairs."

Étienne did not need to be asked twice.

Alone in the corridor outside the study, Spector worked a little of his magic and finally gained admittance to the sealed room. Escapology had once formed part of his act, so he was well-versed in the art of lock manipulation.

Lapine sat at his desk, his head lolling backward in a most unnatural position. It was obvious that he was dead. By the look of him, it was a gunshot that finished him off—a single bullet which entered his left cheek and exited the back of his skull, taking with it a fair chunk of brain matter on its ill-fated journey toward the far wall. A revolver lay on the rug, a wicked twist of smoke spiralling from its barrel.

Spector wasted no time. Being careful to preserve any fingerprints, he examined the room from top to bottom. Everything was more or less as it had been earlier in the day; there was nothing disturbed or out of place. The fire blazed and the two windows were bolted on the inside.

Spector examined the glass panes, but these showed no disturbance either. Beyond them, it had begun to snow once more.

"I must confess to a strange sensation of *déjà vu*," said Spector when Flint arrived some minutes later. Bourdin had returned, panting, having lost the assailant in the flurry of snow. He was now in the salon with Étienne and Juliette. "Someone plainly wishes us to believe this a suicide. The pistol is near enough to the body that it *might* have been fired by the victim himself. But I don't believe it was."

"Typically, I would agree with you. But there's still the problem of the locked room," said Flint. "An *impenetrable* room. And from the way you describe it, it sounds as though you and Étienne heard the shot, so you would have seen a murderer go."

"We were outside the door, and it certainly sounded like a gunshot."

"But the door was locked on the inside?"

"Yes. The key was in the lock. It took me a minute or two to get into the room, but of course there was nowhere a killer could have run to. The windows were locked on the inside. There are no footprints in the snow outside. And I searched the room; there was no place the killer might have hidden himself either."

"The revolver is my father's," Étienne explained. "It was a gift from the Chinese ambassador."

Flint thought carefully for a moment. "I've sent Hook and a few men over to Eustache Dauger's. I want this mess resolved as soon as possible."

"Somehow I doubt Monsieur Dauger will be at home."

Flint looked across at the corpse and shuddered. Then he looked at Spector. "Merry Christmas, Flint," said the old conjuror with a sad, lop-sided smile.

6.

By dawn, both the Lapine and Dauger residences had been fully searched, revealing little of interest. The enigmatic Eustache Dauger was not in residence, but his chauffeur was, sleeping in a small room to the rear of the house. He had shown little resistance to the Scotland Yard investigators.

"That chauffeur is an intriguing character," Spector observed as he smoked a thin, black cigarillo. "What have you found out about him?"

"Not much I'm afraid. He's Rumanian, his name is Miroslav Tcaci." Flint butchered the pronunciation. "But by the time we finally found someone who spoke the lingo we realised this fellow knows about as much as we do. He's never seen his master without the mask on. What do you make of it all, Spector?"

"I'm not sure yet. It might be advantageous to pay a visit to Monsieur Lapine's *other* enemy in London."

"Who's that then?"

"A reporter. I can't help but feel as if he's very closely associated with this whole mess."

It was nine o'clock when Flint and Spector got to the Savoy. An agreeable hour, Spector surmised, for a visit to the eccentric journalist. They strode up to the front desk, the pair of them, and Flint jangled the bell.

"We're here to see Georges Sorel," he announced.

The ghost of a frown passed across the concierge's face, immediately supplanted by a look of suave condescension. "I'm afraid that won't be possible, sir."

"And why not?"

"Monsieur Sorel was taken to hospital in the night, sir. The doctor says he had a heart attack."

In the police car, shrieking and skidding its way along the icy streets, Spector said: "This changes things."

"You're telling me."

"No, I mean, this changes *everything*."

Sorel had been rushed to St. Thomas' Hospital across the river, so that was their next destination. It was mid-morning when they got there, but it proved to be a fruitless visit. After a few minutes' bartering with a square-jawed matron, they were informed definitively that they would *not* be permitted to visit the ailing reporter.

"Mr. Sorel is comatose," she finally said, "and we don't know if he'll ever come out of it."

Flint and Spector shared a troubled glance.

On the ride back to Quentin Crescent, Flint did his best to fathom out the sequence of events. Sorel's role in the murder proved singularly difficult to pin down.

"Of course, we know nothing about his general state of health," said Flint. "It may simply have been a catastrophe waiting to happen."

"No, I don't think so," said Spector. "Sorel may have had heart problems, but he was in a good state of fitness. He told me that he recently cycled the Loire Valley. That's almost two hundred miles. Hardly the sort of undertaking for a man at death's door."

"Well, what then?"

"I think it was shock that made his heart give out."

"Shock at Lapine's death?"

"Possibly. Or something else."

Flint turned in his seat and looked at Spector. In profile, the old conjuror's face had a beaked, saturnine quality. But he had nothing more to say.

7.

The Lapine house was now eerily silent. The police presence had dwindled to nothing, and Étienne and Juliette sat together in silence in the salon. They were both ghoulishly pale-faced in the chilly daylight. Bourdin was nowhere to be found.

"If I may," said Spector, "I should like to examine the study once again. Would that be all right?"

"If you must," said Étienne. Juliette did not answer; just flapped her hand.

"While Spector does that," said Flint, "I've got a few more questions to ask."

Sealed up in the study, Spector commenced a search that was as intense as it was futile. He covered every single wall panel—it took him several hours—but he found nothing. Nothing at all. No tricks or gimmicks or hidden panels. Nothing that would have allowed a killer to escape undetected. He spent a good while on the fireplace, peering up the chimney, but of course there had been a fire blazing the whole evening. No one could have entered or exited the room via the chimney without acquiring more than a few burns for their efforts.

Eventually, Spector had no choice but to concede defeat. It was now almost pitch black outside, and even an old sceptic like him was not immune to the sinister, uncanny atmosphere of a room where murder has recently taken place. He yawned, stretched, and left the room feeling utterly dispirited.

He found Flint still questioning Juliette in the salon. Étienne had apparently retired upstairs. There was still no sign of Bourdin.

The stuffy air of the late Lucien Lapine's study had affected Spector. He had a headache and needed to step outside. Out in Quentin Crescent, the houses were eerily still and calm. One could almost convince oneself that nothing had happened at all. But when he turned his attention to the Dauger house, Spector noticed something almost instantly. It was lights; lights blazing in every window. The house which had been in darkness for so long was now aglow.

"Fire," he said aloud. "The place is on fire. Flint! For God's sake!

Fire!" Almost on cue flames plumed outward, shattering Dauger's windows.

The residents of Quentin Crescent began to assemble in the street to watch the display. Spector caught a glimpse of the Weatherill sisters whispering to one another like naughty schoolgirls. And then: "Look!" someone yelled.

A shape emerged from the flames. It was a man, standing on the roof of the Dauger house, silhouetted magnificently against the inferno. He stood for a moment, his cloak billowing around him, and surveyed the crowd below. Spector convinced himself he could see the flames dancing in Dauger's blackly devious eyes. The next second, the trapped man turned and plunged back into the burning building.

"What are you doing, you damned fool!" Flint roared. But Eustache Dauger could not have heard him. At that moment the roof buckled and the house began to collapse in on itself.

It was dawn by the time it finally burned out. Even in the pink, frosty daylight the air was choked with smoke and soot. Uniformed police officers picked through the wreckage of the Dauger residence. The house had been gutted by the blaze and reduced to little more than a shell of blackened beams.

They found a body—a man's—but it was burned beyond recognition. No chance of an identification.

Spector looked shell-shocked, as though it were he and not Dauger who had been trapped in the burning building. Étienne and Juliette approached him and Juliette announced: "Mr. Spector, I think it would be best for all of us if you left. I hired you to protect my father and you have failed. To save you any further embarrassment, I don't want you to be involved in this investigation any further."

"Now, Miss," put in Flint, "I'm afraid that's not your decision. Mr. Spector is acting as an advisor…"

But the old conjuror was already sloping dejectedly away.

8.

Flint tracked Spector down at The Black Pig, where he occupied his customary seat in the snug. "What was the disappearing act in aid of?" the policeman demanded.

"I don't know what you mean."

"Spector, Dauger—whoever he was—is dead. Burned to a crisp. I thought you might take a bit more than a cursory interest."

"Oh, I'm interested. Very interested. But I needed a little time

and space to gather my thoughts. I believe this case is more compli-
cated than you and I imagined."

"Well, as far as *I'm* concerned," said Flint, "the case is closed.
Whether or not Dauger was really Felix Duchesne, there's little doubt
that he murdered Lapine. His suicide makes sense."

"Yes," said Spector, "I suppose it does. Did you get a chance to
go through Georges Sorel's papers?"

Flint nodded. "Frankly, I don't know what all the fuss was about.
There wasn't much in there to write home about."

"What about Felix Duchesne?"

"Sorel clearly had an obsession with the Duchesne business. But
there was nothing to effectively prove Duchesne died on Devil's Island."

"So you think he was Dauger?"

The inspector shrugged. "Truth to tell, I don't really care. So long
as this mess is finished with."

The old man scrutinised him closely. "I see. Well, I'm afraid it's
not finished with. Not quite."

"What do you mean?"

Spector smiled. "Dinner tonight, Flint. The Lapine place. How
about it?"

9.

Joseph Spector seized control of the Lapine house as he had seized
control of so many theatrical stages in his day. Initially, Juliette had
declined to let him in, but he eventually talked her around by claiming that he had uncovered the truth of what happened to her father.

Étienne, for his part, got into the spirit of things, and emerged
from his room in full evening wear, complete with tails and white
gloves. Bourdin, too, had finally returned. Apparently, he had been
visiting the late Monsieur Lapine's solicitor to discuss details of his
erstwhile employer's will. There was no news of Georges Sorel.

"Well, Mr. Spector," said Juliette, "since you've inveigled your way
into our home once again, you'd better tell us what's on your mind."

They were at the dinner table now. Flint was fidgeting in his seat
and looking generally ill at ease, but Spector was holding sway with
quiet benignity. "Thank you again for agreeing to this, Mademoiselle
Lapine. I am sure it goes against every instinct in your body. I admit
that I failed your father. But I think now, at long last, I can fit all the
pieces together. I can tell you not only who murdered your father,
but how and why."

Étienne's knife clattered against his plate. He looked around him sheepishly. Bourdin smoked a cigarette, his single eye trained on Spector. Flint cleared his throat awkwardly.

"Now is as good a time as any. Flint, are you ready?"

"For what?"

"For the big finish. Étienne!" Étienne jumped visibly when his name was spoken. 'Would you mind removing your gloves?"

"I beg your pardon?"

Spector's voice was ice. "You heard me, Étienne."

"Why should I?"

"Well why *shouldn't* you?" put in Juliette.

"Because it's a foolish request. I'm not going to do it."

"You haven't removed your gloves all evening, Étienne. You are hiding your hands from us. Why might that be?"

"I am doing no such thing. And even if I were, what does it matter?" This seemed to be an appeal to Inspector Flint, but Flint offered no sympathy.

"You don't want us to see your hands because they are burned. Quite badly burned, in fact. You've done your best with salves and bandages, but you're not a medical man."

"That's ridiculous."

"I realised it when you dropped your knife just then. It would be easy to assume I had said something that shocked you. But your body language told me you were reacting to a sudden stab of pain."

Étienne got up and paced over to the fireplace. "This is ridiculous," he said again.

"Prove it."

Étienne did not move.

"You won't remove your gloves because you burned your hands when you were at the Dauger place last night, when you were fighting your way out through the burning beams and all that hideous smoke. Because you started the fire, didn't you? You didn't mean to do so much damage, though. All you wanted was to burn a few papers. But it got out of hand, didn't it? And it was you we saw on the roof, wasn't it, though you wore the mask?"

"The dead body was the driver you hired—Miroslav. Eustache Dauger is alive and well. Because you have always been Dauger, haven't you? Right from the very beginning."

Étienne gave a staccato bark of laughter. "You're forgetting those times Dauger and I were seen together. Out in the street, and whatnot."

"No, I'm not. Perhaps it would be best if we started from the *very* beginning. Specifically, I'm referring to the Duchesne Affair, which took place roughly twenty-five years ago.

"Let's get one thing out of the way. Felix Duchesne was no more a spy or traitor than I am. He was falsely accused. Framed, in fact. He was a handy scapegoat for a cabal of conspirators. Isn't that so, Bourdin?"

Bourdin's single eye narrowed, but he didn't speak.

Spector continued: "I doubt we'll get a word on the subject from Bourdin. But the fact is that both he and Lucien Lapine were bound by their shared responsibility for the downfall of Felix Duchesne."

Over the sudden loud and vocal protests from the assembled company, Spector merely smiled and raised a hand to quiet them. "You don't believe me. Why should you? After all, I have no evidence. My conclusion is based on a logical inference—specifically, the inference that Lucien Lapine was deathly afraid of a journalist named Georges Sorel. So afraid, in fact, that he decided to bring Felix Duchesne back from the dead.

"In his grave, Duchesne is a martyr. But if he is alive and stalking the streets of London, he remains a menace. It was in Lucien Lapine's interest for Duchesne to remain a menace. Word reached Lapine that Sorel had discovered long-buried documents and testimonies that would expose the true extent of his role in the Duchesne Affair. Lapine had no desire to face the ignominy and public disgrace that would inevitably surround the revelation that *he* was in fact the real traitor all along. But he needed to tread lightly. He needed to tease Sorel out into the open. And the best way he could think of going about this was by propagating a rumour that Duchesne was alive, to force Sorel's hand. And so Eustache Dauger was born.

"Lapine couldn't do it alone. He needed an accomplice, and he found one in the headstrong Étienne. Isn't that so, my boy? Étienne would do anything for his father—that much has been obvious from the beginning. You'll note that we never actually saw all three men together in one place—Étienne, Lapine and Dauger."

"But what about when they were in the dining room, and Dauger was prowling around outside?" Flint demanded.

"That was not 'Dauger' we saw in the street at all. Don't misunderstand—there *was* a secret visitor to the house that night, but it was not the masked man. No, whenever Étienne or Lapine himself had face-to-face encounters with Dauger, one or the other was conveniently elsewhere. They cooked it up between them and quite effective it was too, this illusion of a third man. They rented the house and car in the name of Dauger; they hired poor Miroslav Tcaci to serve as chauffeur. Lapine was eager to propagate the idea that he was too feeble for such exploits—hence the little display when he slipped on the ice. That was a carefully-calculated misdirection."

"Very neat," said Bourdin. "But you have failed to answer a very important question. Namely, who *shot* Lucien Lapine?"

"Ah," Spector sighed. "This is where the affair takes a tragic turn. And I mean 'tragic' in the classical sense. Juliette, you must forgive me—you've been absent from this story so far, haven't you? Because they didn't let you in on their scheme, did they? If they had, you would have had no need to hire me, would you? But you really and truly believed this Eustache Dauger was a threat, didn't you? You feared for your father's life." He did not wait for her to agree. "That's why, when Georges Sorel contacted you in secret and requested a meeting, you agreed. You knew Sorel by reputation, and thought he might be a useful ally, little realising that if your father had an enemy, it was he. He was out to expose your father, but you didn't know that. So you arranged for him to visit you. That's why you retired to bed early. He was the man we saw outside, wasn't he? He came in secret, taking advantage of that broken window latch and simply slipping into the gallery. You had given him a map of the house, so he could locate your room, and conduct your meeting with the utmost discretion."

"This is foolishness," Juliette said. "I would never have done such a thing."

"Oh? Just as you would never trudge through the snowy London night to seek out an old magician? Sorel wormed his way into your boudoir with the promise of a revelation that would explode your preconceptions of the Duchesne Affair. He did not disappoint.

"But his revelation concerned an individual who has so far hovered on the periphery of our story. I am speaking of the late Madame Lapine, who headed for an early grave in the aftermath of the trial and fall from grace of Felix Duchesne. We have not heard much about her in all this, have we? A posthumous *persona non grata*. Juliette only mentioned her once; if not for that, she might never have existed at all.

"What might Sorel have told Juliette, do you think? Perhaps he told her of the true nature of her relationship between her mother and Felix Duchesne? The relationship which became apparent from Duchesne's personal correspondence, and which gave Lucien Lapine his motive for framing an innocent colleague? The clandestine relationship which yielded an illegitimate daughter?"

Flint was on his feet. "Good God! You mean *Duchesne* was Juliette's father?"

Spector nodded. "When Juliette came to me a few days ago and asked me to protect her father, she was entirely guileless. For you see, then she believed Lapine *was* her father. But when she was confronted with the incontrovertible documentary evidence of her mother's affair, the persecution of her natural father, as well as the subsequent emotional tortures which drove her mother to the grave, her perception of the matter shifted. It became clear to her what she had to do."

Flint cleared his throat. "That's a lot of speculation, you know."

"Isn't it? A pity that Étienne felt the need to break into Sorel's room at the Savoy and steal the documents which might prove it. It was those he used to start the fire across the street."

"This is slander," Juliette Lapine said, "against both me and my brother."

"I agree," said Spector. "But somehow I doubt you'll do anything about it. Because it's all true. Bourdin told me that he had used sticking tape to seal up the broken window latch. But when Étienne and I examined it, there was no tape. Because you took it, didn't you? You knew the sound of the window banging would draw our attention, so you seized that opportunity to go to your father's study and shoot him dead. In many ways, it's an understandable response. The world as you knew it no longer existed. Your 'father' was not your father at all but a schemer and a liar. He was the one who sent your real father to an unjust fate on Devil's Island, and who drove your mother to an early grave."

Silently, Juliette began to weep.

"But how did she do it?" asked Flint. "The locked room business, I mean."

"Oh, it was deceptively simple," said Spector. "It was the work of perhaps a minute, whilst Étienne and I were in the gallery. When she heard us investigating the window, she crept down the stairs and into the study, where she shot Lapine dead. She used a pillow to mute the pistol, which is why we did not hear the murder. Then, with the deed out of the way, she decided to try and convince us that he had shot himself. This was foolish in retrospect, but in the heat of the moment I suppose it makes sense as a psychological reaction to an impulsive patricide.

"So she set about locking the room, with the key on the inside. All she needed was the sticking tape she had already procured from the broken window latch and two pencils. When we first met, she showed me a pencil sketch she had drawn of Eustache Dauger, so I knew stationery was in no short supply, and that she possessed the thin pencils required for fine, detailed sketches. She taped a pencil to the key blade, so that when the key was inserted into the lock on the inside, the pencil protruded out the other side. Then, with the door closed, she took a second pencil and taped that to the end of the first, creating a 'T' shape. This created a makeshift corkscrew that could be turned from outside, thus locking the door. Then she gave the pencils a sharp pull and they dislodged from the lock, leaving the key in place on the inside."

"Simple as that," said Flint.

"Simple as that. The whole thing took less than a minute, I'll wager. Then she retreated back upstairs with the pencils, tape and—lest we forget—the pillow with a bullet hole. I imagine she destroyed them all by burning—it seems to be a popular solution among the Lapine children.

"Now we come to the *truly* innovative part of her plan. Remember, this was all cooked up on the spot after her fateful meeting with Georges Sorel. Quite an imagination she has! Anyway, Juliette was able to control our perception of the event by giving the impression that the murder took place several minutes later than it actually did—when she was safely upstairs, where we thought she had been all along.

"The trick was worked with the fireplace in the study. You must remember that Juliette's room is directly *above* the study, and though her fireplace has been sealed up so that she might use her gas fire, it shares a flue with the study directly below it. So all Juliette had to do was to remove a brick from her own sealed-up fireplace, and she had access to the flue and, therefore, to the fireplace of the room directly below. But what did she employ to mimic the sound of a gunshot?

"Well, Juliette, unwittingly you gave me a clue to this yourself when we very first met. When you spoke of 'the arts of history, diplomacy and warfare.' The phrase generated an unconscious echo in my mind of Sun Tzu's *The Art of War*. This was completely coincidental, but it was sufficient to set me on the right track. Likewise, the fact that the murder weapon was a gift from the Chinese ambassador. Your father must have spent some time in China in the past. Perhaps he took you with him, or at the very least gave you a sound education in Chinese history. The Chinese invented gunpowder, you know. But before they did that, they used an altogether benign substance to achieve a deadly effect. Bamboo.

"There is a bamboo trellis up the western face of the house. Though this is the opposite side to the study, you could still reach it from an upstairs window and snap off a portion of bamboo. What the Chinese were clever enough to discover all those thousands of years ago was that bamboo grows so quickly that it traps air within its roots. When heated, the air expands. In the right conditions, therefore, a stick of bamboo may have similar properties to a stick of dynamite. Of course you, Juliette, were simply looking to create a flash and a bang to imitate a gunshot when you heard us in position outside the study. A few inches of bamboo snapped from the trellis were more than adequate. These you dropped down the flue into the study fireplace, creating the sound which we naturally took for a gunshot."

Juliette dabbed at her damp eyes with a lace handkerchief. "Of course," she said, regaining her composure, "there's no way to prove any of this."

"We'll be back with a search warrant," said Flint. "We'll find whatever there is to find."

"No," said Étienne, taking his sister's hand, "you won't."

10.

Though the crime itself was as neat and compact as a stick of bamboo, the story surrounding it was not. Georges Sorel, whose heart attack had been induced partially by the stress of his on-foot escape from Bourdin, and partially by the realisation that his meeting with Juliette had led directly to her murder of Lucien Lapine, remained comatose at St. Thomas' Hospital. His tell-all account of the Duchesne Affair would never be published, and it was unlikely anyone would read it anyway. Joseph Spector had a hibiscus flower delivered to the journalist's hospital room, where it was untended and swiftly died.

In spite of Flint's profound efforts, he was never able to muster sufficient evidence to prosecute Juliette or Étienne for the murder of Lucien Lapine or the accidental immolation of Miroslav Tcaci respectively. This irked him greatly. He did not blame Spector for it; he took it as a personal failure. In spite of his wife's frequent admonitions that he must not let it spoil his all-too-brief Christmas break, his turkey that year turned to ashes in his mouth.

Juliette and Étienne left the country soon after that. They returned to Paris, where the death of Lucien Lapine swiftly ceased to weigh on their minds. Bourdin disappeared altogether, though there were rumours that he eventually died in combat fighting for the Spanish resistance. He was a warrior at heart, after all.

Spector received no payment for his involvement in the case.

Indeed, he would have argued that he did not deserve any; he had been hired by Juliette to protect her father. Not only was the man in question not her father, but she herself had subsequently killed him. Quite a turnaround! But all the same, the old conjuror did obtain a single item in recompense for his pains. Nobody knows how he got it, but his gallery of curiosities now boasted a fresh exhibit. It was appended to the wall at head height in the shadowed northwest corner of his study. A black velvet oval, with a pair of narrow eyeholes staring blindly. The mask of Eustache Dauger.

Lethal Symmetry

Part One:
 What follows is an account of the strange fate of Conrad Darnoc, who prized symmetry above all things. He coveted it; cherished it; obsessed over it—hence his chosen name. His greatest architectural creations were exquisite exercises in geometric precision. But his sense of symmetry was not confined to facades—every room, every corridor, every doorframe was utterly symmetrical. And so was he. His tailor made his suits to a unique specification, with a breast pocket on both sides, and a handkerchief protruded from each.
 This was no mere eccentricity—it was an obsession. It consumed every aspect of his life. My name is Bob Markram. Six months ago, Conrad Darnoc hired me as his private secretary. I had been out of work for a while, and the money was good: £888 a year. My only qualification was my name, a pair of palindromes.
 When I met Darnoc at his Kensington home, I knew immediately that the man was a lunatic. But, his demented love of symmetry aside, he was a decent employer—for a time.
 Darnoc lived with his ward, a girl named Hannah. He was unmarried, and the only others in the house were servants. There was the cook, Mrs. Spaulding, a friendly, pudgy-faced widow. She saw herself as a mother figure to the orphaned Hannah, frequently shielding the girl from Darnoc's ire. There was Margaret, the maid, who spent most of her days hiding from Mrs. Spaulding. And there was the driver-cum-gardener, Chisholm. The only one I did not take to was Chisholm. He was a lazy, sullen sort.
 There was one other resident of that strange house: a Persian cat named Horatio, which belonged to Hannah. Darnoc had previously enjoyed convivial relations with the cat, but when it lost an eye in a back-alley contretemps he developed a profound distaste for it. The absence of symmetry, you see.
 Anyway, after three peaceful months, my life in the Darnoc house took a turn for the worse.
 It would be easy enough to blame Reuben Samuels, though I suppose it's not really his fault. After all, one cannot choose with whom one falls in love. When Hannah Darnoc turned nineteen, she and Reuben began courting.

Conrad loathed Reuben with an intense passion. I wondered if perhaps he had entertained ideas of marrying Hannah himself. A rather Victorian arrangement, but such things are not unheard of.

During the subsequent months, the atmosphere in that house grew tense. And finally, one April evening, events came to a head. Before dinner, I visited Darnoc's study. The room was—predictably—symmetrical, with double doors and an oak desk framed by two windows. Either side of the desk was a grand, gilt-framed mirror. Standing in the right spot created an illusion of innumerable Darnocs, seated side by side, on into infinity.

Beneath the mirrors were identical sideboards, and on top of these identical blazing oil lamps. Overhead hung a crystal chandelier in the dead centre of the ceiling. I sat opposite Darnoc and we spoke for perhaps fifteen minutes. After that, Darnoc, Hannah, Reuben, and myself dined together. Margaret the maid was present throughout, assiduously refilling glasses. Horatio sat sullenly on the rug in front of the fire. "He's not been himself all afternoon," Hannah observed. "I wonder if he's ill?" After dinner, Margaret and Mrs. Spaulding went out to the pictures. I don't know where Chisholm was.

The night passed peacefully enough, and it wasn't until the following morning that I realised something was wrong. Darnoc, it seemed, had not been to bed. It wasn't unheard of for him to work through the night. But when the maid tapped on the study door with his tea and did not receive a reply, we began to grow concerned. She came and informed me, and I went and knocked. No answer. I tried the handle—the double doors were bolted on the inside. I went out of the house, and round the garden to the windows. I peered in. Conrad Darnoc was still in his chair where I had left him. But now his head was lolling back, his mouth open.

Chisholm shouldered open the door and we investigated the room. There was no doubt about it—Conrad Darnoc had died alone, in agony and terror. An ugly death. On the carpet between his feet lay his wooden pipe, with blackened tobacco ash spilling from the bowl. The windows, too, were also bolted on the inside. There were now *two* chairs opposite the desk, instead of the one in which I had sat last night. Something else was different, too—something I could not quite identify.

A Scotland Yard man, Inspector Flint, soon arrived with a retinue of constables and a curious old fellow dressed all in black. "My name is Joseph Spector," said the stranger. He spoke softly, but his voice was eerily resonant in the old house. "When Flint told me the

nature of the case—that is to say, unnatural death in a locked room—
I thought it best if I came along."

I accompanied this Joseph Spector into the room. It had been
determined early on that Darnoc's body bore the hallmarks of phosphorus poisoning. There was no suicide note, and apparently no visible
means by which the poison might have been administered.

"He was visited by two others after you left him last night, Mr.
Markram. Note the pair of chairs arranged across the desk from him."

"Hannah and Reuben," I said.

"Yes," Hannah admitted when questioned, "we went in to see him
after Bob had gone to bed. We wanted to talk about things in private."

"'Things'?"

"Our engagement," Reuben elucidated. "Darnoc... wasn't too keen
on the whole thing."

"We were trying to talk him round," said Hannah delicately.

"He had some strange ideas," Reuben continued. "He was threatening to make things difficult for us."

"I appreciate your candour," said Spector.

Reuben shrugged. "You'd have found out sooner or later anyway.
He'd cut off her allowance, and written her out of his will."

"You don't seem all that concerned."

"Money doesn't matter to either of us," said Reuben. "All we care
about is each other."

When the body had been removed, we returned to the study to
watch Spector comb the scene of the crime. I looked around, trying
to pinpoint what it was that disturbed me. Finally, I had it: though
the overhead chandelier was lit, both of the oil lamps had been extin-
guished.

"The lamps are out," I observed.

Spector's eyes snapped toward me. "They were lit last night?"

"Yes," I said. "I remember it. They were both lit while I spoke
with Mr. Darnoc."

"Could they have burned out overnight?"

"No," said Margaret, the maid. "I just refilled them with oil yesterday morning."

"Sergeant Hook," Spector instructed, "please check the oil levels
in these lamps."

The sergeant set about it immediately. "This one's empty," he concluded, "and this one's a quarter full."

"If it's any use," Reuben Samuels offered, "the lamps were out when Hannah and I visited him."

"What does it mean?" I said.

"Possibly nothing," Spector answered. "Or possibly *not* nothing."

With that, Flint came back into the room. "We've heard from Doctor Findler," he told Spector. "Like you said—the tobacco. Laced with phosphorus powder."

Spector nodded. "I thought the pipe was too much of a coincidence."

"But that's not possible," put in Hannah.

"Why not?"

Immediately sensing that all eyes were on her, Hannah seemed to regret opening her mouth. "Because I saw him fill his pipe. He got the tobacco from the pot on his desk."

"This was while you and Mr. Samuels were in conference with him?"

She gulped. "Yes."

"The poison would have taken a little while to start working. You wouldn't have noticed straight away."

"No, it's not that...." She cast a sharp sideways glance at Reuben as she trailed off into silence.

"Hannah means that both Conrad and I took a pinch of tobacco from the same pot at the same time. We both smoke pipes, you see."

Spector's interest was visibly piqued. "And you experienced no ill effects, Mr. Samuels?"

"None."

Spector steepled his fingers. "I see."

Next he questioned Mrs. Spaulding. "Do you keep phosphorus powder in the house?"

"For the rats," she said, "but I keep it under lock and key along with a few other things that could be dangerous. Batteries, oil, things like that."

"How many people have keys?"

"Just myself and the maid, Margaret."

"Not Chisholm?"

"No. He has no need of it."

"Did anybody borrow your key at all yesterday?"

"No, I should have remembered that. I keep it here." She produced it from the pocket of her apron.

Chisholm had his own supply of rat poison which he kept in the shed—but he favoured cyanide, not phosphorus. "How many people have keys to the shed?" Spector asked him.

"Just me," was the curt reply.

Finally, Spector questioned the maid. "Mrs. Spaulding tells me you and she are the only ones with keys to the phosphorus cupboard."

Margaret glanced from side to side. "Yes," she said. "At least, we *were*."

"What do you mean by that?"

"Yesterday, I... I lost my key. I still haven't found it." Mrs. Spaulding scowled at her, and she gulped nervously.

"When did you last have it?" asked Spector.

"I couldn't say."

"Then anybody could have taken it," said Flint. "Anybody at all."

From the corner of the room came the sound of dreadful retching and wheezing. It was Horatio the cat, hitching his neck back and forth in the disturbing way cats do. Finally, he produced a long, murky green-grey tangle of hair. Evidently feeling much better, he trotted away with a happy little chirrup, his tail high and straight. I dropped to my haunches and studied the hairball. Amid the tangle of hair was a most curious object. I sensed Joseph Spector standing behind me. He gave a low chuckle. "Well," he said, "I believe that's the last piece of the puzzle."

It was a key.

"You've solved it, then?" said Flint.

"Yes," answered Spector, "I have."

Part Two:

We gathered in the lounge so that Spector—evidently a theatrical sort—could deliver his verdict on the strange death of Conrad Darnoc.

"What is symmetry?" he commenced. "It is two halves, either side of a central dividing line. In other words, a gift to the professional trickster. Illusion is about manipulating audience perception. The key factor to remember is that if your eye line is instantly drawn in a certain direction, it is almost always the *wrong* direction. With a symmetrical construction, the focus is on the centre. Therefore, we must look elsewhere. What is the *one* aspect of this crime scene which is *not* symmetrical?"

"The oil lamps," I said.

"Correct. While the lamps themselves are identical, and identically positioned, the amount of oil in each is not the same. One is empty, while the other is a quarter full. What does that suggest to you?"

"That one lamp was used more than the other."

"Perhaps. Or perhaps it suggests that one lamp had some of its oil decanted. Enough to ensure that it would burn up its supply during the evening."

"What would be the point of that?"

Spector smiled. "When you met with Mr. Darnoc before dinner, both lamps were burning, isn't that so?"

"Yes."

"And when Miss Darnoc and Mr. Samuels went to see him, both lamps were out. To me, this implies that during the interim, one lamp had in fact exhausted the last of its oil and burnt out. This was a very cynical crime, which played upon the psychology of its victim. Because if one lamp were to burn out, what do you suppose Mr. Darnoc's immediate reaction would have been?"

"To go looking for oil."

"No. His *immediate* reaction."

Hannah said quietly, "He would have turned off the other lamp."

"Correct! This was a man who could not bear the sight of asymmetry. If one lamp burned out, his first act would be to extinguish its counterpart, to restore a sense of order to his surroundings."

"But what's the point of that?" put in Samuels. "I mean, why would the killer want him to go fiddling with the other lamp?"

"Mr. Samuels," Spector said, "when you and he both took tobacco from the pot on his desk, who reached in first?"

"I... I can't be sure, but I believe I did."

"I see. In that case, I think I can explain everything. The question has always been *How did the phosphorus powder get into the tobacco?* Now, I can answer that question. Mr. Darnoc put it there himself." Before the others could protest, Spector silenced them by holding up his hand. "Not willingly. He was tricked into poisoning himself, you might say. Knowing of Mr. Darnoc's eccentricities, the killer could predict his behaviour concerning the lamps. It would therefore be easy enough to coat the switch of one lamp with phosphorus powder. Thus, when Mr. Darnoc gripped the switch between thumb and forefinger, the powder was transferred onto his skin. Then, when he helped himself to another pinch of tobacco from the pot, the poison was transferred once again. The tobacco went into his pipe, and when he lit it this produced deadly phosphine gas that went straight into his lungs, and swiftly killed him."

"Then who's responsible?" demanded Flint.

Spector shrugged. "As far as I can tell, there's only one person who could be responsible. Mrs. Spaulding. She was likely planning to frame Margaret—not knowing, of course, that Horatio had stolen Margaret's key to the phosphorus cupboard. He must have done this around yesterday lunchtime—after all, Miss Darnoc claims the cat first appeared out of sorts during the afternoon. And we know Margaret had her key in the morning because she refilled the oil lamps. That means only Mrs. Spaulding had access to the cupboard in question at the time the poison was placed on the light switch. We must assume the poison was *not* present when Mr. Darnoc switched on the lamps before dinner, otherwise he would have died sooner. Therefore, it seems likely that Mrs. Spaulding decanted the oil and planted the poison *during* dinner. It couldn't have been Margaret because she was present throughout to refill drinks and the like. It couldn't have been Chisholm because, although he was not present during dinner, he had no access to the phosphorus cupboard. Mrs. Spaulding was the only one with the means and the opportunity.

"The other reason is psychological. After all, if a killer is planning to poison a man, surely it would be natural to plant the poison in his food? And who would be better placed to do so than his cook? She knew that if she poisoned his food, the attention of investigators would immediately focus on her. Hence her decision to use poison, but *not* to place it in food."

"But why the light switch?" said Flint. "Why not just poison the tobacco?"

"Because she could not be sure who would use the tobacco pot. After all, both Mr. Darnoc and Mr. Samuels were pipe smokers. And she did not wish to harm Mr. Samuels."

Now Margaret was in tears, while the cook stood icily still. "But why?" said the maid. "I don't see why Mrs. Spaulding would have..."

"I do," said Hannah. "It was because of me, wasn't it? She did it because of me."

The cook spoke at last. "He was going to ruin her life, Mr. Spector. He was going to do everything in his power to stop that wedding."

"Murder is murder," said Spector softly, steepling his fingers under his chin, his pale blue eyes piercing the cook's; a vision of perfect symmetry.

Jack Magg's Jaw

Part One:

When Jack Magg's wicked soul departed his body, it left behind
a heap of battle-scarred flesh swinging from a hangman's rope. The
brutal highwayman faced death with a smile, baring his sharpened
teeth as the life eked out of him.

That was 1740. But his reign of terror wasn't over. In fact it was
only beginning.

Nearly two hundred years later, seven people gathered for a weekend party at Clive Stoker's rambling country house, where each guest's
arrival was met with a chorus from ferocious guard dogs. I was accom-
panying my friend, retired conjuror Joseph Spector. The guest list
included Pamela Rasmussen, whose husband—famed eccentric Odin
Rasmussen—had died seven years previously. The shock of it had
turned her hair bright white.

Then there was Ernest Bland, Stoker's solicitor. Everything about
him was grey; his hair, his face, his conversation. If you glanced away,
you forgot what he looked like.

Next was Canon Villiers and his adult daughter, Violet. Villiers
had wild hair and foggy eyes. I could just imagine him spewing hell-
fire from the pulpit. Violet, however, was disconcertingly perfect. Not
a hair out of place, even on such a humid evening.

Finally there was Vauncey Magg-Boulting, a flamboyant businessman with pince-nez and a Van Dyke beard (or, more appropriately, a
Van Dine). He'd travelled all the way from Maidstone for this, a fact
he reiterated several times.

Stoker himself was benign at first glance. But there was something predatory in the way he beckoned the butler, Gadsby. Gadsby
approached with the pepper mill and ground it noisily over his master's Dover sole.

"I wonder," said Spector, "why you've brought us all here."

"Patience," said Stoker. "All will be revealed."

*

After dinner Stoker led us down a stone staircase to the cellar.
There we found a steel door with a sophisticated timelock. "Behold,"
he said, "my Museum of Murder."

The vault was lit by a single bulb. Free-standing shelves cast long
shadows, each lined with artefacts and handwritten labels. The left-
hand wall was taken up by a painting of a faceless man. "The 'Grey

Man,'" Stoker announced. "Painted in Broadmoor by Edward Manville, the Rotherhithe Strangler. He claimed it was the Grey Man who committed his crimes."

Stoker gave a *précis* of each item. "This is the duelling pistol that killed Lord Nash in 1832. Observe the scorch marks around the barrel. And this locket, embossed with the curlicued 'M,' contains a lock of fair hair from the woman who butchered Jack and Ellen Staveley five years ago; a love triangle culminating in tragedy. The locket was clutched in the dead man's hand. Sadly, "M' remains unidentified.

"And now we creep forward in time. Last year a string of murders shocked southeast England—six girls slaughtered by a madman. Eventually, the crime was pinned on a Sittingbourne lad named Isaac Leach; he protested his innocence right up to his execution several months ago. Here is the damning evidence—a bloodstained fivepound note. Leach was wandering near the scene of the last murder, clutching the note. He always claimed it had been given to him by another man."

Stoker concluded at a plinth in the centre of the vault, where a curve of bone lay on a cushion of black velvet.

"Now, the reason you are all here. My most prized exhibit. Jack Magg's jawbone. I invited four of you here tonight because you've spoken of your wish to obtain it. Eh, Pamela?"

"It was my husband's property," she said, "you stole it from him. It's my rightful inheritance."

Stoker smiled. "And Canon Villiers."

"Your 'museum' is an abomination. If the jaw came into my possession, I'd smash it into dust."

"And Vauncey Magg-Boulting."

"I'm Jack Magg's last descendant. His earthly remains belong to me."

"And Joseph Spector."

Spector shrugged. "I'm simply curious."

"You're being coy," Stoker chided. "Your collection could rival even mine. You'd kill to possess the jawbone, wouldn't you?"

Spector didn't reply.

"Well, you may be in luck. These days, my museum bores me. Hence this little soiree. Tomorrow you will have the chance to bid for Jack Magg's jaw. Mr. Bland's here to ensure everything's above

board. But if you're tempted to help yourself overnight," he said, leading us back out, "I assure you this timelock is utterly impenetrable."

He slammed the door and wrapped his fingers around the timelock
dial. I heard the tick-tick-tick of its rotation as he twisted his wrist
clockwise. When he stepped back, I caught a glimpse of the dial pointing to "7."

"Seven hours. It's three minutes past midnight," he said, checking
his wristwatch. "That means the vault will be completely inaccessible
until three minutes past seven."

"Ladies. Gentlemen," said the butler, appearing at the bottom of
the stairs, "coffee is served." We trailed after him up the stairs to the
lounge, and thenceforth to bed.

"I've no intention of spending the night here," said Vauncey Magg-
Boulting. "Gadsby, telephone a taxi. I'll sleep at a hotel in town. And
tomorrow I shall reclaim my property."

Stoker did not demur. "Do as the gentleman says, Gadsby. Anybody else?"

Shyly, Ernest Bland said: "I believe I shall return home for the
night. It's only a mile from here." Once Bland and Magg-Boulting
had departed, Gadsby took us to our rooms. Pamela Rasmussen's was
first, with Violet Villiers next door. Naturally our host had the master
bedroom. From there we proceeded along a dead-end passage toward
another door. The floorboards gave an animalistic squeal as Gadsby
unlocked it. "Yours, Mr. Spector."

The canon's room was at the end of the passage, whereas mine was
back the way we had come, in a godforsaken corner overlooking the
guard dogs' pen.

*

I passed an uneasy night, waking before six to a chorus of barking.
Gadsby was lurking in the hall. "Your fellow guests are in the cellar,
sir, to await the unsealing of the vault."

"Bland and Magg-Boulting, too?"

"Indeed, sir."

I headed down, my footsteps echoing. The others loitered uneas-
ily as I checked my watch: two minutes past seven. Then I broke the
silence with an apocalyptic sneeze. "Forgive me," I said. "Dust."

At last, the timelock emitted a "click." Magg-Boulting pounced
and eased open the metal door.

"Where's our host?" Pamela Rasmussen was saying. "He should
be here, shouldn't he?"

"Oh," said Spector, his pale eyes catching what dim light there was, "he's here."

We peered into the vault at an alien shape: a body, crumpled at the foot of the plinth.

Clive Stoker had been dead for hours. That much was obvious from the dark, crusty blood pooled around him. His face had been bludgeoned beyond recognition and the weapon—a handcarved bust of Vlad Tepes—lay beside him. Jack Magg's jaw was gone.

An ugly business. Before calling the police, Spector took a good look around the vault. It appeared undisturbed, with one exception—a pair of labels had been swapped around: the duelling pistol and the bloody five-pound note.

*

"There are two other pieces of the puzzle," Spector told me later as we sat facing one another across the kitchen table. "Firstly, this. It was on the floor of the vault, tucked in a corner where it had rolled. As you can see, it's a human tooth—sharpened to a point."

"And the second?"

"This." He produced a wristwatch which I recognised as Clive Stoker's. He must have removed it from the dead man's wrist.

"The time," I said, "it's wrong. Off by about two minutes."

"Indeed. These clues, along with the others we observed together, should tell you the culprit's name and the explanation for the locked-room murder."

I stared stupidly at him.

"All right," he relented, "one last hint. Watch closely."

He plucked an apple from the fruit bowl and bounced it off the stone floor like a tennis ball. I watched it plummet out of sight, hit the ground with a slap and rebound into his waiting hand. He bit into it with a hearty crunch.

Part Two:

"First," said Joseph Spector, "the 'locked-vault' mystery.

"Clive Stoker wanted us to *believe* we had seen the vault sealed. In fact, it wasn't sealed until several hours later—by the killer. I worked this out from the watch. Stoker told us it was *three minutes past midnight*, meaning the vault would unseal automatically at three minutes past seven. But his watch was wrong; out by two minutes. This meant that by rights the vault should *not* have reopened at that time. Therefore it was actually sealed by somebody else, who used a different watch—one showing the correct time.

"As for *how* the illusion was created, consider the bouncing apple. What you really saw was an apple dropping into my lap, accompanied by a tap of my shoe, before I flicked it up with my knee. You *saw* the apple fall, you *heard* an impact. Your brain perceived a correlation between the two. It was the same with the vault. You *saw* Stoker twist the dial, and you *heard* it clicking into place. You saw the pointer levelled against the number seven. But what if it was the *number* and not the *pointer* which had moved? A simple enough device; perhaps a thin, magnetic ring to fit over the dial, covering the real numbers. All Stoker had to do was rotate *it* and not the dial.

"As for the sound, that clue came this morning—when you sneezed. This was caused by the household item which replicated the *sound* of the timelock last night: the pepper mill. This was Gadsby's part in the scheme. His master's instructions were simple enough; a mere matter of timing. Clive Stoker had thought everything through very carefully.

"He hosted the weekend party for one reason—to stage the theft of Jack Magg's jaw, and cash in the artefact's insurance policy. Hence the presence of Ernest Bland—an independent witness. And the other guests… well, he was simply filling the house with suspects. All he needed to do was sneak downstairs while we slept and steal the jaw himself.

"But the killer—who had been waiting for just such an opportunity—went after him."

"So," I said, "which of them was the killer?"

"That was a matter of elimination. It couldn't have been Ernest Bland or Vauncey Magg-Boulting; they weren't in the house overnight. They might have returned under cover of darkness, but not without waking the guard dogs. So they can be excluded.

"Gadsby had no motive—killing his master would rob him of gainful employment. The canon could not have passed by my room without waking me, thanks to that squeaky floorboard. Which leaves Pamela and Violet. This is where things get tricky, and we must resort to the next clue.

"The broken piece of tooth, which I found in a corner of the vault, indicates a scuffle in which Jack Magg's jaw was broken. A rather hasty clean-up operation took place, where the telltale tooth missed the assailant's attention. Therefore the jaw was *not* in fact the motive for Clive Stoker's murder—something else in that vault was.

"Remember that two labels had been swapped around; the duelling pistol and the bloody five-pound note. It seems likely they were knocked over in the same struggle which broke the jaw. That they were replaced incorrectly implies haste, but *also* draws attention to another item—the one *between* them, whose label was replaced correctly. Perhaps the incorrect labelling was accidental, or perhaps it was a calculated manoeuvre to draw our attention *away* from the real reason Clive Stoker had to die."

Spector held up a small metal object—the locket from the Staveley case, with its curlicued 'M.' He flicked it open with his thumbnail, revealing that it was now empty. The lock of hair was gone.

"Pamela Rasmussen couldn't have been the mysterious 'Lady M,' as the shock of her husband's death seven years ago had turned her hair white. The Staveley double murder was two years later, and the lock of hair in the locket was *fair*, not white. Which leaves Violet.

"Her hair was dark and uncannily perfect, in spite of the humidity. This implies fastidiousness, but also something else: a hairpiece. Underneath, she is fair. *She* was the mysterious 'Lady M,' who came to reclaim the evidence linking her to the double murder. And the answer was in plain sight all along…" Snapping shut the locket, he turned it over and I saw what he was referring to. Upside-down, the curlicued 'M' became something altogether different: 'VV.'"

The Indian Rope Trick

IS PRINTED ON 60-pound paper, and is designed by Jeffrey Marks using InDesign. The type is Caslon Pro, which was originally design by William Caslon. The cover is by Gail Cross. The first edition was published in a perfect-bound softcover edition and a clothbound edition accompanied by a separate pamphlet of "The Wager" was printed by Southern Ohio Printers and bound by Cincinnati Bindery. The book was published in November 2024 by Crippen & Landru Publishers.

Crippen & Landru, Publishers
P. O. Box 532057
Cincinnati, OH 45253
Web: www.Crippenlandru.com
E-mail: orders@crippenlandru.com

SINCE 1994, CRIPPEN & Landru has published more than 100 first

editions of short-story collections by important detective and mys-

tery writers.

This is the best edited, most attractively packaged line of mystery books

introduced in this decade. The books are equally valuable to collectors and

readers. [Mystery Scene Magazine]

The specialty publisher with the most star-studded list is Crippen &

Landru, which has produced short story collections by some of the biggest

names in contemporary crime fiction. [Ellery Queen's Mystery Magazine]

God bless Crippen & Landru. [The Strand Magazine]

A monument in the making is appearing year by year from Crippen

& Landru, a small press devoted exclusively to publishing the criminous

short story. [Alfred Hitchcock's Mystery Magazine]

Previous
Crippen & Landru
Publications

NOTHING IS IMPOSSIBLE: *Further Problems of Dr. Sam Hawthorne* by Edward D. Hoch. Full cloth in dust jacket, signed and numbered by the publisher, $45.00. Trade softcover, $19.00.

ALL BUT IMPOSSIBLE: *The Impossible Files of Dr. Sam Hawthorne* by Edward D. Hoch. Full cloth in dust jacket, signed and numbered by the publisher, $45.00. Trade softcover, $19.00.

CHALLENGE THE IMPOSSIBLE: *The Impossible Files of Dr. Sam Hawthorne* by Edward D. Hoch. Trade softcover, $19.00.

SWORDS, SANDALS AND *Sirens* by Marilyn Todd. Full cloth in dust jacket, signed and numbered by the author, $45.00. Trade softcover, $19.00.

HILDEGARDE WITHERS: FINAL *Riddles?* by Stuart Palmer with an introduction by Steven Saylor. Full cloth in dust jacket, $29.00. Trade softcover, $19.00

CONSTANT HEARSES AND *Other Revolutionary Mysteries* by Edward D. Hoch. Full cloth in dust jacket, signed and numbered by Brian Skupin, $45.00. Trade softcover, $19.00.

THE KINDLING SPARK: EARLY TALES OF MYSTERY, HORROR, AND ADVENTURE by John Dickson Carr with introduction by Dan Napolitano Trade softcover, $22.00.

THE ADVENTURES OF THE PUZZLE CLUB AND OTHER STORIES by Ellery Queen and Josh Pachter Full cloth in dust jacket, signed and numbered, $47.00. Trade softcover, $22.00.

THE ADVENTURE OF THE CASTLE THIEF AND OTHER EXPEDITIONS AND INDIS-CRETIONS By Art Taylor Full cloth in dust jacket, signed and numbered, $47.00. Trade softcover, $22.00.

A QUESTIONABLE DEATH AND OTHER HISTORICAL QUAKER MIDWIFE MYSTERIES by Edith Maxwell. Full cloth in dust jacket, signed and numbered, $47.00. Trade softcover, $22.00.

THE KILLER EVERYONE KNEW AND OTHER CAPTAIN LEOPOLD STORIES By Edward D. Hoch with Introduction by Roland Lacourbe. Full cloth in dust jacket, signed and numbered, $47.00. Trade softcover, $22.00.

SCHOOL OF HARD KNOX Edited By Donna Andrews and Greg Herren and Art Taylor Full cloth in dust jacket, signed and numbered, $47.00. Trade softcover, $22.00.

THE SKELETON RIDES A HORSE AND OTHER STORIES By Toni LP Kelner Full cloth in dust jacket, signed and numbered, $47.00. Trade softcover, $22.00.

THE WILL O' THE WISP MYSTERY By Edward D. Hoch Introduced by Tom Mead Full cloth in dust jacket, signed and numbered, $47.00. Trade softcover, $22.00.

Subscriptions

SUBSCRIBERS AGREE TO purchase each forthcoming pub-
lication, either the Regular Series or the Lost Classics
or (preferably) both. Collectors can thereby guarantee
receiving limited editions, and readers wo."t miss any
favorite stories.

Subscribers receive a discount of 20% off the list price
(and the same discount on our backlist) and a specially
commissioned short story by a major writer in a deluxe
edition as a gift at the end of the year.

The point for us is that, since customers do."t pick and
choose which books they want, we have a guaranteed
sale even before the book is published, and that allows
us to be more imaginative in choosing short story collections to issue.

That's worth the 20% discount for us. Sign up now
and start saving. Email us at orders@crippenlandru.com
or visit our website at www.crippenlandru.com on our
subscription page.

TOM MEAD'S
JOSEPH SPECTOR MYSTERIES

"Some of the most ingenious and entertaining locked-room
mysteries being published today."
—GIGI PANDIAN

"I hope to be reading his books for many years to come."
—MIRANDA JAMES

"A master of the art of misdirection."
—PETER LOVESEY

"Pure nostalgic pleasure."
—WALL STREET JOURNAL

"Mind-bogglingly complex . . . Lovely."
—KIRKUS

"An exceptional series."
—PUBLISHERS WEEKLY

AVAILABLE WHEREVER BOOKS ARE SOLD
FROM THE MYSTERIOUS PRESS

Milton Keynes UK
Ingram Content Group UK Ltd.
UKHW041317131124
2821UKWH00037B/181